DEMON RODEO

IT'S NOT JUST BULLS
IN THE CHUTES.

A PARANORMAL SPORTS ROMANCE

GENEVIVE CHAMBLEE

DEMON RODEO

GENEVIVE CHAMBLEE

HOT TREE PUBLISHING

Also by Genevive Chamblee

Chasing the Buckle

Demon Rodeo

Locker Room Love

Out of the Penalty Box

Defending the Net

Ice Gladiators

Penalty Kill

Future Goals

CHAPTER 1

EASTON

"*Good evening from Laran Arena, home of the Piranhas, in the City of the Violet Crown. Tonight will be electric, as the best of the best go head-to-head in a feeding frenzy for a seat in the finals. Fifteen of the grittiest cowboys pair up with the toughest bulls on the circuit for the final Titanium Bull Rider regular season tour stop. There's no mistaking that every rider here has made it this far for a reason. However, the most anticipated ride of the night is no doubt the two-time back-to-back national champion Easton Faucheaux's matchup with the national champion bucking bull, Onyx Alpha.*

"*Easton, who hangs his hat in Tifton, Georgia, is a native of Maringouin, Louisiana, and is one of those cowboys who makes riding look deceptively easy. We've seen him consistently put up big numbers all season and have highlight-caliber rides against ranked bulls. Tonight* is his first time back after his Sioux Falls matchup with El Diablo, a bovine known to wreak havoc on the most skilled cowboys and that showed him no mercy. Something that people don't consider is how smart these trained animals are, and this is what intensifies the challenge for riders. These bulls separate the men from the boys.

"At the end of that ride, El Diablo turned right into Easton's wheelhouse, loosening him up and leaning him back right where the bull wanted him to be. That was all that was needed to buck him off, hooking him in the left side with that massive horn as he went down. Many speculated the injury would sideline Easton for the season. But the naysayers always forget these bovine athletes understand the definition of pain well. What they don't know is relinquishing and fear. Easton's here tonight to conquer this arena and show this audience why he's a national champion. He's been riding well in practice, but let's see what he brings tonight against Onyx Alpha.

"Onyx Alpha is the hardiest bull on tour with fifty-four straight buck-offs and the highest marked rides of the season. He's only five years old but has learned the ropes quickly. In his last appearance, he scored a monster forty-eight points, with fifty points being perfection. Riders have averaged less than 1.6 seconds on him. That's because this beast has the entire package—agility, power, and speed. He weighs over twenty-four-hundred pounds of muscle but bucks like a seventeen-hundred-pound bull. That amount of bulk and weight becomes exceedingly *heavy on the extension of a rider's arm in a hurry. What we've seen with this bull is that he bucks high. He has a lot of forward movement, makes right turns with a lot of whip, and folds up. From the second the gates open, it becomes a matter of survival for the rider as they put their body and existence in peril. And it's all happening now."*

Easton swished water in his mouth before swallowing. Being the last rider always put him on edge. Royal, his best friend and fiercest competition, claimed riding last was an advantage by having the bar set for the score to beat. However, Easton preferred setting the bar and not chasing it. He needed to focus on the ride and not be distracted by the score. It was daunting enough watching the others, regardless of their performance. These were both his friends and his adversaries—people he wanted to succeed but needed to beat. From a stall, he watched their triumphs and failures. Yet it wasn't only the riders he watched.

Each bull seemed to get meaner and more tenacious as the night progressed, and he'd be damned if he hadn't drawn the meanest one of the lot. He needed a big number to maintain the number three spot, but more importantly, he needed to punch the clock to remain in a position to win overall. A buck-off now would put him on the bubble. Even so, his mind drifted to....

"How you feeling?" Marcel, his uncle, flankman,

and coach, asked, slapping him on the back. "You ready for this?"

Ugh! That question again. Did anyone truly expect him to say he wasn't? Did they doubt him? As if he needed doubt from anyone other than himself. But that was another monster entirely. Had all people lost faith in him? His sponsors? His crew? His fans? He couldn't honestly say he blamed them.

"*Oui.*" Easton nodded, his tilted Resistol obscuring most of his face and all of the concern glowing in his eyes. Shards of pain streaked through his side, the medication having little numbing effect. However, there was no need to complain. At this level, most of his rivals were dealing with some sort of pain, and his was not unique. Conversely, he knew he shouldn't be riding, and the Association medic knew it too. It had taken some finagling (a.k.a. a bottle of aged Cachaça he'd won in a game of Texas Hold'em) to get the lowdown on how to manipulate and trick the computerized evaluation system into granting him the approval required to return to competition. What the commissioners didn't know wouldn't hurt them. Truth be told, Easton didn't think it was any of their business. Who were they to tell him what he was capable of? Well, medically, they were supposedly experts, but that wasn't the point. They didn't know his core, his determination. Besides, it wasn't the injury that made Easton hesitate. On the contrary, it was the strange energy in the arena.

He knew the story of eight construction workers who died five years ago when the south side of the building collapsed. Anyone who came into the city limits for more than ten minutes was told the legendary tale at least a half dozen times by gossipy locals. The owners alleged that the building collapsed due to an earthquake. That would make sense, except no earthquake had been documented to have occurred in the area on that date—or before or after, for that matter. Sure, maybe the appropriate equipment that documented such activity malfunctioned. The possibility could be valid. But wouldn't other buildings have had damage? Wouldn't people have felt the tremors in their homes? Or were earthquakes capable of isolating themselves to one spot?

Easton wasn't beyond believing a conspiracy theory of a governmental meteorology cover-up. After all, there existed the whole UFO situation that the media never seemed to want to discuss. And also, what the heck was going on in Area 51 and the Bermuda Triangle? Where were those stories, those answers? Nowhere, because strange occurrences happened and were promptly muted. However, a more plausible answer for the collapse of the arena's south wall was shoddy materials and cheap shortcuts by the multibillionaire corporate owners. But the locals didn't buy into that theory either. Instead, the arena was said to be haunted, and, oddly, there seemed to be evidence to support it. At every event held here, someone died—be it an athlete, coach, staff, fan, or an emergency shelter overnighter.

Maybe Easton would have downplayed the rumor, but someone had the audacity to blast "Black Sabbath" by Black Sabbath over the PA as the riders were lining up for the introduction. Why the hell would anyone play a song about Emperor Evil himself at this place unless it meant something? He inhaled, swallowing a wave of excitement drizzled with anxiety. More than animal musk and pine wafted through this air. Beneath it all lingered a hodgepodge of what-the-fuck.

"You're freaking yourself out," Royal had whispered during the lineup in another attempt to convince Easton that ghosts and *gris gris* didn't exist. "You're letting anxiety created by your overactive imagination best you."

Ha! Easton knew better. When he was four, he'd had what some would call a nightmare but what his South Carolinian mawmaw claimed was an encounter with a boo hag tugging at his skin. He'd awoken soaked in sweat with thick red welts covering his body, chills, and a fever. The doctor sputtered some snake oil garble about an allergic reaction to insect bites, but that diagnosis didn't stop his mawmaw from having a coat of haint paint slapped on both the porch and his ceiling before the sun set that day.

"Ain't no damn bugs left those kinds of marks," she had argued as she handed him a cup of Asosi tea to drink. "Them doctors with all those fancy degrees don't know diddly squat."

He wondered what his mawmaw would say about all of this.

Marcel wagged his finger at Easton. "The devil sho' 'nuff lying. You got that same *bahbin* as Ma."

Tuning back into his present, Easton grunted. "You're one to talk, Nonc. Have you looked in a mirror lately?"

Marcel shook his head, unconvinced, and shoved a pinch of Skoal between his gum and cheek. "All right. Just remember, that's a lot of animal to be straddling if your head isn't where it needs to be."

Easton sighed. Marcel wasn't wrong. Easton needed to lace up his chaps and pull his shit together. His turn to ride would be sooner than not. Atop a thousand-pound beast wasn't a place to allow nerves and other matters to overtake. He drew another deep breath, inhaling the familiar odors of greasy foods, leather, sawdust, and pyrotechnics—the familiar smells of his world.

Marcel continued, "If you're hurting too bad—"

"He's fine," Royal stated, approaching from behind and sporting a pompous grin—as he should, having the lead score for the night. With his middle finger, he plucked Easton's brim. "He's too ornery to not ride and let me win by default."

Easton laughed. "Cocky as always. I'm not the only person who can whoop you."

"But you don't care about anyone else beating me other than you."

"And you assume that I prioritize you enough to care."

"*Ack!* Don't you two ever get enough of bickering like two hens?" Marcel hooked his thumbs in the front pockets of his jeans.

"You love it." Royal beamed.

Grunting, Marcel spun and headed toward the chutes. "I'm going to check on Upton. He's probably setting up."

Royal waited until the older man moved out of earshot and leaned against a gate. "The guys want to hang out tonight, and you look like you could use a whiskey. Apparently, there's a watering hole not too far from here that gives a discount to eventgoers if they present a ticket stub. Since we're the talent, they'll probably waive the door fee altogether. I tried to ask Iznar about it, but it didn't go too well." He shook his head. "I really have to learn Portuguese."

"You've been saying that for years."

"Yeah, I know, but it seems like a betrayal, though."

Easton pressed his lips together. They'd had this conversation more times than he liked to recall, and it never went well. "Your mama was being spiteful."

The muscles in Royal's face strained, and Easton raised his palm to stave off Royal's protest.

"It doesn't make her a bad person, only human," Easton assured. "You shouldn't feel guilty about your heritage and grown people's choices."

"Heritage is history. Past. Duchess is present."

"It's still a part of you, but you insist on sectioning yourself off to be a single unit and deny all the rest."

Royal's stubborn jaw clenched. "I've never denied being half Brazilian."

"You've never embraced it either."

"You're confusing ethnicity and bodily fluids. My donor never did anything for me other than his initial deposit. I owe him nothing."

"No one said you do. But your mother knew he had a family, and she chose to be with him anyway. I'm not excusing his not manning up to his responsibility, but half of you is his DNA."

Easton figured it was the dominant half because Royal looked nothing like his mother. His sultry mint-green eyes beneath indignant eyebrows contrasted her inky black ones and wispy lashes. Likewise, his short, straight toffee-colored hair differed from her long ebony curls. Even his olive complexion didn't resemble Salethia's bronze skin. As far as Easton could tell, the only trait Royal had inherited from her was his full lips that were even on top and bottom and puckered into a kissable pout—a feature Easton tried his damnedest to ignore. However, lately, those lips had been Easton's focus each time Royal spoke, which made no sense. Who obsessed about their best friend's lips? Or eyes? Or everything else about him being a delicious morsel to sink his teeth into?

He dragged a lingering gaze over the long lines of Royal's lean frame and wet his lips. These pervasive thoughts hadn't always been a thing. Nonetheless, over the past several months, Easton couldn't shake them, and his stomach somersaulted in Royal's presence. *What's wrong with me?* A streak of guilt barreled through his body. He'd no business to be thinking of Royal that way. *Concentrate.*

"She shouldn't be offended if you learned some things, especially not a language," Easton continued. "You have siblings who you've never met."

"Half."

Easton shook his head. "I've never met a half-person."

"That doesn't say much, considering the shitty company you keep."

"Present included, no doubt."

"Listen, I didn't walk all the way over here for your lip."

"*Pff.*" Easton snorted, mocking Royal's feigned

affront. "You pranced from two chutes down to gloat on your way to the locker room. I could spit that far."

Royal smirked at the accuracy.

Clang! A chute door burst open, and the crowd roared as a feral bovine rocketed forward and into a spin, scarcely clearing the fence. Its rider was flung frontward toward the broad head, then snapped back like elastic onto the sleek hide before being hurled to the dirt. One point six seconds. Bullfighters sprinted to distract the animal while the rider rolled clear of the dusty hooves.

"Damn, Brown needed that ride," Easton commented, watching the rider scramble to his feet.

"We all do," Royal replied with a sigh. "So, are we going out later or no?"

A wicked grin crept across Easton's lips. "Assuming I'd want to be seen in public with you."

"Who wouldn't want to be seen with me? Face it, I'm the best thing that ever happened to you, *baw*."

On point. Shuffling, Easton turned his profile to Royal to prevent his expression from revealing the truthfulness of the statement. Unfortunately for him, he hadn't been quick enough, and Royal's brow quirked.

To cover, Easton added, "And all this time, I thought it was the bull manure I've been smelling."

"Not an answer."

"Fine. It's a date."

Royal chuckled. "I'm the best date you've had in months."

Also true. Easton's cheeks flushed. "Ass!"

"Yeah, you can watch it as I walk away. Swish, swish."

The lines in Easton's face scrunched with concern. *Does he know?* No, he couldn't possibly. He'd wallop the fire and brimstone out of Easton and then stomp him in the mud if he did. And with Royal's recent winning, he had more than enough to make bail—not that either of them needed another run-in with the law. It wouldn't be threats of juvie hall this time. But honestly, what teenage boys didn't go joyriding in a "borrowed" pickup, sneak a few bottles of shine, skinny-dip at the lake, roll a lawn or two, and occasionally moon a passerby? Besides, they had filled the tank up with gas and run it through the Soapy Suds carwash before returning it. But this would be different because Royal would beat him—as in for real mud stomp him to hell with a rocket in the crack of his ass like the Fourth of fucking July.

Hollywood could produce and film all the *Broke-back Mountains* they wanted, but it didn't change the fact that there was no such thing as gay cowboys—total myth. Well, maybe they existed in some remote closet in a desolate, alternative universe but definitely not in professional bull riding—the superlative of masculinity. He'd have better luck milking a unicorn.

However, what was this malarkey being conjured in the indentions of his subconscious brain anyway? Just because he sprang a boner at the thought of his male best friend and fantasized about being the zipper on his jeans didn't mean he was gay, did it? It was purely coincidental that he'd never been attracted to women, right? Sure, he'd dated a few, but just to cease his matchmaking mother's nagging. Besides, it only made sense that he felt drawn to Royal. They had been best friends since their sandbox days and grew closer each year. Royal had helped take care of him during his recent recovery, taking time off from events and risking his rank. No one knew him better, and they shared everything. So what if they once had jerked off together after watching porn? They had been kids then. Nineteen. A couple of bayou boys blowing off steam. Plenty of guys did it. Right? It wasn't like they had jerked each other off.

In fact, Easton had read an article written by a sexologist in a reputable magazine that there was even a term for that sort of thing. Buddybating, it was called, and it was a rite of passage of sorts. No, communal masturbatory experiences were as common and old as the beginning of time, dating back to the ancient Romans and Greeks—and maybe even predating then. Experts declared it to be so. Who was Easton to question experts—ignoring the fact that he questioned the Bull Riding Association's experts? *No, not hypocritical at all.* He didn't have a post-doctorate in human behavior. Hell, he'd barely made it out of high school—not that he'd attended the best school district. Yet a cloud of doubt fogged his brain.

But playing the devil's advocate and assuming there was something more to the flummoxing sensibilities, Easton was sure it was all one-sided. Royal loved the ladies, and the ladies loved him. Why wouldn't they? Royal had always been a walking smoke show—one of those teens who puberty discriminatorily skipped from stinking cute to undeniably dashing overnight. Instead of zits and residual baby blubber, Royal had broken out with abs and biceps. His strong jawline had sharpened, and his playful eyes had deepened with mischief and mystery. Over the course of one summer, he'd sprung up six inches and his voice metamorphosed to 1-900-bedroom-sexy. His hands, feet, nose, and teeth had never fallen out of proportion with the rest of him. In fact, with each passing year, he became more devastatingly dashing and debonaire. In short, he was the guy all the other guys detested while longing to be in his presence. Royal was as regal as his name proclaimed.

And his rodeo skills.... Wow! They were insane. Pure natural talent, although Easton believed it had more to do with Royal's ambition than innate skills. He simply wanted to win more than others did. He was on a mission to prove to the universe that he was somebody. Because despite Royal's outward cockiness, Easton detected the truth beneath the mask. He recognized that Royal didn't see himself the same way the rest of the world did. Instead, he saw himself as unwanted and tossed away. While Easton loved Royal's mother dearly, he resented that her actions had fucked with his broski's head. As a result—at least partially—Royal sought validation in the beds of women. And there were plenty of them.

Every night, a line of precious darlings in tight jeans and thin T-shirts waited for him at the exits, and Royal didn't turn them away—well, not on most nights. Sometimes, he opted to hang out with Easton, and the two talked for hours while sipping cold beer and staring at the constellations. Stargazing was a secret passion they shared.

Growing up, Easton had had trouble reading. He'd also had a terrible stutter. Royal, as a brilliant eight-year-old, suggested Easton read Greek mythology stories aloud, since they had an abundance of big words—or big to a couple of eight-year-olds, at least. What Royal had meant was the complexity of the names. Since all their peers also wrestled with pronouncing the names, Easton hadn't been self-conscious about his reading skills. And low and behold, it had worked. Both his reading and confidence improved.

Subsequently, due to mythology being tied to the stars, it was only a natural progression that his and Royal's interests turned celestial. So, yeah, they'd sneak off to a quiet open field and lie shoulder to shoulder while finding the various constellations. Over the years, it had grown into this thing that they didn't share with anyone else—their secret.

Easton's mouth dried. They had secrets *with* each other but not *from* each other. At least that had been the case until recently.

If Easton confessed his feelings, Royal would think he was Mad Hatter crazy and laugh him so far under the stalls that even the cockroaches wouldn't be able to find him. Royal wouldn't understand this. How could he? The embarrassment Easton might could stand, but the risk of destroying their friendship was not a gamble he was willing to take.

"Hey." Royal rested his hand on Easton's shoulder, the warmth of his fingers sinking into the skin beneath Easton's shirt, and cast a speculative glance that seemed to peer into Easton's soul. "What's with that look? I'm joking."

"I know."

"*T'es sur de sa?* You seem... I don't know... on edge."

"It's nothing." Easton glanced down at his boots.

Royal stepped closer and lowered his voice with concern. "You don't have to ride tonight. No one would blame you. Your total is enough to push you through."

"I'm fine."

"I'm serious, Easton. I don't want you getting hurt again. Last time—"

"Was a fluke." Or at least it better have been. Even if it weren't, he'd convinced himself that it was. Allowing fear to creep in and rent space in his head was career suicide. Pain served as a reminder to never permit his past situation to reoccur. "Besides, I know what you're doing." Easton flashed his most arrogant smile. "No need wasting oxygen to convince me to sit this one out so you'll have a clear shot. I'm so squashing your ass, so get ready."

Royal returned the hubris and waggled his eyebrows. "Apparently, you haven't recovered from the concussion. You're still delusional. This one is mine." He clapped Easton on the shoulder before heading to the locker room.

CHAPTER 2

ROYAL

When it came to rodeos, things rarely went as planned despite how well they practiced. Bulls were unpredictable, venue owners dicey, and weather temperamental. Rolling dice or reading the best gunpowder tea leaves imported from Sri Lanka often yielded better odds than gambling on how a ride would go. For several days, ever since learning of this show, a pit had developed in Royal's stomach. And it wasn't because of Easton's rumblings about the location. Royal had heard the stories and listened to the old hands tell their tales. He'd wandered through the corridors and felt the cool breath of death skate over his skin. These weren't stories created to add character to the place or pique tourist interest. These stories had teeth, or more accurately, the whole damn skull. There was a body count.

Inside the arena, he couldn't see the night sky, but he knew a new moon hung there bright and bold, beckoning for the extramundane that lurked a cat's-whiskers-length beneath the surface on any given day and inviting that capriciousness into a place exactly like the one he was standing in. Frankly, it gave him the heebie-jeebies. Of course, he couldn't let on to anyone, especially not Easton, that he knew the myths weren't myths. What many defined as myths were merely deniable truths and circumventing renunciations of the uncomfortable—all the prickly mess people didn't want to accept. And he couldn't allow anything to distract him. He needed to study these bulls—not their film but them in action. They reacted to more than the chute and the rider. Animals were keenly more aware of atmospheric weirdness than humans. In fact—

Clank!

Royal snapped out of his thoughts and stared at the bovine charging into the center of the arena. He'd ridden that mean son of a bitch, Caldera, two weeks ago in Belcourt, North Dakota—another odd night filled with.... Royal didn't even know how to explain that night or even if he wanted to. One minute, he'd been enjoying a cold brew at a local choke-and-puke, and the next, he was storming down the highway on foot in the rain to a motel with a janky AC. It all had happened quickly—so quickly, in truth, that Royal didn't know what was happening and felt transported to another realm. A handshake of introduction between Easton and the newbie had been all it took to zap every particle of cheer out of Royal's night.

Although Maddox Pyrite had arrived on the circuit three months ago, Royal had never met him. Oh, Royal had seen him ride, and Maddox's technique was damn spectacular. The boy had skills, but he'd come out of nowhere. *Poof!* There he was. No one seemed to know anything about him, and he pretty much kept to himself. He showed up just in time for the lineup, tipping his hat as acknowledgment, and slipped out— sometimes with a curt wave—seconds after the final results were announced.

It had been a pattern until that night when he'd shown up at the bar with his shiny gold hair, sparkling blue eyes, skintight jeans, and hot body-ody that screamed Instagram model and looked yummier than a Scooby Snack. Of all the empty chairs in the joint, he'd strolled over to the table Royal shared with Easton and their usual crew and had asked to join. Everything red—red flags, red carpets, red curtains, red rover, red M&Ms—had flown like banners in Royal's head. However, before he could turn the unin- vited intruder away, Marcel cheerily agreed and scooted over to make room. To make matters worse, instead of dragging a chair to the end of the table, Maddox had squeezed in beside Easton. Just plopped his ass down like he was supposed to be there.

Royal sensed it immediately. Maddox's gaze. His smile. The way he'd shaken Easton's hand. It wasn't the way one should react toward a comrade. But if Maddox thought he could waltz in and.... And what? Well, for starters, he could kick rocks wearing open-toe shoes.

Royal refocused on the action in the ring, shifting his weight and attempting to convince himself that he wasn't bothered by the likes of Maddox Pyrite, who obviously had a thing for Easton. Well, the joke was on Maddox. Easton wasn't into men, and Royal should know. Not only had he known Easton forever and had watched him hook up with oodles of women, but Easton had also been unresponsive to Royal's advances when they were younger and coming into their own. Sure, at one point, Royal had thought there was a possibility that Easton's pendulum swung in the opposite direction, but he'd been wrong. He'd allowed those fantasies to drop long ago... sort of.

Royal scratched his chin. Okay, so maybe there hadn't been *oodles* of women, but there had been some. Enough. However, none ever panned out to be serious. But rodeo life was hard that way. It was difficult to maintain a lasting relationship when on the road forty weeks out of a year.

Oddly, watching Easton go after women hadn't been difficult to accept. No one could change how they were sexually hardwired. But watching Maddox make a play for Easton chapped Royal's ass. He couldn't stomach it and had chosen to storm out that night. Since then, Maddox had been finding ways to slither around Easton—always with some lame excuse that Easton either didn't see through or wouldn't. No one else did either. But how could they not? Were they all blind? Or was Royal crazy? No. He dismissed the last thought. He wasn't imagining things. It didn't matter whether Easton chose not to or couldn't see Maddox for the flesh-eating bacteria he was. Either way, Royal's duty as a best friend and wingman was to protect Easton—to always have his back, front, side, diagonal, and every other angle.

Really, what did anyone know about Maddox other than he could ride a bull (and probably more than one species)? He could be a serial killer busted from prison. Okay, probably not. The rodeo circuit would be too high-profile for someone on the lam—at least for a rider. Maybe hands would go unnoticed, but riders were constantly in front of cameras for interviews and promotions. However, he could be on parole.

Royal frowned and rested his palms on the gate rungs. He'd warn Easton later tonight—subtly, of course—over a round of Jägerbombs at whatever taphouse they ended up at after the show. For a cowboy, Easton's feelings were tender and required a delicate touch, which was precisely why some rabble-rouser like Maddox needed to keep his distance. Since he'd cropped up on the scene, Easton had been acting differently. Royal couldn't put his finger on it, but something was off. Coincidence? Maybe. Royal wouldn't bet money on it, though. That's why he'd gone to great lengths to ensure an invite to the bar tonight wasn't extended to Maddox.

The buzzer sounded, and the crowd cheered at the rider's effort, but it was ultimately a failure. He'd lasted longer than most but not long enough. Watching always fostered conflict in Royal. In his heart, he wanted his circuit buddies all to do well, but in his purse, he needed them to tank. In bull riding, being good wasn't enough to make a decent living. Anything outside of being in the top five wasn't worth rolling out of bed. And anything besides the top three had zero bragging rights. Sometimes—oftentimes—in the end, pride was all a rider had—reflection on the glory days when his body wasn't too broken to climb on a beast one more time. Sadly, no rider knew when that day would be. It didn't come at a certain age or number of years as with most nine-to-fives. The end came when the body said, "Enough."

Royal peered at Easton's chute. Medically, he shouldn't be riding tonight. Everyone knew it, but those weren't words to be spoken. However, there existed a world of difference between *shouldn't* and *couldn't*. Technically, he didn't suppose anyone in his right mind *should* be climbing onto animals with horns that could gouge out one's liver at the correct angle. *Who does that? Maybe Hannibal Lecter for an entrée with his fava and Chianti.* Yet if Easton stood a chance of having any kind of season, he had to go out there, hurt or not. That was how it worked. Welcome to the world of PBR. So, if Easton felt confident, Royal had zero doubts in his ability.

Onyx Alpha reared in the chute. *Damn that bull.* Already causing trouble. *Easy,* he mentally reassured Easton, as if the two had telepathic abilities. Out loud, he said, "Take control, East! Handle that!"

Inwardly, Royal grunted. Control was something he should be practicing himself instead of allowing his emotions to get the best of him. He'd had a hellfire of a time explaining (a.k.a. lying about) his little hike/tantrum down the highway. He'd created some cockamamie story about having alcohol-induced dehydration leg cramps—an innovative way of saying the booze made him do it. The guys seemed to have bought it. At least, Royal thought they had. Maybe. Hell, they were all half drunk anyway. If they questioned him, he'd claim the tequila had twisted their memory.

The chute flung open, and Onyx Alpha burst out

with a hard buck. Royal had said it a hundred times. That was one mean-ass bull. Its hooves pounded into the dirt, spawning a pygmy haboob, and....

Royal stiffened as a wave of discomfort shimmied down his spine.

What the actual fuck?

CHAPTER 3

EASTON

"Are you listening?"

What? "*Oui,*" Easton lied, snapping back to attention. He tightened the strap of his helmet and then climbed the gate. From the top rung, he stared down at Onyx Alpha. Its hide glistened a shimmery ebony as if slicked with crude oil. Swinging a leg over, Easton placed his foot on the animal's back, and it reared upward as if climbing out of the chute. The arena lights flickered. "For all that's unholy," Easton mumbled, pausing to allow the snorting bull to settle before reattempting his mount.

"Woo-wee!" Marcel exclaimed. "*Gardez-donc.*"

Easton clenched his stubbled jaw as he repositioned himself over the bull and handed off his rope.

"Handle that," Royal yelled, his voice rising above the noise of the arena.

Easton questioned how he had heard him so distinctly. And no, it wasn't his imagination. He'd know that erogenous baritone that melted every part of him that mattered anywhere. As many times as Royal had leaned close to whisper a private matter in his ear, causing Easton to nearly cream his pants, there was no chance of him mistaking it... unless it *really* was his imagination. *Am I losing my mind?*

Onyx Alpha reared up again, swiftly catapulting Easton back to reality. The bull's snorts stirred the sawdust in the chute, and its back hooves banged against the steel. Again, Easton steadied himself— more his nerves than his body—and gritted his teeth.

Shit! Now isn't the time for drifting thoughts. Focus.

Easton's gateman threaded a rope through the rungs over the bull—a measure to discourage movement. However, it did little to deter the bull from lying back and rattling the gate.

Ornery bastard!

"You and I are going to have to come to an understanding," Easton muttered at the bovine as he shook down his bell. "Cos this right here isn't working, *sha.*" The bull snorted as if in response, but Easton steeled his jaw and proceeded to wrap the rope around his gloved hand until tight. "Let's do this *fais do do,*" he stated, giving the nod.

The chute yanked open, and Onyx Alpha lunged forward straight into a spin, its hind legs perpendicular to the ground. *Ah hell!* A sharp pain snapped in Easton's back as he was jolted forward, narrowly missing the animal's curving horns and his free hand millimeters from a disqualification. His hips skidded left when the bull's hooves dug into the arena floor, the momentum propelling dirt pellets into Easton's face, before whipping in the opposite direction. Plumes of warm exhaust billowed from the bull's flaring nostrils. In the swirls, a figure formed in the vague shape of a human. Sunken, slanted eyes glowed scarlet on an angular face with a hooked nose and bulging blue veins. It floated toward Easton's face, its tendril-forked fingers clawing for his throat. "Cheater," it seethed.

Blood drained from Easton's face, and his throat parched. *Bitch!* That was no hallucination before him. "Stay back, demon!"

As the shape was about to make contact, Onyx Alpha launched forward, shearing the dust cloud and the contained figure. The animal whirled in a way that should defy gravity, and Easton swayed—uncertain if due to the motion or the vision.

"Get over him," Marcel shouted. "*Lache pas las patate.*"

Get over? Fuck getting over the beast. Easton didn't want to get *under* it. Adjusting his weight, he hoisted himself up as best as he could as the bull dove again. Sweat slid into his eyes, stinging and blurring his vision—as if he needed to append an additional layer of difficulty. Another hard landing and Onyx Alpha lost its footing. Time blurred a second—not even enough of a span for panic to register—into infinity. Easton felt his grip slip and body sail through the air, flipped ass over head as the bull crashed down on its hip. An instant later, Easton slammed into the earth, jolting the breath from his lungs, and rolled several times before coming to a stop. Disoriented and wheezing, he staggered to his feet on instinct and hobbled toward the first glint of steel. Coolness seeped through his sock, bringing his awareness to the loss of his boot. Yelling and hooves pounding behind him alerted him to the danger of the charging beast that failed to be corralled by bullfighters.

"Oh, God!"

"He won't help," an unearthly voice cackled.

Gripping a gate rung, he didn't have the strength to pull up. Mercifully, sturdy arms hauled him over and out of the way.

"Did you see it? That thing?" he asked, inhaling a robust scent of mint. "Did you—"

"Shh!"

Easton's gaze slowly tracked the length of the powerful arm to the intense face of its owner. When their eyes met and held, he heard the soft groan.

"I got you," Royal soothed, his voice practically a

whisper. Something curious glinted in his wide eyes that evoked the same in Easton.

Yes, you do. A faint blush stained Easton's cheeks at the realization that Royal was holding him longer and tighter than he should. He wanted to extend his hand and stroke Royal's jaw. Instead, he said, *"Merci."*

CHAPTER 4
ROYAL

Je vous salue Marie, pleine de grâces...

Seconds before Onyx Alpha rammed the gate, Royal managed to lug Easton to safety from the bull and whatever the fuck it was that he thought he saw hovering in the dust above the arena floor. Perhaps when his pulse ceased racing, he'd be able to make sense of what he'd witnessed. But for now, he'd settle for Easton being out of harm's way. Thank the heavens Easton had gotten up. Many cowboys wouldn't have—at least not immediately. But adrenaline spurred spectacular feats.

Onyx Alpha trotted around the rink in a victory lap —victorious in that it had successfully tossed Easton like a rag doll. However, Easton had held on by the hair of his chinny chin chin long enough to be scored. It was ugly, but ugly counted. Ugly earned a payday.

Royal's eyes darted to the jumbotron for the replay. "*Hrump*," he grunted. On the screen, the dust looked like dust. No weird form. No distinct shape. Just dust.

"You okay?" Marcel huffed, climbing the steps with a gaggle of the crew following to the bleachers where Royal and Easton were.

Shit! Royal still had Easton in his arms. Quickly, he let go and stiffened.

"*Pshaw*. He's fine," Royal quipped, taking the lead on whether it was true or not, and he doubted that it was. But he'd felt Easton trembling and knew his friend would be *honte* and mortified if anyone suspected he'd been rattled. Plus, Royal wasn't sure how permissible it would be for Easton to state what he'd seen. People may think he'd whacked his head one too many times and stick him in an asylum. At the very least, he wouldn't be allowed to ride until cleared by a shrink, and God only knew how long that would take. Again, it required a certain amount of insanity to willingly mount a two-ton beast that wanted to draw blood. Admitting to seeing apparitions would short-list him to a padded cell. Nope, floating supernatural entities were best kept quiet.

"He wanted to show off his acrobatic skills," Royal continued. "Besides, he landed on his ass. He's got some cushion back there."

"Hush it." Marcel waved him off. "East, talk to me."

"Yeah, I'm good," Easton answered, straightening himself and diverting his eyes from Royal, the color slowly returning to his face. "*Ça marche.* Just got the wind knocked out of me. All limbs accounted for and balls intact."

Marcel nodded. "Your mama will be glad to hear that." He reached out his hand to Easton, who was still on the floor. "She nearly skint me alive last time I had to tell her you'd been hurt. Chewed my butt good. I'm surprised I have any left. Had me swimming in the head, I tell you. She'll be wanting grand-youngens."

"It would be funny to see you walking around like the Headless fucking Horseman," Upton snickered. "With your Stetson on your shoulders all yaw ways and shit."

"Quash it," Marcel griped, pulling Easton to his feet. "You always yacking your trap when you ought not. All of yas." He cast a glance at the men around him. "I don't know why I stick around."

"I already said. Cos you love us," Royal replied, standing. "We are the beacons of sunshine in your life. We're your oxygen and the wind in your sails. The gold at the end of your rainbow. The—"

"Pains in my rump is what y'all are. And you—" He pointed at Upton. "—need to watch your mouth. This is a family-friendly event."

Uh-huh. Where parents bring their crumb-snatching

tax deductions to watch us get slung about like a third grader's boogers.

After looking Easton over, satisfied nothing was broken or out of place, the lines in Marcel's face relaxed.

Royal planted on a smile to lighten the mood, but not because he felt it. His legs still felt wobbly, and a lump was lodged at the base of his throat. That could have gone so very wrong. Easton shouldn't have ridden. Royal shouldn't have covered for him. That bull was too damn mean for this sport, and that *thing.... What was that?* A shiver raced up his spine. *Pull it together.*

He focused on the jumbotron. A score of 94.6 scrolled across the bottom—good enough for a solid second. He turned and grinned at Easton. "Told ya you wouldn't outride me, *baw.*"

"Yeah, yeah." Easton dusted himself off. "Easy to say when you pulled a docile calf."

Royal laughed. "Don't be jelly cos you couldn't own that dainty little sugar dumpling you pulled." He glanced at Onyx Alpha still prancing around the ring. "He's *so* agreeable. You must didn't whisper sweet nothings in his ear."

Easton made a face, stifling a smile. "*Embrasse mon cul.*"

"All right, all right," Marcel interrupted. "Let's get

back to the locker room. I want the doctor to check you to be on the safe side."

Upton grunted. "No sides are safe."

"I'm fine," Easton protested.

"It's not a horrific idea," Royal said mildly. However, the quick glare from Easton let him know his words were seen as traitorous.

"No. I'm not having any doctors prodding and poking on me. I'll take it easy for the rest of the night."

"Now you listen here," Marcel bit out. "That's exactly how little problems develop into huge problems—by not checking."

"He seems to be okay, but I'll stay with him to make sure he's not seeing double or anything," Maddox offered.

Where had he come from? Royal frowned and cast an incinerating gaze at the unwelcome bystander. *Who asked you anything?* "*J'ai ça.* I got this," he repeated in English, realizing Maddox hadn't understood.

Maddox smiled coyly. "Brown said you guys were going out, and I'm sure East..."

East? Who gave you permission to call him that? You don't fucking know him like that.

"...wouldn't want you to change your plans. I was planning on staying in, so it's really no problem. We can hang out, watch TV, and get to know each other better."

You son of a—

Marcel nodded. "Well, I guess that would be better than nothing."

The hell it is.

Folding his arms across his chest, Royal protested, "He doesn't need a babysitter. I'll stay."

Maddox's eyes narrowed, and his mouth quirked in a humorless smile. "If he doesn't need a sitter, what does it matter who stays with him? Besides, I'm certified in basic first aid."

Royal noted the deceptive saccharine quality in Maddox's tone. *Why you—*

Before Royal could respond, Easton nodded. "Maddox is right. You shouldn't change your plans because of me. You deserve to celebrate your win."

"Good. That's settled," Marcel stated, bringing the matter to a close. "Let's finish this shindig up."

No, nothing's settled.

"I'll meet you at the hotel," Maddox confirmed.

That slithery, no-good, conniving bastard!

CHAPTER 5

EASTON

Easton glanced back at the cloud of dust drifting above the arena floor. It should have settled by now but hadn't. Why was no one else freaking out about what happened? Bulls throwing riders brought drama, sure. But damn apparitions manifesting from the earth promoted drama to another galaxy. People should have been racing out of the arena, screaming their lungs out. Popular word, that—*should*. Was anyone counting all the shoulds that should have happened? Easton wondered.

Onyx Alpha, snorting, still evaded the bullfighters attempting to corral it into the holding pen. It trotted around the perimeter as if it was proud of its accomplishment and king of the rodeo. Easton supposed that was true—the bulls were the stars of these roughstock events and the cowboys the supporting cast—nobility but not royalty. But honestly, he was thankful Onyx Alpha was evading the pen. As long as the bull remained in the rink, the promoters couldn't set up for the awards; hence, Easton could avoid going back down there for the time being. Whatever had risen from wherever—likely the bowels of hell—had returned... at least temporarily. And temporarily was sufficient as long as it was enough time for him to clear the hell out of this place. If that made him chick-enshit, then so be it.

He took a step, and pain streaked from his lower back to the base of his skull. There it lodged. Now that the adrenaline had begun to fade, the intensity of the pain started to register. It would take more than a couple of aspirins to rid him of this. He'd need a good, long Epsom-salt soak, plenty of camphor liniment, and a shot of apple cider vinegar mixed in pure cherry juice. He wouldn't smell that great, but as long as it worked, he didn't care if he smelled like a bucket of month-old striped polecat urine. He preferred to stink with Royal by his side, and if not with him, then alone. Not for one nanosecond did he doubt Royal would put his needs second to Easton's. He always did. Lately, though, Royal seemed to do that continuously, and that wasn't fair. Easton couldn't—wouldn't—ask Royal to sacrifice his night on his account. Besides, Maddox didn't seem like a bad guy to hang out with. Although....

Easton studied the blond newcomer. For some reason, he got the feeling that Royal didn't care much for Maddox. And if Royal was concerned, then perhaps he should be concerned as well. Then again, Royal was often distrustful of new people. He had a small select group of friends and an even smaller number of relationships. On reflection, Easton couldn't recollect Royal having any serious romantic relationships. The longest he could recall lasted possibly a month, and that had been years ago. And the only reason it had lasted that long was due to the girl having appendicitis, and Royal had hung around for her recovery. Royal had said it would have been shitty to dump her while she was laid up. Frankly, Easton hadn't thought waiting had made getting dumped any less shitty. It only prolonged the inevitable—sort of along the same lines as requesting an extension for filing taxes.

Easton reckoned all of this stemmed back to the jacked-up relationship between Royal's parents. However, Easton wouldn't concern himself with that festering sore at present. If having Maddox as a companion shut Marcel up, then that was how it was going to be. Doctors were not an option.

All bull riders got injured at some point in their career. The world had seen Easton face-first in the dirt before, but this was different. Gritting his teeth, Easton took another step and then another. *Don't be a pussy. Eyes forward. Shoulders square. Walk.* His knees buckled. *Okay, hobble—but don't fall.* The locker room was approximately twenty feet away. He needed to make it there on his own—not only to get Marcel off his back but to prove to the crowd that no bovine would ever get the best of him. Promoters and sponsors needed to see that he was solid. He made another step, plastered on a weak smile, and waved at the crowd. *I'm a chameleon. You'll think I'm fine even when I'm not.* Purposefully, he didn't look in Royal's direction. He knew his best friend would see straight through the act. And if that happened, Royal would call his bluff the minute they entered the locker room. Easton didn't have sparring with Royal in him tonight... or with anyone, for that matter. He needed to get his head together to process this shit show of an evening. He took another step and winced before he could control his expression.

"*Quoi y a?*" Royal asked, his brows pulling into a tight line of doubt.

Don't look at me. Please look away. "Rock," he lied, diverting his eyes and praying the fear he felt wasn't visible on his face. He couldn't admit what was truly wrong. "My boot."

"One of the bullfighters will grab it," Marcel reassured. "They have their hands full. That's one ornery bull."

"They should shove your boot under its nose,"

Royal joked, glancing at the arena. "That stench would chase anyone away screaming."

"Or drop 'em on the spot like chloroform," Upton added.

"They can't do that," Cody, Easton's gateman, chimed in for the first time. "Every animal rights advocacy group would hang all our asses for animal cruelty."

Easton's lips rebelliously curled into a smile. "Fuck y'all."

"Language," Marcel warned.

Royal laughed. "You're wasting your time on these barbaric fuckwads. There's no reforming them for civilization. They eat with their feet."

Marcel narrowed his eyes. "You got one more time, Royal. Just one more."

Royal laughed harder. "All right. Simmer down, old man. I'll behave."

Easton shook his head. "Heads up, everybody. Watch out for a lightning bolt. It'll be coming in hot."

Yes. Distract, distract.

The lighthearted bantering removed Easton's focus from walking, and before realizing it, he'd reached the locker room. But once he hauled himself inside, the fury raging inside his body unleashed. He flopped onto the bench closest to the door and released a slow but silent breath of relief.

"Here you go."

Easton glanced up at the hand extending him a bottled water and muttered a thank you to his gateman. *I could be him.* Cody was one of the broken ones. Two years ago, a bovine, Rumpy, had trampled him, leaving a hole in his skull. Cody had made a remarkable recovery, healing much faster than any doctor had predicted and showing no lasting effects. Miracles happened daily. Of course, he could be like Easton and was hiding them, but Easton didn't think so. Cody seemed to function with no pain. However, the doctors had warned that another head injury could kill him instantly. That hadn't scared Cody, though. Easton knew this from the way Cody eyed the bulls, that gleam of longing mixed with sadness. He was itching to climb back on. The reason he didn't was his wife. She had threatened to divorce him and take their babies if he ever rode again. So, he'd relegated himself to coaching and helping at events, grasping to have some small part of what he'd lost.

The doctors hadn't given Easton that drab of a prognosis, but he felt they were close to uttering such poppycock drivel. Therefore, he had to be careful. He couldn't give anyone an excuse to permanently sideline him, and that meant not curling up on the bench at present and screaming in agony the way he wanted to. *Suck it up, sugarplum.* Now that he was seated, pain soared through his body in thumping waves. Nausea rose to the base of his throat. *God, please let me make it back to the hotel.*

He opened the water and sipped as the bustle continued around him—other riders inquiring if he was okay and congratulating him on qualifying, event makers ensuring he would be able to attend the closing ceremony, Marcel being Marcel. And at his side on the bench, Royal fielded all the questions, handling matters as usual.

Where would I be without you?

CHAPTER 6

ROYAL

What a crazy night.

Royal sipped his beer at the bar and attempted to focus on his current environment. The bar was crowded but not shoulder to shoulder. A decent band graced the stage, and the beer on tap wasn't abysmal. Plus, there was no shortage of buckle bunnies. In all, it turned out to be one of the better after-work establishments. However, his mind kept floating to Easton alone with Maddox in the hotel room. What was going on there? What was Maddox doing? Touching Easton? *I'll choke the son of a—*

Quit it!

No, he couldn't allow his thoughts to drift to that dangerous place. That rabbit hole was best left unexplored. It wasn't a hole—more like a groundhog tunnel that kept going and going. Popping his head up in the wrong spot could get it whacked slam off. No, he needed a distraction.

"Royal Guérin," called the familiar voice over the bluegrass song.

Royal looked up from nursing his beer and at the smiling face. "Abilene Bailey." *Ah! Distraction on cue.* He opened his arms to welcome an embrace from the travel blogger. "What has you in these parts?"

"Why, I came to see you boys ride, of course. Quite the show tonight."

He nodded. "Yes, it was, but I can't believe you came all this way for us."

"Honestly, I wasn't going to, but you know that arena has a reputation."

Royal's smile soured. "Don't tell me you came to see one of us get killed."

"No. Don't be that way. You know I love you guys."

"Well, that's kind of a fucked-up reason to come."

"It's a job, Roy. Someone has to write it."

"That someone certainly doesn't have to be you."

Abilene twisted her face in an unflattering series of lines and wrinkles. "I don't know why you detest my job so much. I never criticize yours. It's not always teacups and roses with neat little petits fours on the side. I write the story at hand the same as you ride the bulls you draw."

Royal couldn't disagree. That was a fair assessment. Abilene was one of the few women who got it—

who would crawl in and out of his bed without questions, expectations, or complaints. She was pretty perfect in that regard, and Royal was certain that her job had carved her that way. Her career was important to her. With all the traveling she did, plus her ambition to be famous and desire to see the world, she didn't have time to settle down and pump out a houseload of babies. However, time was what one made it to be. Royal figured it probably had more to do with want. Many of the men on the circuit had family, and many more of them teetered on the edge of divorce. The rodeo lifestyle wasn't for everyone. In reality, the circle was small, which was why Royal needed to appreciate his. Abilene, in an odd way, was part of it, yet he couldn't help being rubbed the wrong way by some of the articles she printed.

Yes, she considered herself a travel blogger—writing about the places she visited. But those weren't the blogs that paid the bills, although Royal knew she would never admit it to him because he'd made his feelings known. No, her bread and butter were the freelance articles she sold to gossip sites using a pseudonym. Royal had figured out her secret last year after an article about him appeared in *Chaps & Chutes* magazine. In the article, it mentioned his trademark blue spurs being the same color as grape hyacinths. Perhaps it had been an odd coincidence, but Royal found it curious that the article would compare his spurs to that particular flower when the only people he'd ever mentioned it to were Marcel, his mother, Abilene during pillow talk, and, of course, Easton. His mother never gave interviews, and he doubted Marcel would have remembered. Easton wouldn't have a reason to mention it. When Royal reread other articles about himself from this same author—Dusty Rooks—a pattern of small details became apparent, and the only reporter who would know about them was Abilene.

Yet, to her credit, Royal had to admit that Abilene wrote the least salacious articles, providing mostly facts without all the fluff. Of course, she did her bit of exaggerating too. And while Royal considered her a friend, he had to consider her an online journalist first. Therefore, he had to be careful of what he allowed to slip. He knew she would eventually get around to asking about Easton tonight, and there was no way he could relay what had really happened in the arena. *Might as well get ahead of it.*

"You're right," he said, pointing to the empty stool next to him. "Let me buy you a drink. Have a seat." He waved to a waitress before his companion could respond. "It's been a grisly night, but it always is with tough bulls. It's always a mixture of luck and skill. Luck was on the side of the beasts tonight, but fortunately, no one got injured."

Abilene quirked her brow. "No one? Is that why Easton's not here tonight—cos he's not hurt?"

"He had other plans." It wasn't a complete lie. Not exactly the truth, the whole truth, and nothing but the truth, but he didn't imagine it was anything that would hurl him into the depths of purgatory either.

"Oh?"

"You know bars aren't his scene."

"Since when?"

Damn, she's going to dig. "Since forever. He hangs out to be social, but truth be known, he prefers to curl up with a good mystery book." He studied the blogger's face. She wasn't sold. "And off the record?"

"Sure," she agreed, her eyes sparkling with interest.

He could trust her, especially since what he was about to feed her wasn't juicy. "He's been taking online courses. The boy has homework."

"In what?"

"Business and broadcast."

"Really?"

"Darling, we can't do this forever, you know. There has to be an exit strategy."

"Easton's thinking about quitting?"

Shit! And this was why he disliked talking to reporters. They could read into and twist anything.

"That's not what I said. It's never too early to begin planning for the future. Procrastination is no one's lover. You can't tell me you're not stuffing away a few coins a little on the side."

A waitress approached them. "What can I get you?"

"I'll have whatever he's having," Abilene responded.

"I'll take another beer and a scotch neat."

Abilene waited until the waitress was out of earshot before angling her head and speaking. "You're in a mood. You going to tell me what's bothering you?"

Royal's lips twitched. She could read him better than most. "It's just one of those evenings. The road gets lonely."

Abilene tipped her head toward Royal's and curled her lips seductively. "Would you like for me to make it less lonely?"

Would he? The fact that his response wasn't automatic or his enthusiasm several notches higher should have given him some indication. Over the past several months, crawling in bed with random hookups had become less and less appealing. But, on the other hand, why shouldn't he? What, or rather, who did he have waiting at the hotel to scratch his itch?

"Maybe later. I need food in my gut first. I'm a growing boy, you know."

Abilene inched forward and hooked her fingers in Royal's front pockets. "I'll have you *growing* for sure."

His dick didn't even twitch. *Damn. It's going to be*

one of those nights—a night that he'd have to concentrate extra hard to make *stuff* happen. But did he want to exert that kind of effort?

He smiled sweetly and nodded in an ambiguous acknowledgment. He'd worry about it after a nice juicy steak. It would buy him time. And who knew? Maybe something would happen between now and then that would make him more *responsive*. Besides, there were worse ways he could spend his evening. He could be stuck in a room with Maddox.

Dammit!

He didn't need the recurring thought of his best friend spending the evening alone with Maddox Pyrite in his head again. That was the entire point of the alcohol. He downed the remainder of his beer.

CHAPTER 7

EASTON

Easton settled into a hotel chair by a window with several slices of pizza stacked on a flimsy paper plate. It wasn't the most comfortable chair. Then again, the hotel wasn't some posh five-star resort with marble lavatories, bohemian chandeliers, exotic wood floors, Persian rugs, velvet-lined furniture, and a garden view. It was three-star at best. Plus, his body was in no condition to differentiate between lumpy furniture and the knotted muscles that were beginning to ease with drugstore-brand pain medication, creams, and patches. He stunk of menthol and witch hazel to high hell and back, but it served as a better alternative to other options.

The idea of taking anything stronger made him wary because that was how addictions began. For now, he decided to stick with the over-the-counter meds instead of hitting the hard stuff in his suitcase that doctors had prescribed. His father had traveled down that murky path—though for different reasons. However, Easton didn't suppose the cause made any difference if the outcomes were the same tragic ones. It was far too easy to plunge into the trap without any biological predisposition being added to the equation. All he needed to do was linger around a stall for a smidgen too long by himself, and the pushers would find him. It was no secret—although the circuit media reps kept it on the down-low—that many of the veteran riders depended on the services of pharmaceutical entrepreneurs. Hopheads on bulls wouldn't be good for the family image the tour promoted—a wholesome, clean, healthy sport. Proud cowboys taming wild beasts.

Eh. That wasn't exactly the truth. The bulls were trained to be "wild," although the training did play off their beastly instinct and bred-in temperament. Aurochs weren't being rounded up from the unexplored Western frontier as was sometimes implied. These were domestic animals trained to buck off anything on their backs. Horning and stomping the trigger—a.k.a. riders—came as a package deal. So, when a bovine harmed a rider, it truly wasn't the animal's fault. Likewise, when a rider got injured, it was his—or her—job to suck it up. The risks weren't unknown.

Easton didn't judge those who turned to extra help in coping with the pain. He understood the why. He, too, felt the temptation to have it instantly taken away. The body could only withstand so much. But he'd also seen the damage and destruction of prescription drug addiction. The cons outweighed the pros. He consciously chose to manage his pains with soaks, home remedies, and OTC medication until he could no longer physically endure them.

"What do you want to watch?" Maddox asked, plopping into the only other chair in the room and aiming the remote at the flat-screen on the media console.

"Doesn't matter. Anything." Easton lifted his limp pizza to his lips and suppressed a frown. He'd eaten enough on-the-road take-out pizza to tell by the way the crust sagged that it would taste a step above licking Styrofoam. But beggars couldn't be choosers, though Easton wasn't convinced of the sentiment's accuracy anymore. Sometimes, the choice was to accept nothing in opposition to mediocrity. However, tonight wasn't that night for him. "Thanks for picking this up and bringing it back to the hotel."

"No problem." Maddox smiled. "Actually, I'm glad you needed me to."

Easton's brows bunched.

"I don't mean I'm happy you got slammed, but I'm

thankful for a chance to get to know you better. We've never had a chance to talk before now."

"What do you mean? I'm always around."

"And always surrounded by a ton of other people I don't know. Everyone already seems so close."

"We are," Easton agreed. "We've been together a long time—a gaggle of Maringouin boys, even if some of us don't live there anymore. We're like family. Well... some of us—a lot, actually—*are* family. Blood-related. It's why I think bull riding may be genetic. I can't remember a time when I didn't know the rodeo. I started roping—well, tossing a rope at sheep in a pen —when I was three. I can't say my mama was too happy about it, though she never tried to stop me." He took a swig of soda. "You have family in the business?"

"Only a distant cousin. He lives somewhere out in California, I think." He paused to bite his pizza. "Heck, I don't know. That was years ago."

"I take it the two of you aren't close."

"I only met him a few times when I was a kid."

"You have siblings?"

Maddox shook his head. "Not unless fosters count. I have plenty of those. I got bounced around a lot."

Easton froze and swallowed the contents in his mouth around the large lump that suddenly formed in his throat. "Shit, man, I'm sorry. I had no idea. I didn't mean to—"

"You didn't do anything. The past doesn't conveniently change just because it's not all rainbows and sunshine. Or sunshine and rainbows—whichever comes first." Shrugging, Maddox dragged his hand through his hair.

"I think that would have to be the sun, since rainbows are reflective light on the rain."

Maddox grinned. "Listen at you, my little meteorologist. So smart."

"I don't know about smart. I do climb atop a bull every night."

Maddox softly chuckled. "I suppose we all will get points deducted for that, but what profession doesn't have hazards?"

"True, although most don't have the hazard of death."

"Maybe. Or maybe it's embedded in all jobs. Ever heard the saying 'working yourself to death'?" Maddox didn't wait for Easton to answer. "Any job can be strenuous or, at the very least, stressful. If it takes enough toll, it doesn't matter if you're a firefighter or librarian. A job can kill you—be it from high blood pressure, heart attack, cancer from a toxic material, or falling off scaffolding. Death makes all things equal. Some hazards are just more visible than others."

Easton thought for a moment. "I've never thought of it that way."

"Do you ever think of dying when you're riding?"

Looking up from his pizza, Easton stopped chewing. "No," he stated firmly. "If I had those types of thoughts, I wouldn't be able to ride at all. Do you?"

"I don't know. Maybe. Honestly, in the moment, I don't know what thoughts go through my head. It's only when I'm at the exit does the world come into focus again to make sense, yet while I'm up there, I'm aware of everything." Maddox shook his head. "I know it sounds bizarre. I can never explain it well enough to make anyone understand."

"No, I get it. It's the same for me. Maybe it's that way for all riders. Once you're out there, it's second by second, and God willing, you get through it."

Maddox studied Easton evenly. "Are you religious?"

"I was brought up that way, sure. I don't really practice any organized religion anymore. It's pretty challenging doing that with being on the road all the time. I'm not about to waltz into any ol' church concocted up on a hill. They claim to be Christian and to love thy neighbor, but not all of them are welcoming. Plus, it's no guarantee what they're preaching. It may be some whack-a-doodle shit that says if we don't eat anchovies farmed by purple aliens from Stonehenge, we'll all grow a second butthole. No offense to anyone, but I'd prefer not to end up in a place pulling rattlers out of baskets or being tested if I can float with a fifty-pound weight on my chest. But yes, I believe in a higher power, good and evil." He paused, then added, "And other mystical spirits. How about you?"

Maddox hunched his shoulders. "I don't know. Sometimes. I have questions."

"It's okay to question, especially if it challenges something that we thought we knew. It prevents us from getting... comfortable." He paused again. "From taking things... relationships... for granted."

Maddox's brow rose. "Relationships?"

Why had he said that? Easton felt the heat growing on his face. "You know. How we interact with the world.... People."

"People? Or a specific person?"

Oh my lanta! How had this conversation swerved this far this fast?

"I guess in general."

"You guess?"

Easton gulped. He couldn't shake the feeling that Maddox may be fishing for something. But why? "I didn't have anyone specific in mind." The hell he didn't! "Did it sound like I did?" *Careful what you ask.*

Maddox shrugged. "I don't know. Maybe. I would think someone like you would be seeing someone."

"What do you mean, someone like me?"

"You know, a good-looking rodeo star. You're bound to have tons of groupies."

"Naw," Easton tittered, shaking his head and shifting. "Buckle bunnies aren't my style. And if I can't find time to make it to church once a week, there's no way I could manage a relationship."

"Not even with someone who's on the tour?"

"Uh...." Easton shifted again. *Tread lightly, as in tiptoe, through this minefield of fucking tulips.* "You mean like one of the energy drink models?"

"Sure. Could be one of those."

What the...? Easton tilted his head, uneasy with Maddox's tone. *Is he hinting at something?* "They're hired to do a job. I'm certain they get tired of being hit on all the time when they're simply trying to earn a paycheck. It borders on workplace harassment."

Maddox smirked. "You go, Mr. Woke Women's Advocate."

"It has nothing to do with being woke or advocacy. Everyone deserves respect."

"True. I didn't mean to imply otherwise. I only meant being on the road can get lonely."

"That's why it's important to have friends on tour with you. Someone who makes the downtime tolerable."

"Like Royal?"

Uh-oh.

"You two seem close."

"We are. He knows damn near everything about me. But how could he not? We've known each other since grade school."

"But there are things that you don't share with him."

"I didn't say that."

"Yeah, you kinda did."

Shit! "Well, no one tells anyone *everything*."

"So, you have secrets?"

Shit, shit, shit! No, this wasn't a conversation he desired to have. He pulled his best game face and emitted what he hoped to be a convincing chuckle. "I guess you're not the only person not good at explaining things." He finished off his pizza slice and stood. "I need to use the commode." He didn't, but he did need an escape to regroup. How the hell had he gotten himself into this mess?

Maddox nodded, but Easton could tell by his expression that he didn't buy the excuse. *Well, hell.* "On second thought, I think I'm going to call it a night. The ground never gets any softer when you land on it."

Disappointment flooded Maddox's eyes as he stood. "Um, sure."

I'm acting like an ungrateful ass. Stop it. Don't be a tool. He didn't have to spend his evening with me. Be gracious. "Thanks for understanding and for hanging out with me. I appreciate it. We should do it again."

"Really?"

"Of course. You're one of us now."

Maddox's expression brightened, and Easton felt his conscience ease.

CHAPTER 8

ROYAL

Abilene's nimble fingers drifted down Royal's spine and halted at his waistband while her other hand massaged his chest. "I have to leave early in the morning to be in Tucson tomorrow, but I have time tonight if you want to go to my room now."

A wave of discomfort churned in his belly, and he trapped her roving hand beneath his on his chest. "Not tonight, doll. I just remembered I have some paperwork to complete."

"Paperwork?" Frown lines deepened on her forehead. "At this hour?"

"Yeah. Some sponsorships and business stuff I need to get taken care of."

"And you have to do it tonight?"

"I need to, yeah. I've been putting it off." It wasn't a whole-ass lie, just a bit of creative fabrication. He had been dragging his heels for days about the paper-work but had buckled down and finished it all earlier in the afternoon. All that remained was a brief look-over before uploading the documents to his shared drive, and that would take all of ten minutes. Additionally, there was no rush to get it sent tonight. He had until noon, and even then, he could request an extension if needed. But he didn't need it, and it wasn't pressing. So, what was his hesitation to accept Abilene's offer? No, not hesitation. Rejection. He'd turned her down. His mouth had opened and blurted a ridiculous excuse to avoid being with her. But why? Why had he done it? Nothing about Abilene's abilities was unappealing. She'd certainly satisfied him in the past.

He eased back and shook his head. "I know. It's a bummer, but you know how some of these companies can be." And still, his mouth continued doubling down with the lie. "If you don't jump when they want, they move on to the next person."

"Yeah, but—"

"Now, didn't you just rake me over the coals about how you never complain about my job?"

Her mouth formed a seductive pout. "Oh, all right. If you're determined to be no fun tonight, I'll have to find someone else to play with."

Royal didn't doubt the blogger would have any

trouble in that area. She had an entire bar of horny cowboys who would delight in her talents.

"My loss." He smiled and stroked her cheek. "Next time." A few seconds later, he was out the door and standing in the newly paved parking lot, alone with the fetidness of asphalt and his unwelcome thoughts.

For a moment, he stood motionless, taking in the long rows of pickups, trailers, and campers. Ironically, compared to the inside of the bar, the silence and stillness were deafening and allowed the strident screams of his subconscious to barrel to the forefront. These thoughts were so violently blaring and swift that they failed to register in his consciousness long enough to make sense. And at this point, with a basket of trepidation mamboing a jig on his shoulders, he didn't care to explore the meaning. He wanted silence. He needed silence. He needed the world to shut the fuck up, if only for a nanosecond.

"Hey, what you doing out here, creeping around in the dark?" Marcel asked, stepping from between two double-cab trucks.

So much for his wish for silence being granted. Apparently, his fairy godmother had resigned. He sighed. "Being one with nature, I suppose."

Marcel's eyebrows knitted together. "What the Sam Hill is wrong with you, boy? You've been acting more peculiar than a bee-stung gelding ever since we left the arena."

Royal contemplated his response options. The truth wasn't happening—not that he was exactly sure what that was. Being glib would have been his usual go-to, but Marcel was wearing his serious face and would light into him. Royal could do without that battle. He could lie and deny it, but he doubted he could be convincing. Besides, he didn't like lying to Marcel, or to anyone, for that matter. But hadn't he done that minutes ago with Abilene? His bologna had a name: h-y-p-o-c-r-i-t-e. Therefore, he settled on trying his luck with being ambiguous and sidestepped with an immaterial half-truth.

"The closer it gets to the end, the harder it is to celebrate. I want to win, but I don't want to jinx anything."

Marcel approached and slapped Royal's shoulder. "I know you do, and you have a good chance this year. Having a few celebratory drinks has nothing to do with your riding. It's pride that's the sin. But you've always been cocky, so you've nothing to worry about. God has forgiven you for being who you are, and the rest of us don't pay you any mind."

Royal smirked. "What the frickety frackerty frick kind of comfort speech was that?"

"Well, I didn't know I was supposed to be swaddling you." Marcel allowed his palm to slip from Royal's shoulder and flashed him a paternal smile.

"You crusty ol' coot," Royal muttered with a grin.

"I'm going to head back to the hotel—get my money's worth. I got coupons for free bottled water at the front desk."

Marcel grinned back and headed toward the entry. "Knock yourself out with that. But Cody told me there's a better band playing on the other side of town. We'll probably head over later."

Success. Conversation averted. Hi ho, back to the hotel I go. No more delays.

He began walking but faltered after a few steps when he heard a crunching sound. He spun around to the source of the sound, peering toward the rear of an F-150 hitched to a travel camper, and spotted one of the new rodeo hands leaning against it. Royal recognized him as Gerald's—one of the stock contractors—kid.

"Whatcha doing there hiding?" Royal inquired.

"The same as you. Being one with the night."

Royal smirked. "Eavesdropping, eh?"

The scrawny boy stiffened. "I was doing no such thing. You were out here in the open, talking all loud as everything. Anyone could hear you."

Royal's smirk widened. He recognized—and appreciated—the youthful condescension masking insecurity. "What's your name, kid?"

"Jerry. Gerald Junior."

"Well, Jerry, Gerald Junior, a honky-tonk parking lot is no place for someone your age."

Jerry puffed out his chest. "You're not much older than me."

"Yeah, well, I'm old enough to be legal, and you're not. How old are you, anyway?"

"Fifteen."

"Fifteen," Royal repeated with a grunt. The boy didn't look a day over twelve. "I remember that age. I won my first junior rodeo."

"I know. You rode Rumpy. He's one of our best sires now. He sired El Diablo, Tomorrow's Promise, Onyx Alpha, and Future Dismay. You rode Future Dismay a few weeks back in Topeka."

Royal's jaw dropped. "I'll be damned. I knew there was something familiar about that bull. I even told Easton it felt like I'd ridden him before. Bulls are like popping your cherry. You don't ever forget."

Jerry giggled, drawing Royal back from the memory and to reality.

Oops. "Don't tell your papi I said that," he continued, remembering he was talking to a minor.

Jerry's gaze dropped to the ground, and a soft chuff escaped his lips. "He won't care."

"I highly doubt that."

"What do you know about it?"

Ew! The amount of bite in the youth's words caught Royal off guard. "Nothing. Just that fathers care."

And who is this, challenging from my mouth like Dr. Benjamin Spock?

Jerry's contrite gleam darted from the ground to Royal. "Oh, is that why you let your old man speak to you the way he did just then?"

"First, Marcel isn't my old man. Second, what do you mean, the way he talked to me?"

"He called you a boy. Don't you find that offensive? Racist?"

"Not coming from Marcel, I don't. He calls anyone younger than forty 'boy' when he gets riled up. It doesn't matter their color. It's the way he talks. And if I said something to him about it because it bothered me, he'd stop or, at least, try to. Hell, he's been doing it so long, I don't know if he can. He'd probably choke on his tongue." He envisioned the image of prying Marcel's tongue from his throat and shuddered. "I wouldn't want to have to explain that to anyone. But this isn't about me. Does Gerald know you're out here?"

"Yeah."

Royal arched a suspicious brow. "Now, why don't I believe that?"

"You should."

"Gerald said it was okay for you to wander around?"

"Well, no." Jerry shuffled. "But he didn't say it wasn't okay."

"Uh-huh. So, what did he say?"

"To wait for him in the camper."

"Then that's what you should be doing." He jerked his head toward the Airstream and folded his arms across his chest. "Go on. I'll wait until you get inside."

"I could wait until you leave and come out again."

"But you won't."

"Why not?"

"Because you're going to give me your word that you won't."

"My word?"

"Yep. It's the most important thing a cowboy has."

Jerry shifted his weight and glanced at the ground again. "I'm no cowboy."

"I've seen you taking care of the stock, rounding 'em up and all. Hell, those animals get taken better care of than most people—the best fortified feed on the market, prompt veterinary care, and stalls clean enough to eat off the floor, although I wouldn't recommend going that far. Seems to me you have the right fine makings of one. Besides, being a cowboy means doing things—sometimes hard, other times not so much—even when you don't want to, but you do it because it's the right thing. We have to look out for each other because out here, we're all we got. That's cowboy code. If something happens to you, we're all responsible. My head will be in a guillotine as fast as your papi's. And well, I kinda like my head connected to my shoulders. It looks good that way, and I paid fifteen whole dollars for this haircut."

Eyes bright, Jerry grinned a genuine smile, and Royal returned it.

"Okay, then," Jerry replied, walking to the door of the camper. "Night."

Royal tipped his hat, waited for the door to close and click behind Jerry, then began walking. He glanced over his shoulder at the bar entrance. "What a dick," he muttered, thinking about Gerald. *Fathers are supposed to care. What kind of father leaves his teenager in a travel trailer in a bar parking lot while he gets drunk inside?* Yet Royal had defended him. What kind of hypocrite—for the second time—did that make him? Was there even more than one kind, or was a hypocrite just a hypocrite? He was the last person who should have been lecturing anyone about the goodness of fathers. His mood sank from bad to worse.

Yeah, it was fair to identify his mood as foul. He certainly wasn't happy. He hadn't been happy since Easton had been slung off his bull.

Easton. Royal quickened his step, determined to return to the hotel. He wouldn't be deterred again, except...

"Mr. Guérin?"

Royal spun around. "*Oui*, Jerry?"

"Do you think you could get me a cheeseburger or

something from inside? My dad said he would when he finished eating, but that's been over an hour ago."

That son of a bitch!

"I'm getting pretty hungry." The boy reached into his pocket and pulled out a fistful of crumpled bills. "I got money."

Royal shook his head. "Sure, c'mon. I saw several burger joints up the street a ways." He waited until the boy had jogged up beside him before he spoke again. "Put that away." He nodded toward Jerry's extended hand. "Your money's no good with me. Text your papi and tell him you're with me."

"Yes, sir."

"And it's not sir or Mr. Guérin. I'm Royal. All my friends call me Magnificent Supreme Emperor, but for you, I will make an exception. You may call me Your Majesty."

Jerry laughed, and Royal chuckled in return.

The hotel would have to wait a little longer.

CHAPTER 9

EASTON

EASTON STEPPED OUT OF THE SHOWER AND WRAPPED A towel around his waist. His first shower had been to wash off the stench of bull, dust, and sweat. The second had been to rid him of smelling like a side-hustle after-hours clinic. Staring at himself in the foggy mirror, he sighed, his breath more aperiodic than he'd expected. Despite the heat, his muscles were beginning to stiffen. However, on a better note, his headache had faded to an intermittent thump. And while he was recovering physically from the evening, his nerves continued to oscillate, and his thoughts spun to make heads or tails of any of it. But lately, when had anything made sense? Perhaps a good night's rest would put everything into perspective by the morning.

He padded out of the bathroom to the main room

and crawled between the king-size bedsheets. He'd grab his pajamas in a minute, but for the time being, he merely wanted to stretch out and enjoy the pillow-top mattress. Well, it probably was more like a foam eggcrate special from the dollar discount, but Easton was afraid to look beneath the fitted sheet to find out. Then again, why should he? If Baby Jesus lay on straw, who was he to complain about a ratty convoluted polyethylene topper? He'd bite his tongue and count his blessings.

Circuit life could be costly, especially when one wasn't winning or the turnouts were lackluster. Budgeting was key because Lord knew winning streaks could turn on a dime. In the time it took to manage a thought, the fate of a ride could be decided —whether he'd be leaving the arena with bank or in the back of an ambulance.

Most nights, Easton stayed in Marcel's RV with his uncle, two cousins, and Royal. But sometimes, they all needed a break from being cooped up in such a small space with one another. Easton was glad tonight was one of those nights.

Truthfully, they could afford more—much more. But Marcel argued that just because they didn't have to scrape together three quarters and a dime to buy a Moon Pie from the vending machine didn't mean they should be boastful and shove how well they were doing in the other riders' faces—especially when so many of his comrades were struggling.

"Humility grows character," his uncle preached. Easton agreed with this philosophy and didn't mind. The RV was homey, and sharing hotel rooms kept him bonded with the others. Besides, a serious injury could eat through savings faster than Pac-Man could chomp through power pellets.

As usual, Easton had booked a room with two queens to save money by splitting the cost with another cowboy on the tour. Tonight, though, the hotel computer said otherwise and decided to flip him the middle finger. Easton had been too tired to argue with artificial intelligence and the human whose actual fault it was. Of course, no one ever wanted to assume responsibility for fuckups. Inevitably, a drawn-out segment of round-robin and finger-pointing would have ensued. With the day he'd been having, Easton had preferred to forgo the drivel, accepted the king-size, and would foot the entire bill.

Seconds after closing his eyes, the door beeped and then creaked open. From the sounds of the familiar shuffling, he deduced Royal had drawn to be his roommate. Or maybe Royal had simply asserted it, removing himself from the room assignment drama. Although his group had whittled the process of room determination down to a science, it could be a hassle some days, since science wasn't always exact. Dalton snored like a lawnmower, and Sullivan suffered from night terrors that usually ended with someone running from the room. No one wanted to bunk with either of them, and rarely did fate twist so that they roomed with each other. As a method of decision-making, the group drew playing cards with the lower card values gaining the first choice of roommates from those who had reserved rooms. But tonight's additional *scientific* hitch was of a king-size nature.

"Well, I take it we're not going out tonight," Royal huffed, dropping his duffel bag on the floor. "There's a decent—depending on your definition—band playing tonight. I thought after you rested up a bit, I could convince you to change your mind and we go have a listen."

"No one's stopping you."

"I'm not getting stuck with babysitting Upton all night, and that's exactly what will happen if you're not there."

"He's going through a rough patch is all. Sadie's pregnant."

"Again? Damn."

Easton peeled open his eyes and stared at Royal. "Don't judge."

"Uh-huh. Maybe this time, it'll be his." He looked around and waved his hands as if in a showroom. "What's this? Where's the other bed?"

"What do you mean, where? Do you think I ate it? It didn't come with one."

"There's no pull-out? Nothing? Just two chairs?"

"Your counting skills continue to amaze me."

"*Brasse mon cul,*" Royal murmured.

Easton chuckled at Royal's mock insult of kissing his ass and realized he should have apprised the guys of the situation so they could have adjusted room selection. Should have. However, his mind had been all over the place during check-in, and the thought hadn't crossed his mind until now.

"Then quit bitching. There's plenty of room. There's not a problem unless you say there's one." Not exactly true, but Easton decided to stick to that story, since he'd uttered it for some reason. He was bound to have one huge, protruding problem. At least in the dark, the problem would be hidden.

"Fine," Royal huffed. "I'm going to shower."

"Don't forget to wash behind your ears," Easton teased in his best motherly voice.

Royal slapped his own rear. "Kiss it, I said."

Royal

OI-VAY!

Royal shuffled into the compact bathroom and kicked the door shut with his heel. *One bed?* He'd attempted to play it cool, but an unexpected flurry of nerves had struck him the instant his eyes had landed on Easton's form snuggled beneath the quilted duvet. Nothing about this was new. He'd seen Easton tucked in bed more times than *Sesame Street*'s Count von Count could count. So, what was different tonight? Why did he have this bizarre—was there even a name for it—coiling in his belly? All he could do was hope he'd been careful not to allow his voice to give away his emotions as he chattered on about... what had they talked about? What had he said? *Probably something idiotic.* That was usually how it worked when he suffered conversation amnesia—almost the equivalent of a cheap tequila blackout sans the alcohol.

He twisted the water knob in the shower as far as it would go to build up steam and listened to the splashing water echo off the subway tiles and a shower curtain that looked as if Norman Bates would pop out and yell, "Hey, honey, I'm home." Perhaps a hot shower would cleanse the atmosphere and wash off whatever demon's breath had latched itself onto him.

What a weird fucking night.

But there had been one positive. Maddox hadn't been in the room when Royal returned. Perhaps Easton had sent him packing. Hit the road, Jack.

Naw, not East. He's too nice. But I would have. I'd have

heaved that incendiary out on his ass. No, I would have never allowed him in. Feed a stray once, and they are bound to come back.

Royal studied himself in the mirror that was beginning to fog. *What do we have here?* The reflection staring back seemed foreign. *Liar,* it mocked. *Such a liar.*

Despite his reluctance to admit it, Royal knew the problem. He'd known for years. He was a gay man pretending to be—no, *masquerading as* sounded less duplicitous—someone else. He wasn't simply in the closet. He was in a fucking cellar with the dead bolt latched. Coming out should be simple, especially in this day and age. At least that was what many people would assume. But it wasn't simple. For all the wokeness, talk of social justice, and disillusioned folks with their heads in the it's-all-in-the-past-so-don't-mention-it sand, hate still existed in the world in terrifying ways—microaggressive boxes of candy-coated sweetness. And for Royal, it would mean fighting a battle on multiple fronts—something even more people wouldn't understand. Sure, a gay man these days wouldn't turn many heads—usually. In certain communities and cities, a synthetic magnetic eyelash wouldn't have been batted. A gay cowboy, well, that was a horse—or in this instance, bull—of another color. Cowboys were expected to be rough, rugged, and straight. Yes, it was an antiquated stereotype, but not one easily shaken.

Okay, he was a gay cowboy. That wouldn't be too difficult to manage, right? Perhaps had he been a ranch cowboy, it would have been less formidable. But one riding bulls…. Many sponsors wouldn't go for that, and the Lord knew how many people peeped him any given day of the week. There were always reporters, photographers, and promoters lurking around stalls and vending machines. Regardless of what one may have thought, lucrative endorsement required more than winning. Winning all the gold belt buckles in the world didn't mean a damn thing without the proper image. Bull riding was associated with masculinity. And while many gay men were the epitome of masculinity—and this also depended on the definitions—the stereotype remained that gay men were effeminate, based on outdated heteronormative gender roles.

In Royal's mind, a man who went to work daily, provided for his family, showed compassion for his fellow man, and could be fair without being judgmental were the qualities of masculinity. How much a man could bench-press, demand attention like a screaming two-year-old with diaper rash, grow a knoll of unkempt facial hair, beat his chest, scrape car grease from beneath his nails, manifest controlling asshole syndrome, and exhibit other toxic behaviors had absolutely nothing to do with it. Men could care about their appearance, cook gourmet meals, sew, dress well, be tidy, and all that other stuff without losing masculinity points. Some would deem these traits to be resourceful. But not in his world, his reality. No, he'd be dropped like a porcupine experiencing a psychogenic attack. He dared anyone to wrap their head around that.

So much of his livelihood depended on sponsors. He didn't expect he'd be kicked off the tour, although that could happen. Bias that obvious would make the tour susceptible to discrimination and civil rights violation lawsuits.

Sponsors, conversely, could be sneaky-snake slippery about reasons for withdrawing endorsements. They could drop him or not renew without giving cause. All they needed to say was that they decided to go in a different direction. Case closed. End of story. Point-blank and to the period. No one would question the direction. It wasn't like any commission was whipping out its morality GPS. Besides, knowing something and proving something were two different things.

Plus, who would fight them? Big sponsors had money, power, and hotshot attorneys to squash any litigations brought against them. They created "give-up" culture. In reality, lawsuits were negligible. The industry would simply pay off greedy ambulance-chasing attorneys to settle for what was mere pennies, allowing itself to continue business as usual. Knick-knack paddywhack, toss the casualties a bone.

And then there was the obvious. Royal was a man of color—half Creole with a prominent African heritage and half Brazilian. The tone of his skin drew instant hate from some people—people he didn't know or had ever met. Despised for breathing and having been born. Told to leave the country that his mother's ancestors had been born in and helped build since 1734. But for Royal, it went even further than that. Because of his Brazilian heritage, he wasn't fully accepted by the African American community. And because of his African American heritage, he wasn't fully embraced by the Hispanic community. Even within the Creole community, he was rejected by some for having too dark a skin tone for their liking. Racially and ethnically, he was displaced. His sexuality, he could hide. His race, he couldn't. Every day, he awoke with the hardships race brought.

Being a gay person of color took matters to an entirely different stratosphere. Unless one had been there, it wasn't something Royal could explain. The LGBTQIA+ community had its own hierarchy and pecking order. Once again, race issues reared their ugly, atrocious head. Even in the gay community, some looked upon him as inferior.

There was only so much hate a person could take.

Each day, he fought hate—some blatant, others

hidden. Did he sometimes get scored lower in rounds because of the color of his skin? Sure. Could he prove it? Nope. Would anyone admit it? Absolutely the fuck not. And what good was bringing it up? He'd only be told that he was paranoid or a sore loser or felt an incessant need to place everything beneath a micro-scope to bring in the race card. People didn't care for the truth unless it suited them. Therefore, Royal lived with it on the daily. He wouldn't address it, but it didn't mean it didn't affect him. It didn't mean he didn't feel it. He accepted the shit because if he didn't, he would spend most of his time dealing with it and nothing else. Besides, when the people in charge of resolving issues were the ones causing them, there was no recourse.

Some things were a part of everyday life. They didn't disappear because they were unpleasant or made someone uncomfortable. There wasn't always a "manager" to call and air grievances to. Sometimes a person had to suck up all the bitterness through a straw and swallow. Doing so didn't demonstrate weakness. On the contrary, it required self-discipline and strength. Thus, as the proverb went, when life gives lemons, make Tom Collinses. Well, maybe that wasn't exactly how it went but close enough. However, fresh lemonade required straining before consumption.

But Royal wasn't done tacking on the bullshit.

His coming out would affect other people's livelihoods. He had crew members who worked for him. Plus, he sent money to his mama. Well, not directly to her. She would never accept a cent from him. Royal had an arrangement with her oncologist to pay for her chemo treatments. As far as his mother knew, her medical bills were being paid by a special hospital grant. It was another lie, but one he imagined would be forgiven. How could he in good conscience jeopardize any of their situations? Because that was exactly what his coming out would do.

And lastly, there was perhaps the largest consideration of all: Easton. Not only could Royal potentially end his own career, but he could also place Easton at risk. People would question the nature of their relationship. And even if they didn't, there would be people who would pressure Easton to turn his back on him. Easton wouldn't, of course.

Would he? No, not Easton. He wouldn't care if I'm gay, although he might care if he knew I'm crushing on him. More than crushing. Not the point.

If Easton was pressured to turn against Royal and didn't, Easton's fans and sponsors could potentially turn against him. Royal couldn't allow that. He wouldn't. He could never directly or indirectly hurt Easton, and he wouldn't allow anyone else to either, which was why Maddox sniffing around perturbed him. Okay, so that wasn't the only reason, but a problem was a problem.

Oh sugar-honey-ice-tea! What a colossal pile of foulness.

At the end of the day, week, month, and year, it was Royal's prerogative and no one else's which battles he picked and chose to fight. The notion of him deliberately choosing not to address these matters was beyond comprehension by the people who generally were accepted and embraced in most settings. They had the luxury to kick back with their feet propped on a hassock, complain about the unfairness of life while eating Persian Osetra and sipping Lafite Rothschild, and attempt to dictate his behavior because of what they expected and wanted. While they didn't have to live his life, they still thought they knew how to best live it.

As the captain of his ship, Royal wasn't required to please every crew member. He didn't aim to. And even if he tried, he'd fail. There was no pleasing everyone, but he could satisfy himself, and what satisfied him most was keeping Easton safe. That was his focus among all the other noise when it cropped up. And oh, it would crop up. It always did. Through it all, Easton had always been there with his kind eyes, shy smile, and faint speckle of freckles across the bridge of his nose. Granted, he didn't always understand Royal's plight, but he damn sure tried. Royal respected and appreciated that. How could he not? Easton was a person who sought the good in everyone, who searched high and low to find one redeemable quality in even the worst of people. It was a great quality to possess, except it made him vulnerable and susceptible to those with ill intentions.

Royal watched as the mirror completely fogged and his reflection became nothing more than a blur.

Calm yourself. Act normal.

He had to get through sharing a bed with Easton tonight. Of all nights to have a single bed. Who had he pissed off in a past life to deserve this type of torture? What the fuck? Not to mention, he couldn't bring himself to think about the brouhaha earlier in the arena. How did he begin to wrap his head around that shit?

This town!

But it wasn't only this town, was it?

He released a long breath before stepping into the shower.

CHAPTER 10

EASTON

Royal slipping into the bed woke Easton. He didn't suspect he'd been asleep long, but he felt notably better—not great, but at least functional. While a marathon wasn't in the running, he didn't feel like he'd be wheeled into the morgue either. His pain had dulled to tolerable, but the room had cooled significantly, and chill bumps prickled his skin. He squirmed beneath the sheets, pulling his knees toward his chest.

"You okay?" Royal asked.

"*Oui*," he replied, shivering. "It's refrigerator mode in here."

"I know. I cut it off. You had it set to subzero."

"I didn't—" The protest died on his lips as his back began warming from the heat radiating off Royal's torso. Subconsciously, he shifted and scooted back as if being pulled by a magnet. *What am I doing?* He shuddered, then stilled at the bodily contact as Royal's arm settled on his and provided immediate rewarding warmth. *And what is he doing?*

"You *are* cold," Royal affirmed.

And you're naked! Easton's breath hitched. *We both are! What the...?* "Did you think I was making it up?" *If you needed verification of my temperature status, you've gotten it. So, why is your arm still where it is? No, this isn't weird at all. And no, I'm not getting a boner. I'm not. I'm not. I'm not.*

"That was an ugly ride you had tonight—too ugly."

"I made my eight seconds, though." *Barely, but barely counted. How the fuck is he so calm about this?*

"That's not the point. You could have been hurt... again."

Answer him. Don't think about his dick against you.

"We all get hurt. Nothing new about that."

"Naw, it's different. Something's up with you. Your mind was miles away before climbing on, and that bull sensed it. It flung you like snot from its nostril."

Oui, plenty is up... straight up. Damn, Royal!

"It was the arena. There's some bad juju in there."

"Don't hand me that crap." Royal shoved Easton's shoulder, forcing him onto his back. "And don't dare lie to me," he demanded, staring down at his best friend. "You've been acting weird for months. I deserve to know when something is bothering you. *Quoi, ça dit?*"

Easton hesitated, his breath shaky. Quickly, he bunched the sheet as best he could over his crotch to conceal his state. Biting his lip, he weighed whether confessing would make matters worse. "You really want to know?"

"I do."

He parted his lips, but the words lodged in his throat. "I just don't feel myself, like there're things I need to figure out."

"Like what?"

Easton shook his head. "That's the problem. I don't know. Something's changing, but it's not."

"You're not making sense."

"I know that too." Easton's gaze dropped as he gave a pathetic sigh, then sucked in a long breath. An empty feeling of incompleteness coiled in his gut. "You know how there are things you just know about yourself? Like when someone asks you how do you take your coffee or what side of the bed you prefer? You don't have to think about it. Somewhere in life, you figured it out, and chances are, you never realized when this happened. Now imagine one day, for no reason all, those default choices evaporate. Suddenly, you're unsure."

Royal's face lit with understanding. "Ah, I think I know where this is coming from. After a bad injury, lots of guys reconsider, and getting a rank bull the first time back doesn't help."

"That's not it. Or maybe it is. H-E-double-hockey-sticks, I don't know, Royal. *Je suis de'pouille.*"

"Shh. You're no mess—or at least no worse than the rest of the universe. Try to get some sleep. I'm sure things will be clearer in the morning." Royal's tone softened to such a level that Easton almost didn't hear him mutter the next sentence despite Royal's mouth being close to his ear. "For both of us."

"*Quoi?*"

"*Pas rien.* Pay me no mind."

Yeah, that's not going to happen.

"I'm talking loopy too." Royal continued. "I guess I'm more tired than I thought."

Is that all it is? Although he wondered, he didn't dare ask. Instead, he lay motionless, drinking in the silence as he awaited the Sandman to return and desperately flipped through his mental Rolodex of any image that would nippily diminish the bit of a problem happening in his crotch.

Correction. It wasn't a *bit of a problem*. It was a whole-ass *situation.*

Royal

I'M ONLY WARMING HIM UP. HE'S COLD. BODY HEAT IS effective. Perhaps if he repeated it enough times in his head, he would convince himself, and if he remained still, neither of them would feel his semi. *Yeah. Uh-huh. Down, boy!* Easton shifted and…. *Salleau prie! Good gravy and butter!* His insides buzzed as if he was on the lift hill of Kingda Ka and about to straight plunge into negative G-force without a seat belt. *This was a bad damn idea.* He needed to release his embrace. This… whatever it was… had gotten far out of control, and he had no one to blame—again—but himself. *This is the second time you've had Easton in your arms tonight. Let go,* he ordered himself, but his muscles refused to obey. And his cock…. *Oh, heaven above!*

Royal inhaled a few deep breaths to settle himself. He attempted to swallow, but his throat had gone bone dry. Did he not just have this absurd conversation with himself in the shower? Had his brain left his body? Had he contracted amnesia? *Welcome to Clownville.* He needed to take his own fucking advice and go to sleep.

Screwing his eyes shut, he forced his mind to focus on counting sheep. *Mary had a little lamb, little lamb….*

Easton lightly elbowed him in the chest. "I'm not a baby."

"*Quoi?*" Royal opened his eyes.

"I don't need you humming me a lullaby."

"I wasn't—" He interrupted himself, realizing

what he'd done. *Oops.* "I didn't mean.... It wasn't for you."

"You want to talk about *me* acting strange, but what about you? Your Mercury is out of retrograde."

"My Mercury is where it always is."

"What does that even mean?"

"It means we both need sleep. It's been a long night." He resisted maintaining eye contact any longer and rolled over, turning his back to his bed companion. There was no way he could continue meeting Easton's gaze and not have his hard-on flare up even more. He was struggling enough as it was. *Come on, sheep. Do your thing. One, two, three....*

He felt Easton rise.

"Royal, about tonight. In the arena—"

A shiver raced up Royal's spine. *Uh-uh. Not going there. I will not discuss it in this bed. I won't discuss it outside of my head. Nope, I'm not gonna do it, Sam-I-Am-Not. There's not a single poached green egg or slice of honey-baked ham on this plate. This isn't going to be a repeat of Sioux Falls.*

"What about Sioux Falls?" Easton asked.

"Huh?"

"You said Sioux Falls."

Shit! He'd done it again, spoken what he thought he'd only thought. He really must have been tired. Either that or he was developing a split personality.

"*Pas rien.* I ate some oysters earlier. I don't think they're sitting right with me."

Easton chuckled. "In that case, be sure to keep the covers tucked tight around you. I don't want you fumigating this room. That's not how I wish to die in my sleep. I can only imagine the epitaph: 'Gone too soon, smothered by flatulence.'"

Royal laughed in return. "Inhalation. Smothering suggests I shoved your head beneath the blanket and held it there."

"Well, isn't that just a lovely thought?" Easton relaxed on the mattress. "Forcibly gassed. That would make it premeditated instead of manslaughter." A moment of silence passed before he spoke again. "I wouldn't blame you, though. It would be the only way you beat me this year."

"You did hit your head tonight. *Dors.*"

"All right. *Bonne nuit.*"

One sheep. Two sheep. Three…

CHAPTER 11

EASTON

"No, ma'am," Royal answered the reporter. "I don't ride or train on any bull that has had hotshots or spurs used. Bucking straps are lined with fleece to prevent burns or chafing. Much care is taken not to harm these animals, which, by the way, are trained athletes. They are handled with the same respect as traditional and legitimate ranch work. They are rotated between events to allow them plenty of time to recuperate and rest, fed a healthy diet twice a day every day, and given ample space in transport trailers with dividers to reduce fighting. As with any sport, rodeos—bull riding in particular—are evolving and progressing. Not everything is perfect, but it's being worked on. Without animals, there is no rodeo. It takes years of training to get them to compete at this level. That's an enormous financial investment. Therefore, it serves no one's best interest to mistreat them."

Easton leaned against a stall railing as he watched Royal give an interview addressing protesters. Interviews had never been a favorite activity for Easton. In truth, he shied away from the microphones and cameras. However, dealing with these kinds of interviews, he wholeheartedly detested. He had spotted these protesters before they'd entered the fairgrounds and suggested they hang back for a while.

"We'll go in the back," Marcel had declared. To which Royal had huffed and marched into the den of haters. Typical Royal. It was the quality Easton admired the most about his comrade. Royal never failed to defend the things or the ones he loved. The heated and poignant questions flew at him, and unfazed, Royal responded with matched zeal, as if he'd been ready for this fight today. Perhaps he had been. All morning, he'd seemed edgier than usual. Then again, Easton shouldn't have been shocked by this. Royal hadn't slept well. Easton had felt him tossing and turning for much of the night. Something was bothering him, and Easton didn't fancy the idea that his brohan was holding back a secret. *Ack! Secret.* There was that word again. He and Royal didn't have secrets. *Well....*

"He's taking a huge risk with those reporters, don't you think?" Maddox inquired.

"How so?"

"Those protesters are looking to shut us down. One wrong word and he gives them the ammunition to do so. How come he can't ignore them like the rest of us? Why does he have to act like he's some intergalactic hero?"

Easton's expression soured. "Because that's who he is. Besides, he's leading the winner's board. Who better than him?"

"I suppose." Maddox didn't sound convinced. "It only seems unnecessary. Ignore them and they go away."

"But they won't stay away. Problems, no matter how hard or how far you try to push them down, always find a way to resurface."

I should know.

Maddox shoved his hands into the front pockets of his Wranglers. "Do you truly believe he'll get anywhere with that crowd?" He jerked his head toward the gathering assembled around Royal. "They're not here to be reasoned with or listen to alternative points of view."

"That's where you're missing the point. Royal isn't trying to change their minds and convert them into rodeo lovers. He's putting the truth out there for those who may not know. Do you have any idea how many people have only heard one side of the story? If there's only one version out there, that is what people will accept. There is no other choice."

"Again, what difference does it make if there are a thousand choices but they've already settled on one?"

Drawing in a deep breath, Easton inhaled the scents of churros, sausage, and cedar. Oddly, the motley of aromas reminded him that he was both on the road and at home—which, on second thought, seemed appropriate, since the road had practically become his home.

"When I was coming up, I used to hear about a school that was a reformatory for delinquents. All the old folks used to threaten to send us kids there when we misbehaved. The school had a reputation for having the worst of the worst students. But what no one ever talked about was the teachers or the educational program they developed. Those teachers took the time to teach those students. They asked questions and found answers. They didn't base their methods on the hearsay that the students were lost causes or a barrel of bad apples. Today, that school is known for its superior training. It's a privilege to attend. The majority of the graduates win scholarships to Ivy League colleges. That's because it was never what the rumors claimed it to be. The students weren't delinquents. They had learning disabilities that interfered with their functioning in a traditional classroom setting. Once that was realized, appropriate changes could be made. Little by little, year after year, the teachers had been releasing the stats to the public until one day, they couldn't be ignored. Rodeos don't have the prettiest of pasts. There's plenty of truth to the accusations. But just because something once was doesn't mean that it must remain that way, that it can't develop into more."

Maddox tilted his head. "Are you only talking about rodeos?"

Easton's cheeks heated. "Um...."

"These fuckers who supported slaughtering a year-old bison colt bred in captivity as part of a conservation breeding program are okay with allowing kids to watch it being skinned, hacked to pieces, and fed to tigers in the name of population control yet have a problem with me on the back of a bull. I can't stand narrow-minded folks," Royal griped, rounding an open gate. "If you don't want to know the answer, don't ask the question. Bunch of keyboard-wannabe gangsters. They'll Billy Badass in packs or behind a screen but piss themselves before saying it alone to my face."

Maddox snorted. "Yeah, well, all you did was stir the hornet's nest."

"Then it needed to be stirred," Royal quipped in return.

"For the rest of us to get stung," Maddox bit back.

"I assumed you'd be accustomed to having a little prick."

"Hey! *Sa c'est assez,*" Easton interrupted, stepping between the two men who'd both taken steps toward each other. "This isn't the place for this."

"*C'est pas ma faute.* Tell it to your new friend," Royal snapped. "He's the one who started the bull."

"I'm just calling out your attention-seeking grand-standing," Maddox retorted.

"Trust me, I get enough attention by winning."

"Oh yeah? Did what you did up there win you anything?"

"Listen, bub, there are groups that legitimately care about the treatment, welfare, and conservation of animals and do good work. I respect them. But this isn't one of those groups. They are politically moti-vated and need to be on someone's watch list."

"You're just saying that because you made matters worse. They are ten times louder now, and that's on you."

"No one's to blame," Easton interjected.

Before Easton could respond further, Royal stomped off down the midway toward two of the event promoters who alternated pointing between clipboards and empty stalls.

"*Y'ou t'es parti?*" Easton called at Royal's back.

"*A l'ouvrage.*"

"Oy."

Maddox's brow furrowed. "What did you say?"

"I asked him where he was going. Sometimes when he gets in a mood, he does something stupid."

"Imagine that," Maddox mumbled. "So, where did he say he was going?"

"To work. In other words, to do something stupid."

Maddox grunted and then shrugged. "So, do you want to hang out a bit?"

Easton didn't. He wanted to follow Royal and talk, but he'd seen that dark glint in Royal's eyes. It meant he needed time alone to decompress from whatever was agitating him. More so, Easton still felt dickish from the way he'd treated Maddox yesterday, and Maddox seemed like he could use a friend.

"Sure. I'm not busy until later. Balor asked me to meet him around four."

It would be three days before he rode again, but promoters had requested riders to come early to do PR. Now Easton understood why. This gig wasn't solely about selling tickets. It was about selling politics. He sighed. Just another day in rodeo life. Sometimes, the simplest thing he did was climb on the back of a bull.

"What do you want to do?" Easton asked.

"I saw a sign for a Supercross race. I don't know if you're into that kind of thing."

He wasn't, but it didn't mean he couldn't get into it. In the past, he'd had plenty of opportunities to attend. After all, Supercross was a sport fairly common at these types of county festivals. One night it would be concerts, the next monster trucks, and the next rodeo—anything to keep the people coming back and appealing to as many interests as possible. If protesters caused attendance to drop and interrupt cash flow, there existed a real probability that the rodeo wouldn't be invited back. The pushback wouldn't only be from local oppositional animal rights groups but also vendors who would suffer collateral damage. But from Easton's understanding, dirt bike racing was receiving some flak for safety concerns at these events too. At the very least, he could attend to show support for fellow athletes.

"Sounds like a plan," he replied, dragging his eyes away from Royal and back to his current companion. For the first time, he noticed a depth of concern in Maddox's expression. "Hey, don't let those protesters get to you."

"How can I not, and how can you remain so unconcerned?"

"It's all a part of it these days. Our profession doesn't start and stop at eight seconds in an arena. That's what the fans come for, and that's what they see. Every city has challenges, and we deal with them as they come. Sometimes, they're the same. Other times, they aren't. Some get resolved, and others not so much."

"All I want to do is ride bulls. It's all I ever wanted."

"I dare to say every rider on this tour feels that way, but that doesn't stop reality. Not everywhere we go will greet us with open arms, but we go where the promoters direct us. It's our job to keep the sponsors happy."

"Well, I'm glad it wasn't like this in Austin."

"I don't think we were any more welcomed there," Easton huffed, reflecting on his last ride and that thing in the dust.

"What do you mean?"

The memory made him queasy, and bile collected in the base of his throat. "It's nothing," he replied, shaking away the image. "Let's go find some tickets to the race."

CHAPTER 12

ROYAL

Royal climbed up and perched himself beside Marcel on the top rail of the weathered fence covered with peeling whitewash from having been painted far too many times without sanding down the chips. A refreshing breeze that brought with it the pungent scents of juniper, moist soil, and farm animals tousled the short wisps of hair peeking from beneath his hat and tickled his warm skin. He didn't have to guess why Marcel had selected this particular spot to consume his lunch. It resembled his ranch in Ville Platte.

"Where'd you get off to?" Marcel asked, squirting mustard from a packet onto his jumbo corn dog.

"I spotted a library not too far from here as we were driving in. I walked to it."

"What is it with you and libraries all of a sudden? Seems every time we get close to one these days, you're breaking your neck to get there. It's like you're obsessed."

"Now, that's a stretch."

"You don't have a card to check anything out, and you couldn't have had enough time to read any books. No one prints newspapers anymore, and everything else you see on that phone of yours. So, what's the appeal?"

Royal chuffed. "Wow! I go to a bar, and you say nothing, but I go to a place of learning and information and get the third degree. Interesting logic you got going on there. Maybe I wanted to read a nice fairy tale or research how to clone my good looks. Precious and relished stuff that is—like spinning gold. But no, you make it sound all clandestine and grim."

"Don't play me, boy. You're up to something."

Royal frowned. Marcel knew him too well, but that didn't mean Royal would admit anything.

"Paranoid much? Can't I just want to broaden my horizons?"

Marcel snorted. "Riiiight. Where's your twin?"

Royal shrugged. Everyone always expected him to know Easton's whereabouts, and he did 99 percent of the time. He could guess now, and chances were, he'd be correct—well, not about the *where* but about the *with whom*. For that reason, he didn't want to think about it. "No clue. He wasn't in the camper when I got back from visiting at the children's hospital."

"How'd that go?"

"Absolute around-the-world stupid. When Brown asked me to go with him, I had no idea he'd planned to have media there like some Publisher's Clearing House sweepstakes winner's ambush. Instead of it being about the children, it was about how many photos he could wrangle for his social media. Had I known, I never would've gone. Taking advantage of sick kids that way is shitty."

"Go a little easy on him. He's been struggling and could use some positive press."

Royal conceded with a noncommittal "Hmm" and softened his tone. "It still was shitty."

"You and that mouth. One of these days, I'm going to dunk your head in a trough and scrub your tongue with lye."

"Didn't you do that once already?"

"No, I was trying to baptize your ornery butt, but apparently, it didn't take. Rolled right off and polluted the waters. That's why eels exist today."

Royal laughed and realized it had been the first time all day that his glowering mood had lifted enough for him to find humor in anything. Tipping his head back, he closed his eyes and allowed the sun to beam on his face. A minuscule bit of tension eased in his shoulders. "Marcel, when you were competing, did you ever wonder about what you were giving up?"

"I'm not sure what you mean."

"Seeing those kids today got me thinking. We never know how much time we have with each other. You'd think doing what we do, I'd have a deep under-standing of that. I've seen people trampled into so many Humpty Dumpty pieces that Gorilla Glue can't hold them together." He spoke easily, almost offhand-edly. "So, it would make sense that we would value how precious time is and share how we feel with the people we care about, yet much of what we do and say is to make other people comfortable or satisfied. It's not necessarily the truth."

Marcel bit into his corndog and thought for a moment. "You've always been one to speak your mind. Lord knows you don't have much of a filter."

"I say what's proper for the franchise."

"What? You don't believe your own words?"

"I believe them, but it isn't all I believe."

Licking mustard from his lips, Marcel observed Royal evenly. "What are you getting at?"

"Sometimes what a person wants and the choice a person must make are at odds with each other."

"If this is about you winning the championship, you know Easton will understand the same as you would if he wins."

"No, it's not—" Royal stopped himself and pushed back the mixed emotions of making a full confession. No, he couldn't have this conversation, especially not with Marcel, who would never understand the words on the tip of Royal's tongue. Jumping jackrabbits, he struggled to have it with himself. He needed to find a balance between the warring of his logic and his emotions. Rubbing his palm over his face, he pondered when he'd become such a coward at taking a risk. *When it involves Easton, that's when. Better go along with what he's thinking.* "Yeah, you're right."

"Look, both of you boys have trained hard, and you both deserve it. But there can only be one winner."

"Now, if that doesn't sound like a line ripped from an exorbitant testosterone-riddled dystopian horror novel, I don't know what does."

His gaze bounced along the wooden fence to the end, where it abruptly stopped at a veil of trees and met barricades to prevent festivalgoers from going farther. On the other side, between branches swaying in a gentle breeze, he caught a glimpse of a small pond. The area looked peaceful. If Easton had been here, Royal would have suggested they go for a stroll the way they often did at home when they wanted to rid themselves of troubles and hopping on a bucking animal more than ten times their body weight wasn't an option. But Easton wasn't here. He hadn't been at the camper or with Upton at the practice arena. Cody hadn't seen him either. Royal had asked a half dozen people of Easton's whereabouts, and no one had seen hide nor hair. His text messages had gone unanswered, which wasn't all that unusual. Easton had a bad habit of forgetting his cell. However, what happened to be too coincidental was that Maddox was conspicuously MIA as well. The glower on his face returned.

"What do you know about that Maddox character?" Royal asked, pleased that his tone remained steady despite his eyes glinting precariously. "He seemed to have popped up out of nowhere."

"No, he's been training for a while but working mostly the smaller shows. With Bob and Frank both retiring, it opened up some spots. He's good. Consistent. Definitely someone you'll want to keep your eye on."

Oh, I'm definitely doing that.

"But I don't think he's a main concern. He can stay on, but he doesn't have much in the way of showmanship."

Royal grunted. *I'm not so sure about that.* The man positively had some sly moves—like a third weasel on Noah's Ark.

"You worry about doing what you do," Marcel continued.

"Again with the solid advice. I could've gotten that from a fucking fortune cookie."

Marcel paused midbite and scowled at Royal. "That mouth!"

Chuckling, Royal hopped off the fence. "Yeah, yeah. Lye soap. *Je va vous voir plus tard.*"

"Not if I see you first, but I hope by then you'll have a better attitude."

Royal hoped for that as well. This funk wasn't what he wanted. However, if he was honest with himself—and there was no reason for him not to be—this entire tour was jacked the hell up. He was living his dream, right? Leading the pack. Yet he couldn't say he was happy. Each day brought more melee and another pile of crap to step in. He needed a spreadsheet to keep track of the mounds of bullshit. Easton had gotten hurt. Gerald was a deadbeat, forcing Jerry to be a latchkey kid. Protesters were trying their damnedest to hurl him into the unemployment line—or the entrails of hell, whichever came first. At this point, it remained a coin toss. Supernatural elementals emerging from fucking floors. Chronically ill kids being exploited for clicks and views. And an asshole moving in on his man.

He froze in his stride at the last thought. *His man?* Not his boi but his *man*. When had he begun thinking that? And what a dangerous thought it was.

"Roy, wait up," Upton called, jogging to catch up, Cody and Wade trailing not far behind. "Didn't you hear us hollering after you?" he huffed once at Royal's side.

"Naw. My mind must have been on other things," he answered, pulling himself together.

"I'd say. You were walking a mile a minute. Where's the fire?"

"Nowhere. What's up?"

"We were about to go shoot some darts. Wanna come?"

Royal smirked. "Now, you know those balloons are underinflated to deflect the darts. It's nothing but a gamble."

"Which is why we have a pot going," Upton replied smugly. "A dollar a balloon."

"You're going to pay somebody to take your money and then pay someone else for someone taking your money?" His tone dripped with derision. "Real smart."

"If you're not afraid of losing," Upton retorted, "what difference does it make? Don't be chicken."

Placing his hand on his hips, Wade flapped his elbows and clucked like a chicken.

"If you blow all your money, I'm not spotting you supper."

"You cheap ass." Upton smirked in return. "But you don't have to worry about that because I'm going to smoke you."

"This is so dumb," Royal muttered, glancing at Wade and Cody, who were both sporting equally smug grins. He waffled between practicality and wiping the condescending smirks off his companions' faces. It was a no-brainer. "Y'all have less going on in your heads combined than the Headless Horseman, but you're on."

The gaggle ambled down the congested midway, shuffling between rowdy adolescents shoving each other for attention, cheery parents carrying sticky-fingered toddlers with dripping ice cream cones, and senior couples reliving memories of their youths. It didn't take long for the quartet to find a darting booth, and they weren't the only ones. As they approached the booth, Easton and Maddox were being handed darts. Each laughed and carried on as if neither hadn't a care in the world.

Disgust flickered across Royal's face, and his spine stiffened to the degree that he thought it might snap. He'd strongly suspected the two were together, but seeing it leveled up.

"Hold up there," Upton yelled as Easton drew his arm back to throw. He rushed up to the pair and began explaining the bet.

While Upton spoke, Royal's eyes narrowed to slits as he icily stared Maddox up and down, and his chest swelled with irrational fury. He felt his upper lip curling in a snarl to reveal his gums and his jaws clenching. *Get away from him.* Yes, Royal recognized his irrationalism. But did he care? In a word, in that moment: fuck no. Easton was his... what? His *man? No, no, no.* Damn, it was getting old and tiresome, repeating these conversations with himself. He could not afford to keep having those kinds of fantasies invade. *Fantasies? Fuck!* He'd advanced to a new echelon in a matter of minutes. *Get yourself together.*

"Where have you been?" Royal demanded, hissing between his teeth. *Shit! So much for getting it together.* Royal had intended it as a nonchalant inquiry, but it had come out sharp and pointed. He'd never been one to emulate others, but he was performing a damn good caricature of a Neanderthal. He'd failed to disguise the venom in his voice. All his companions' heads snapped toward him, and they glared at him with stupefied eyes and slack mouths.

Easton folded his arms across his chest. His voice was firm, but his eyes conveyed warmth with zero hint of hostility. "Maddox and I went to the races. You could have come, too, had you not stalked off earlier."

"We had a good time," Maddox added.

Royal's vision flashed red, crimson, scarlet, and some more shades on the Sherwin-Williams paint wheel that he didn't know the name of. *Who asked you?* Slice open the wound, and pour in a bucket of salt. He did not want to hear about Maddox and Easton's date. *Whoa! Date?* How the Nancy Drew had he made that leap? *Reel it back.* He needed a diversion—something to keep his mouth shut and mind occupied from venturing to unsanctioned places. He reached into his pocket to retrieve a few loose bills and slapped them on the booth railing, his eyes glittering with temper and his lips harboring a pout. "Give me what that pays for," he directed the festival worker. "I need to show these skinny boys what a dispensary of whoop-ass feels like."

"Oh, you think so?" Easton questioned, his easy tone returning. A crafty smile curled the corners of his mouth. "Let's see what ya got, *sha*."

The festival worker set twelve darts in front of Royal and stepped out of the throwing path. Royal selected a dart and rolled the brass barrel between his fingers, measuring for weight. "Prepare to be cremated."

As expected, the dart was light with a dull tip and long shaft. The odds weren't in his favor—about five thousand to one on a good day, but he'd gotten himself into this pissing-on-an-electric-fence contest, and there was only one way out. He focused on a red balloon, envisioning it as Maddox's face, and released his shot. The dart made contact, but the balloon only bobbled.

Figures. Deceptions always hung around longer than they were wanted.

He released a windy sigh, deflated but still determined. Yep, he was bound to be out of a lot of money before the night's end.

EASTON

"Uh-huh, uh-huh! Who's the man?" Wade sang, dancing a slaphappy jig while hoisting a hulking neon toucan over his head.

"Not you," Royal replied, his expression somewhere between "I hate you right now," "You're an idiot," and "I'm going to hurt you if you don't stop playing in my face."

"Hater," Wade chuckled, lowering the stuffed animal but still swaying from side to side. "I'm the man. I'm the man."

Easton interrupted Wade's gloating. "Dude, you won by default."

Wade puckered his lips. "Of course you would take his side." He jerked his head in Royal's direction. "A win's a win."

True, but in this instance, Easton wholeheartedly

agreed with his ride-or-die. All of them had bombed at darts. Those balloons weren't going anywhere except in the opposite direction of the dart. The slightest breeze from the incoming miniature missiles had the inflatables bobbing north, south, east, and west, and the janky darts wouldn't fly in a straight line if straight was the only path that existed.

That had been okay with Easton because it meant they all would go home with egg on their faces—equal-opportunity humiliation. He couldn't think of a better way to waste thirty bucks than knowing his friends had been suckered as much as he had. Plus, the carny worker had made a small fortune from them. While Easton didn't treasure parting with money, he also appreciated how difficult it was for some of the game vendors to make a living. They could go for days or weeks without a single customer. Of course, Easton didn't know this worker's situation, but it didn't matter. He and his friends had been able to work off some energy while managing a kaka and a ki ki.

Well, almost everyone.

Royal and Maddox had ended up in some twisted, ostentatious competition that transcended the actual game. Yeah, they had played along with everyone else, but they only seemed to have wanted to compete with each other. Then the unthinkable occurred.

Easton had never witnessed anything like it, and he'd participated in more than his fair share of dart games. What had become a type of lightning round had been like the scene from the movie *Ghostbusters* when the main characters—spoiler—crossed their streams to take down the Stay Puft Marshmallow Man. Royal and Maddox had released their darts at the same time, aiming at different targets. Both projectiles veered off their trajectory path, collided, and wedged on either side of the same balloon, stabilizing it, which allowed Wade's throw a half second later to burst it. Thus, in their quest to best each other, they had bested themselves and allowed Wade to sneak in the winning throw. The only thing that had been more comical than everyone's mouth gaping open to catch flies had been Royal's sputter of obscenities and hand gestures. His look of disbelief crumpled Easton over in stitches.

But now, as they walked, Royal had grown silent, his eyes distant as if he was lost in thought.

What are you thinking?

The crowd had grown noticeably thicker. Easton wondered if it was due to people getting off work or if there was a big attraction happening.

"Let's go in here," Maddox suggested, stopping in front of a grayish tent.

"In there?" Easton asked, raising a brow.

"Sure, why not?" Maddox continued.

"Because," Upton argued, "some of these folks be messing with stuff they don't know."

"C'mon," Maddox countered. "It's just for laughs."

Unable to determine if the tent's coloring was due to age or mildew, Easton focused on the plastic double-sided foldable signboard of a palm with an Eye of Ra in the center. A Hamsa hand, he believed it was called. Or maybe not. He wasn't well-versed in those sorts of things. For some reason, the sign reminded him of the classic *Sinbad* movies of the 1970s.

"I don't know," he hedged. "I have to be at the pavilion soon."

"You've got plenty of time," Maddox rebutted.

"Well, okay," Easton caved. "But we can't stay long."

"Have you gone stupid?" Upton piped up, his mouth twisting in odd angles. "Marcel will slap you naked and hide all your damn clothes if he finds out you've been messing around with a fortune teller."

Probably.

"Who's going to tell him?" Maddox challenged.

Easton answered. "No one, because you're going in too." He jabbed his index finger on his cousin's chest.

"Oh no." Upton vehemently shook his head. "I'm having no part of this."

Easton turned his focus to Royal, who'd remained silent.

Royal held up his hands. "Don't look at me. It's your funeral."

"Yours too. Either Nonc won't believe you watched me go alone and will slaughter you, or he'll snuff you because you did. Either way, you're gourmet worm food." Easton began walking toward the tent opening.

"Shit," Royal muttered, grabbing Upton by the arm.

"What are you doing?" Upton protested, attempting to snatch his arm from Royal's grip.

"You know how *Titanic* ends. You're part of the band. Now let's go."

"But I don't want to be Jack," Upton whined.

"Jack wasn't part of the band," Easton clarified.

"So? Who gives a shit? He still became a floating frozen sardine popsicle for the humpbacks."

Royal gave him another tug. "Bring your ass on."

"We're doing this?" Cody asked, following Upton. "We're *really* doing this?"

"Quit ya bellyaching, Miss Celie," Royal replied. "You bet not tell nobody but God."

Upton shook his head. "This is such a bad idea. I mean, the worst. See, this right here is how Stephen King novels begin."

"I can't believe what a bunch of pussies you all are being," Maddox chastised, pushing aside the canvas at the entrance. "What can happen?"

Royal grunted. "Does that question ever have a positive answer? We're not about to play ring-around-the-rosy or whoever going under the mulberry bush."

Easton had no time to contemplate a response. The smells of sweet tobacco, incense, and Irish whiskey immediately drew his attention. The inner tent canvas was covered with colorful fabrics and scarves. Sparkly beads and gems dangled from the top. In the center of the area was a round wood table festooned with luminescent crystals, baubles with the icy shimmer of diamonds, and what looked to be handmade candles. Around the perimeter of the room were long tables covered with trinkets and crushed dried flowers stuffed into glass bottles for sale. At the rear of the tent was a second opening. Beside it was a life-sized resin Khmer-style seated Buddha teaching mudra. Smoke drifted from its lap to the top of the tent. A middle-aged woman wearing a maxi dress and bangles up to her elbows on both arms suddenly appeared at the entrance.

"I see I've drawn a crowd." Her tone was casual and her voice pleasant. "Lots of energy in this room."

"And body funk," Royal mumbled under his breath.

Easton rolled his lips inward to keep from laughing.

"We've come for—" Maddox began.

"I know why you've come." The fortune teller walked slowly in front of them and looked each of them over from head to toe as she passed. She stopped in front of Easton, closed her eyes, moved her hands around either side of his head, and hummed. "I'll take you first."

"No," he protested and pointed at Maddox. "He—"

"You," she snapped. "You need me more."

Easton would have laughed, but there was nothing humorous in the woman's stare. "O-Okay."

"Come." She headed toward the second entry.

Easton followed, second-guessing each step. He shouldn't be here. What had he been thinking?

Royal followed, but the fortune teller stopped him at the second entrance and lowered her voice. "Don't worry. I won't do that. That has been assigned to you."

Royal nodded and took a step back.

What the hell?

The inner area was much cooler and darker than the previous one. The table in the center was much smaller and draped with purple linen edged in gold lace. A smaller and shorter table cluttered with an array of objects was positioned beside it.

"Sit," the fortune teller instructed, gesturing to a metal folding chair.

Why am I doing this? Obediently, he plopped down in the chair.

The fortune teller extended her hands, which were patterned with henna and looked too wrinkled for her age, palms up over the table. Understanding, Easton placed his hands on hers. She began by inspecting the back sides of his hands. She flipped them both over multiple times, running her finger along his thumbs and pressing at the tips before releasing her grip. Her head jerked backward sharply as if she'd been punched by a phantom hand, and her eyes glowed with a fierce repudiation. Observing Easton's astounded expression, she smiled wryly. "No, this will not do." She turned to her right and tapped a carved wooden box that had a brass handle.

Easton strained to see the box that was partially obstructed from his view by a stack of rolled astrological charts. The engravings on the box looked to be ancient rune symbols. But what did he know? They could have been cat claw marks.

The fortune teller lifted the top, revealing a turquoise lining with a pink satin pillow nestled in the bottom. Atop the pillow was a stack of worn tarot cards that she removed and slapped onto the table.

"Take them," she ordered, nodding at the cards. "Put your nondominant hand on the bottom and your dominant hand on the top and shuffle them. Once you're satisfied, cut the deck into three sections, and then restack them in any order you want."

The majority of his brain once again told him to walk away, but something else kept him planted in the metal chair that wobbled and creaked each time he moved. He paused briefly before doing as instructed.

After hovering her hand in a clockwise motion over the deck, the fortune teller lifted the cards one by one and placed them face down on the table in a pattern. The first card she placed vertically and the second horizontally across it. The next went below and another to the left. Easton watched, mesmerized, as she peeled each card from the top of the deck and positioned it on the table, her bangles clacking rhythmically. In total, she placed ten cards. She pointed at the center card, the first she'd placed. "This represents you," she said, flipping it. "Two of Cups."

He had no idea of the significance but nodded anyway.

She flipped the horizontal card and paused. "Hmm."

Hmm? What do you mean, "Hmm"? What's hmm? He stared at the image that looked to be a cross between Adam and Eve in the Garden of Eden, Botticelli's *Birth of Venus*, and Michelangelo's *David*.

"The Lovers," she finally stated. "This is what crosses you."

"I—"

"Shh." She flipped another card. "The Five of Wands. Inverted." She peered up at him without raising her head. "You have someone in your life who you care about very much, but you're conflicted."

The tiny hairs on Easton's arms began to stand.

She continued. "Two of Wands. Inverted Ten of Swords. Death."

"Holy shit! I'm going to die?"

"We all are, honey. Someday. Calm yourself."

Calm? How can I be calm? I'm going to die.

"The Death card doesn't always mean literal death. From what I'm seeing so far, it doesn't look like it this time either. Often, it means a change or an ending—possibly to a relationship or friendship. However, you're also entering a new season." She tapped one of the cards. "Trauma. Looks like you've been hurt... recently, and you're not healed. You're out of sorts, and it's affecting your emotional availability to others." She flipped another card and made a soft tsking sound. "Queen of Cups. Inverted. So much self-doubt and feelings of vulnerability. I think.... No, let's see." She flipped the remainder of the cards, reared back in her chair, and studied the entire spread. "The Two of Cups," she said, pointing back to the first card, "indicates that you have someone in your life who balances you, your equal, but.... Hmm."

"What? What is it? Why do you keep saying that?" Easton had scooted to the edge of his chair, and both his legs bounced restlessly.

"I sense you're hiding part of yourself, and that's causing a division. It seems that you're at a crossroads, and you need to decide whether you want to move forward and follow your intuition or allow other forces to hold you back and detain your growth. Choosing what you feel isn't going to please everyone. You will lose something important. It will be painful—like being hit by a freight train—but you can't allow fear to continue to be your cloak and hide in the midnight shadows. There will be new people and opportunities at another station. Some you may already have encountered, but they'll get on board if you allow them a ticket."

Easton rubbed his hand along the rear of his neck, smoothing the hairs that were now standing up there as well, and frowned. "You just said a whole bunch of words and nothing at the same time. What does any of what you said mean?"

"Oh, I think you know deep down. You not taking action may be destructive." She retrieved a pewter vase from the side table, removed the lid, and held it in front of him. "Put your money in the offering vessel."

He started at the vase that looked more like an urn. *It's a vessel, all right.* "How much is it?"

She told him the price, and he paid, adding a tip. Why the tip? He didn't know. She hadn't told him anything that he wanted to hear. Had she told him anything that he hadn't known? Had she clarified the situation? Had he even been entertained?

He stood to leave.

"Send in your friend—the one with the centuries-old reincarnated soul."

Reincarnated soul? Well, she can't be talking about Upton, and I doubt she means Maddox. Wade barely has any soul. Dude can't dance worth a lick and amasses enough static energy crossing a carpeted floor to fry anything inside him to a pork skin crackling. Cody? Naw.

Cody's wife wouldn't be having any reincarnation bullshit. If she thought for one second that anyone other than Cody was crawling in bed with her, there would have been a WWE smackdown a long time ago.

His process of elimination left one person: Royal.

He exited to the outer area, where the air not only felt warmer but cleaner, yet he shivered. Only Royal remained.

"Where is everyone?"

"Just outside." Royal nodded toward the tent opening. "The cell reception isn't good in here, and Upton wanted to livestream his last will and testament—or testimony, as he called it."

"Why aren't you with them?"

"Who do I want to talk to on the phone?"

"Cinderella's ugly stepsister? I don't kn—" He stopped his protest. There was more to this story, but there wasn't time to explain if everyone was going to have a turn before his call time at the pavilion. "She wants to see you next."

"I bet she does. What did she say to you?"

"I have to buy an Amtrak ticket."

"*Quoi?*" Royal cocked his head as if he'd suddenly pulled a muscle. "To where?"

"Georgia, I guess." He jerked his thumb toward the entrance to the inner area. "Go on. She's waiting for you."

CHAPTER 14
ROYAL

His turn. A rash of goose bumps spread down Royal's arms, and his palms grew clammy. He didn't fancy a turn, but he had to—not because he agreed to it but because he'd spent the last fifteen minutes trying to hear what the witch—yes, witch—was saying to Easton. His intentions weren't to be disrespectful, but he knew what she was. And she knew he knew. He'd sensed it the instance he'd crossed the threshold, even before he saw the otherworldly shadows reflecting in her eyes or the apotropaic hexafoil-shaped birthmark peeking from beneath the tumble-tangle of long curls that once had a luster.

While Easton had been inside, Royal had lingered at the second entrance and strained to hear the conversation. However, a persistent low tinnitus—perhaps from a radio, but it had sounded eerily like keening—rendered their words incomprehensible. Even after kicking his companions out of the tent so he could better eavesdrop, he hadn't been able to decipher a single word. He'd heard the muffled voices but nothing distinct. He needed answers.

No use wasting time. He slipped between the part in the canvas and marched to the vacant chair across from the witch, his shuffling and stealthy steps scuffing the matted tall fescue. The succulent smell of earth mingled with other scents, and an odd sense of déjà vu erupted. In response, a warm tingling sensation fizzled across his skin like a fine sheen of sweat as his eyes settled on her. Folding his arms across his chest, he sat. He'd neither the inclination nor the patience for idle chat.

"All right," he demanded. "Tell me."

The witch's lips twitched and curled slightly at the corners.

HE WANDERED OUT OF THE INNER AREA——THE WITCH'S LAIR —swimming in an ocean of dark emotions and massaged the rear of his neck where tension had roosted. Not that her words had comforted him—in truth he could argue that they'd been troublesome— but at least he now knew, had affirmation. However, had he needed confirmation? And at what cost? His energy felt drained. He shouldn't have allowed her to touch him, permitted her ring-spangled fingers to rub over his palms. That was a gateway opening, how one allowed iniquitousness to absorb into the skin like a disease and became a vessel to—

Or maybe none of it was true. Practiced witches could conjure false images and cause people to see, hear, and believe things that weren't real. They could, when it suited them, employ a more flexible approach to reality with a gaslit justification. Disgust flickered across his face.

"Hey," Wade said, drawing Royal out of his thoughts. "Why such a forlorn face? She tell you how ugly your wife is going to be or something?"

His companions laughed, and Royal attempted to muster a smile. However, his facial muscles felt too tired to expand or contract, and he managed what he presupposed was an emotionally detached expression. His entire body sagged, drained and fatigued. He longed to curl onto a mattress and sleep, to recuperate.

"Naw, he looks spooked to me," Maddox chirped, accompanied with a glib smirk and a condescending gleam. "Did the little old lady who lives in a shoe tent scare you?"

Burrowing maggot!

Royal parted his lips to give Maddox a piece of his mind, but his ringing cell phone preempted it. He wasn't in a talking mood and would have ignored it.

However, he'd reserved that ringtone for his mother, and she rarely called. *Screw him.* He grimaced, stepped away from the group, and swiped his screen.

"*Que se passe-t-il?*" he answered as a greeting.

"*Pas rien,* sweet pea. I'm calling to ask you."

"Nothing's wrong, Duchess."

"Are you sure?" she asked in a motherly voice that reminded him how much he missed her. "I was in the garden, finally getting around to planting some okra, when suddenly there was a gust of wind. In with it rolled a smell sort of like but not quite the cherry tobacco you and Easton used to sneak out back and smoke that you thought I didn't know about." She chuckled softly. "It was sweet but not exactly pleasant. Familiar in a way. The more I walked, the stronger the smell got. I followed it down the path toward the bayou. Did you know half of the stepping stones have sunk?" She didn't pause long enough for him to answer. "And the broom sedge has taken over. But anyway, I followed the scent to the bench you built in woodshop, and my heart nearly stopped. A pair of your riding gloves was lying on top, unmoving by the breeze. Why, I was out there yesterday, and I didn't see anything on that bench. But there they were, folded nice and neat. I figured there had to be a reason I'd see them now."

Every pore on Royal's skin twinged as if they'd been debrided with steel wool, and his entire body tightened. Spooked? Yep. His mother wouldn't fabricate such a story if it wasn't true. Words rolled and stuck to the edge of his tongue with the spiky sensation of an unpeeled kiwi. He couldn't speak them— not those words.

"Naw, I'm fine. Everyone's fine."

He didn't consider this a lie—merely a skirting around an abbreviated dissemination of all factors. Physically, he was healthy. Fact. His mental state, on the other hand, was sketch, but he needn't include it to answer a broad open-to-interpretation question. His mother hadn't specified that she meant mental health too. Plus, Easton wasn't fine. Royal knew this, but Easton had proclaimed to be. Therefore, Royal needed—at this moment, at least—to accept Easton's statement at face value. Oh, these tangled damn webs. The bottom line was, Royal couldn't worry his mother. He wouldn't.

"Maybe a bit anxious about riding tomorrow night," he continued. That part was 100 percent true. "But it's always like that. Marcel always says a little bit of nerves is a good thing. It keeps us aware, allows us not to become complacent or overconfident. It keeps us safe."

"Marcel still taking good care of you, then?"

"Oh, yes, ma'am. He rations us processed food and water barely needing iodine tablets and sometimes even beats us with a belt instead of the horsewhip."

His mother laughed. "You cheeky thing. I don't know where you get it from. Certainly not me."

Rolling in his lower lip, he sighed. "Perhaps the other half of my DNA." A nervousness churned in his stomach as a beat of silence passed.

She emitted a noncommittal "Hmm" before speaking in a polite and creamy tone that masked a slight coolness. "Perhaps. Back in my day, we didn't learn a lot about genetics in biology, but from what I remember, DNA is like a church collection plate. Each of your relatives puts something in. By the time it gets to the end of the row, it's full and it doesn't matter who added what. It all goes to pay for the church."

That was his cue to drop the subject and move on. This wasn't a hill he was willing to die on—at least not today. His eyes smoldered with regret. "*Oui*, Duchess. You said you were planting okra. Planning a big garden this year?"

"Not much. Just some cabbage and collards, and maybe some tomatoes and corn. The peppers look like they're trying to come back from last year. Food is so expensive these days, and you never know what they're putting in it. This garden gives me a small peace of mind."

"Well, I'm happy you have something to keep you busy. I know how much you enjoy yardwork."

"You know what I enjoy more?"

"What's that?"

"Hearing my baby's voice."

Royal smiled. *"Je t'aime, aussi,* Duchess." He concluded his conversation with his mother and returned to the group.

"How's Salethia?" Easton's inquired. "Everything okay?"

"Yeah. Sure."

"You don't sound sure. She's not worse, is she?"

"No, nothing like that. She—"

"Hey, what's that?" Upton interrupted.

Fucking rude. "What's what?" Royal replied.

"That in your hand."

Royal glanced at the folded pages that had been shoved into his hand by the witch as he'd exited her tent, and a hot flush splintered from his chest to his face, neck, shoulders, and back. He'd forgotten about that. Well, not so much forgotten as had been distracted.

"Uh... nothing."

"Aw, did your girlfriend write you a love letter?" Upton sang as he attempted to snatch the papers from Royal. "Let's have a look."

"J'ai dit que ce n'était rien," Royal growled, his voice deeper than usual and tone infused with wrath.

"Whoa, dude." Upton took a step back and threw his hands up in surrender. "It's not that serious. Simmer down."

Easton raised a brow. "Roy, are you sure everything's okay?"

Of course it isn't.

"*Oui*, I'm just tired. Sorry, Upton." He stuffed the pages in his pocket. *Out of sight, out of mind, right?*

"No probs."

Only, there were probs, starting with the way Easton was staring at him. Royal needed to smooth this over.

"By the way, Cody," Royal stated, changing the subject, "it's your turn. But don't take all day. We need to get moving if Easton's going to make it to the pavilion on time."

Cody shook his head but stalked toward the tent. "You better be glad that blood is thicker than water. I swear, East, if we weren't related and I didn't think I was in your will, there's no way in hell I'd do this."

Dude, you have no idea.

CHAPTER 15
EASTON

Despite more than a decade of friendship, sometimes Easton didn't know what to make of Royal's moods. Total enigmas. While he was left pondering at the moment, he knew something was off—very off—this afternoon. However, he couldn't put all the blame on Royal. He felt off too. It wasn't like he hadn't had off days in the past—although this felt different—but previously he'd been able to talk to Royal about it. He could talk to Royal about anything... except this. When had that started? Him not being able to confide in Royal? It was another question that required answering but something he'd have to sort through later. *Showtime.*

Easton slapped on a plastic smile that he hoped passed muster and didn't make him appear too goofy and stepped onto the podium, the camera lights nearly blinding. He paused to allow the photographers to his right to snap a few shots before turning to his left. *Fulfill the duty.* He counted to ten and then took his seat at the judges' table. Out of all of the promotional events he'd been asked to participate in, this was hands down the most uncomfortable and absurd.

Balor Adder, one of the tour's promoters, had warned them all that this stop would be unconventional. However, even in the most remote regions of his imagination, Easton wouldn't have ever guessed that Balor would assign him to be a judge in a beauty pageant of all things. Easton hadn't been aware that beauty contests even existed anymore. Correction. He'd been instructed by Balor to refer to it as a talent competition, but Easton didn't constitute strutting down a makeshift catwalk in five-inch heels and a string bikini as talent. Then again, he'd never attempted to walk in stilettos. He had to admit, it did look a bit daunting. However, that was neither here nor there. While four of his other tour companions delighted in the opportunity to be judges, having gleefully slapped one another on the back and made more than one inappropriate comment, Easton couldn't help feeling icky about it. Sure, if the pageant contained a bona fide talent segment, Easton would have felt better about it. But the *talent* portion consisted of a group line dance in Daisy Dukes and colorful tank tops. The only thing missing was a water hose. And that would have been okey dokey if that had been all there was to it. Of course it wasn't.

What disturbed Easton the most was that he'd gotten wind that some of the participants were as young as sixteen. What parent would allow grown men to rate their teenage daughter in a bikini? Who? Why? The whole thing felt gross. To boot, the prize for winning would barely cover the cost of a burger and fries at the festival.

Easton looked at the audience with disgust. Where were the protesters now? Why was no one saying anything about this?

Glancing over his shoulder, he spotted Royal standing on a landing and watching. He bore an equally appalled expression, and Easton felt a need to apologize. Royal's intentions had been to return to the RV and take a nap. He'd changed his mind and only had come to be Easton's moral support after all the pig, cattle, and horse manure hit the industrial fan with Balor.

"You're going to love this," Balor had proclaimed, chewing on the end of a fat cigar. "Everyone does. It's a town favorite, the highlight of the festival."

"No. This has nothing to do with bull riding. I'm not doing this, Balor."

"Now, Easton, don't be unreasonable. It's wholesome, clean fun."

"How is it wholesome? Look at what they're wearing!" Easton waved a flyer that had been attached to the door of the judges' check-in booth. "Hand them a tray with a malt liquor and it's a titty bar. Look, the decision for anyone who wishes to participate is theirs to make." He waved his hands. "Knock yourself out. But I shouldn't be compelled to make an unethical choice about something that isn't morally in line with my values."

"Morally in line? This hasn't anything to do with morality. No one's dying. That's what's wrong with you young people these days. You're too sensitive. I don't want to pull rank here, but...."

Hosh-ah-fee, hosh-ah-fee, hosh-ah-fee...

From that point onward, Easton had tuned out. However, he must have had one of *those* expressions on his face, because Royal stepped in then to do the heavy lifting by having a conversation with Balor and the other promoters. It had been all in vain, though. A diametrically opposed chasm between what promoters considered acceptable as to what Easton found copacetic remained worlds apart. He had been set to bow out but decided against it after Balor had made it clear that the pageant was supported by local businesses. If the pageant didn't occur, all donations and sponsorship funds would have to be refunded, which, in turn, would mean the festival couldn't break even. Therefore, the festival would close immediately. For some families, the festival was their source of income that would allow them to survive during the winter. They needed this pageant. Thus, his participation was needed for the greater good. The ick factor was smeared all over this.

Easton couldn't explain why, but for whatever reason, Balor insisted Easton be a judge. It made no sense. Easton had never expressed any indication that he'd be interested in this sort of thing. Yet here they were. Balor then had uttered some drivel of an excuse that a substitute judge couldn't replace him since Easton's name had been used in advertising. It sounded like gobbledygook bullshit to Easton, and he didn't understand how his agent had dropped the ball, screwed the pooch, and allowed this to slither past. Who thought he would be on board with this? He questioned if promoters would rather shut down the festival than allow someone to take his place. That's when he'd consulted Royal, and Royal had seemed nervous.

"I don't know if we can risk it," Royal had said. "Balor's being a real hard-ass. We agreed to promoting, and Balor is sliding this under the guise of a promotional event. But if you want to refuse, I got your back."

Of course he did. There was never any question about it. No matter what type of disagreements they had, at the end of the day, Royal was always there for him. Whatever snit Royal had been in earlier, Easton had witnessed it disappear the instant he'd been informed of the assignment.

Oh yeah, Balor had been wise not to inform him in advance of the specifics of the itinerary.

This town! Easton shook his head.

Technically, no laws were being broken. Being hypocritical—to proclaim to fight for animal rights but not human rights—wasn't illegal. All participants —reportedly—were consenting, and no one was being steered around on dog leads. An entire town openly cosigned a misogynistic culture of silence and disguised it as some customary artistic expression—a method of hiding in plain sight. The mayor along with the city's aldermen, supervisors, sheriff, and chief of police were all in attendance, sitting a couple of hundred feet from him. There was no one to complain to and nothing to be done. And even if there had been, in a few days, Easton would be long gone. Who would follow up? Besides, it seemed to be a paradox of power. The more he pushed, the harder the promoters would push back. There was no way to win.

The best he could do was to get through it because it was his job—at least for the time being. Grin and bear it, as the idiom went. He planned to keep his eyes on his score sheet and look up as little as possible. Then he would not think or speak of it again. This fight ended here tonight.

A twinge of nerves coiled like barbwire in his

stomach, and he glanced at Royal for an extra dose of reassurance. His tentative scrutiny was met with a nod. The small gesture caused a calm to begin spreading through him.

Soon, music began pouring from overhead speakers, and a line of contestants filed onto the stage. Thankfully, they were covered in tasteful—well, mostly tasteful—costumes. The featherless ostrich costume was a bit strange, and the jar of wax costume, he didn't get in the least. Other than that, they were all fine. Many of the contestants winked and blew kisses at him and the other judges to entice additional points. Little did they know, he deducted for such behavior. He knew he should be at least a little turned on, but everything in him remained flatlined.

However, that hadn't been the case last night in bed, had it? In effect, thinking about it now stirred…. *No, no, no. Not again.* He shifted in his chair. And that was the real problem, wasn't it?

"Who doesn't like looking at pretty girls?" Balor had chastised almost accusingly.

The question transported Easton to his grammar school days when a helmet had been crammed on his cranium and his body shoved onto a peewee football field. "Oh, look at how cute," football moms had crooned.

How cute indeed. Easton huffed at the memory. He'd been scrawny then, his protective pads weighing nearly as much as his body. The other players had dwarfed him. His first play in, he'd been tackled so hard—because even at that age, flag football wasn't a thing in the South—that for a brief moment, his world went black. It wasn't because he'd been knocked unconscious. No, that would have been merciful. In that scenario, he would have been carted off with "Awws" and "Poor dears" by the onlooking mothers and fed ice cream for his troubles. But that wasn't what had happened. No, he'd tumbled right off the field and rolled under the draped water stand on the sideline where the chinch bugs, cutworms, and boll weevils were hiding. The impact had tipped the table over, and Easton was left looking like the Wicked Witch of the East after meeting her demise with a farmhouse. Only his cleats and striped tube socks had been visible. Needless to say, the coach benched him. That was when the real humiliation began.

Due to the compact area, Easton had been forced to sit on the bench behind the cheerleaders for the duration of the game. "Who dat talkin' 'bout beating those giants? Who dat? Who dat?" It had been one of three cheers the squad had learned. Over and over, Easton had had to endure listening to the chirping voicers chanting the cheer. For the next twenty-eight minutes that felt like a lifetime to a seven-year-old, he'd had rustling pom-poms and flapping pleated skirts waggling in his face.

After the game, his father had clamped his huge hand on Easton's shoulder and grumbled, "Well, at least you got to watch some pretty girls, eh? Wasn't that fun?"

No! Just as he didn't find his current situation appealing. *Who dat indeed, Balor?*

Even if it could be proven that every pageant contestant was of legal age, Easton wouldn't have enjoyed watching them. If he dug a little deeper—which he didn't relish doing—there were aspects in his life that he never thought about, or rather, never allowed himself to consider. Why had he never had a girlfriend? Dates, sure, but never a girlfriend. Why? His standby answer was that he was focused on training and his career. He didn't have the time. But was that the truth?

If he lied to himself, he could make it the truth.

How could he get to his age and not question? Because in a lot of ways, the excuses he deluded himself with were true. He had focused on training and his career. Hours were spent working on ranches and riding mechanical bulls. He had plenty that kept him more than busy. It was easy to hoodwink himself and selectively ignore any contrary evidence. Plus, when he spent nearly every waking moment with a person who got him and was his other half, what need was there for him to want more? His life was full. He didn't have to think about certain things, didn't have to question. Didn't have to look any deeper than surface level. But if he did, he'd have to admit that he didn't have time for a girlfriend because he didn't make the time for one. What's more, he had never wanted to.

As the participants paraded around the stage, doing pirouettes and fouettés, Easton reflected on how he'd gotten to this emotional stage. When had the circumstances changed between him and Royal? If he'd been marched in front of a firing squad and told to answer to save his life, he would have been riddled with bullets. He contemplated for another moment. Perhaps the *when* didn't matter. Perhaps the *why* didn't matter either. Maybe it was an issue of mindfulness where he needed to transcend attempting to analyze his thoughts and simply go with them without question. Because frankly, trying to understand it was getting old. He continuously hit the same walls. Origins could possibly be overrated. He didn't remember learning how to walk or speak, yet he had. Not remembering hadn't affected his language or mobility. But then...

One afternoon, a normal day like so many others and much like today, he'd noticed for no reason at all. Hot and tired from cleaning stables, he and Royal needed to clean themselves up before entering Marcel's kitchen for lunch. As always, they strolled to the side of the barn to use the water hose to rinse away the grime and some of the stench. Royal had peeled off his sweaty T-shirt, revealing bronze skin and rippling muscles like a Michelangelo sculpture, only with a much bigger cock and gleaming with sweat.

At that moment, Wade, who'd also come up from Maringouin to work on the ranch, snatched Easton by the arm, nearly dragging him off balance. "What are you doing?" He'd sneered.

Startled, Easton had grown pale, his voice shaky. "*Quoi?* What are you talking about? I'm going in for lunch."

"You were staring." He'd jerked his head toward Royal, who was bent over with his back to the pair, water dashing over his head from the hose.

From the splashing of the water and the passing tractor, Easton assumed Royal didn't hear Wade's accusation, as he never turned around.

"I wasn't," Easton had denied.

"It sure looked as if you were. You'd better be careful, or people will start to think you're some kind of weirdo."

That evening, he'd asked Jolie Troye to the movies. She'd squealed in acceptance. He'd taken her to the movies and the Dairy Barn after, where they'd ordered vanilla shakes and cheeseburgers. Most ranchers went there on dates. Royal had been there with some delectable cutie on his arm whose name Easton hadn't bothered to ask. He'd purposefully not glanced in

Royal's direction, draped his arm around Jolie, and leaned in close. He'd done all the right things, all the things he was supposed to do. He'd even kissed Jolie, for what it was worth. He'd shown the world, fooled everyone—including himself.

Easton had rammed that memory down and slung it into the vault of repressed memories. Now Balor's words had it lurching, clawing its way to the surface.

I won't do this. Not today. Not now. It was nothing.

"Those were some hot babes," Wade commented on their way out of the pavilion. "That number twelve had a nice ass."

Easton shrugged, unable—or rather, unwilling—to respond and thankful the ordeal had ended. He hadn't been gawking at any asses. His intention had been to vote for the contestant who looked the most mature. However, with the teased hair, pounds of makeup, and padded pushups, they all had looked midtwenties plus. *Eeny, meeny, miny, moe.* As fate would have it, the last contestant—Statue of Liberty costume—gave a riveting answer to a rather mundane and ignorant interview question and spoke of a desire to become a mechanic. Her response hadn't won huge cheers from the audience, but it had seemed honest, unlike the others who indicated desires to be models or would donate their salaries to the conservation of mosquitos or some wacko armadillo droppings. He voted his conscience, and that was all he could have done. Now he was going to—

"Look, they have barbecue," Maddox chirped.

"They always have barbecue," Royal uttered, squinting against the fading sun. He raised his hand and motioned to someone down the midway. "What festival do you know doesn't?"

Easton shielded his eyes with his hand and peered to see who Royal was signaling. A teenage boy trotted toward them.

"The one in L.A. didn't," Cody offered.

"That wasn't a festival. That was a...." Upton waved his hands as if air-drying them. "Well, I don't know what exactly it was, but it wasn't a festival, that's for damn sure."

"It's their version. They do it differently out west," Brown chimed in.

The teenager joined the group, and Royal stared at the paper tray he was holding. "What in tarnation is that abomination?" Royal's face twisted as if gnats were swarming his space.

"Crunchy cheese chips with ranch dip, chili, sweet relish, anchovies, and green olives."

Cody contorted as if he were nauseous. "Do the what to the what?"

The expression on Royal's face eased only the tiniest bit. "That better not be your supper. Is it?"

"Looks like an emergency-room disaster if you ask me," Brown added, pressing his palm against his chest as if making a pledge and puffing out his cheeks.

"It was the shortest line. No wait."

"I can see why," Cody mumbled.

Shaking his head, Royal took the food and tossed it in a nearby trash can. "Uh-uh. You're coming with us."

"But I have to get back to the animals. I only have thirty minutes."

"You'd be better off eating wood chips than that crap. You'll go back after you consume something halfway decent or at least FDA-approved," Royal stated authoritatively.

"But—"

"Listen, that right there?" Royal pointed at the discarded food. "That is going to require some home-owner's insurance for when you blow out a toilet a mile high. Mark one that Kaopectate can't fix. Don't worry. I'll explain it to whoever needs it explained to when you go back."

Easton arched his brow at the tone. Granted, Royal always had been good with non-adults, but he preferred to spend his time with people of drinking age—something about children being a poor emotional investment.

The boy's eyes, clouded with uncertainty, met Easton's.

Easton smiled. "Yeah, we're about to choke down some Arkansas barbecue."

"We're in Oklahoma," Royal corrected.

"Are we?"

"*Oui*." Royal paused. "I think."

"This is Kansas," Wade said. "Arkansas City."

"That's what I said," Easton clarified. "Arkansas."

Wade shook his head. "Not the state. The city."

"That's all fine," Cody interjected, "but we're in Kansas City."

"So, *I* was right," Wade replied, pointing a finger at himself. "Kansas."

Cody shook his head. "No. Missouri."

"Oh, for fuck's sake!" Royal blew out a frustrated breath. "Does anyone know where the corn nuts we are?"

Brown grunted. "Does it matter? They all begin to look the same after a while."

"Careful," Cody warned. "That almost sounds like burnout."

"Naw, my flame's not going out until after I do Barretos."

"What's Barretos?" Maddox asked.

"Only the largest and toughest rodeo in the world," the teen answered.

"And you call yourself a cowboy?" Royal snorted,

the veneer of any semblance of civility having vacated his tone. "Even the kid knows. But then again, it's only for *real* men."

Shots fired.

Maddox's lips pressed into a hard line. "Oh really? Have you done it?" His voice oozed with cynicism.

This is getting heated. Easton sensed more than witnessed the self-control Royal was exercising over his own temper. *One wrong word and he's going to explode.*

"No, and I don't know why he hasn't," Brown replied before Royal could. "Especially since he has people there."

Uh-oh. Shit just went sideways.

Royal's jaws clenched, and Easton could practically see Royal's breath strangling in his throat.

You just had to add that last part, didn't you? Damn you, Brown. You know better.

"Brown, don't make me break my foot off in your ass cos—"

"That food is smelling good," Easton interrupted Royal, hoping to change the subject before the conversation deteriorated further. He glanced at his best friend and nodded. *I got you too.*

CHAPTER 16

ROYAL

"I don't get why you don't like Maddox," Easton said, opening the door to the RV.

"I never said I didn't." Royal appreciated Easton's nonjudgmental directness, but it didn't mean Royal would own up to the allegation, because that would mean admitting jealousy. And jealousy was the master key to Pandora's pretty, ornate box. Oh, and how that box sparkled with glitter, gems, and all kinds of stardust. He entered the RV after Easton, allowing the door to shut behind him.

"You didn't have to. It's apparent. Everything you say to him is contentious. You're spewing enough pettiness to strangle a mean girl and her right-hand minion."

"Roy contentious?" Marcel mocked, lifting his hat from a table. "Naw! Say it isn't so."

"No one asked you, old man," Royal said with a sneer but without the faintest edge of irritation in his tone, his verdant eyes shining.

Marcel chuckled, unoffended. "The truth be golden." He arranged his hat on his head. "Okay, you two are on your own tonight. Upton's bull rope has somehow gone missing, and we can't get one shipped in time. He, Cody, and I are going to drive down to Houston and pick up one."

Royal scratched his chin. Although he'd shaved that morning, between his rush and dull razor heads, he could feel stubble. "That's quite a drive."

"Well, now, that's why the three of us are going— so we can take turns driving." He swiped the brim of Royal's hat. "Use your head sometimes."

Rolling his eyes, Royal plopped down onto the bench sofa, the pillows giving a small puff beneath his weight.

"Where did he lose his rope?" Easton asked.

Marcel made another face. "Boy, sometimes I think the two of you share a quarter of a brain. If we knew where it was, it wouldn't be missing, now would it?"

"Damn, you don't even give us credit for a whole brain, starting us out in fractions."

Easton blushed. "Yeah, I guess that was a dumb question."

"You don't have to guess. Don't be modest. Be

certain and own it fully. It was downright stupid," Marcel responded.

Royal snickered. "It's so touching how benevolently nurturing and endearing your sentiments are to us."

"You've been reading the big boy dictionary again." Marcel grabbed his keys from a table. "We should be back by tomorrow afternoon. Don't forget, you both are doing the breakfast segment on the morning show. East, they want your jacket zipped in the front to show off the logo, and Roy, you're to wear one of the new caps. Right after that is a podcast interview, and then East, you have Walk Down Main Street."

"What's that?"

"Exactly what it sounds like. They're going to get some footage of you walking through the old part of town where a lot of the sponsored businesses are. It shouldn't take long. Buddy will pick you up, since I'm taking the truck. There are a couple of other things, but I wrote it all down and left it on the counter. You two should be all right. Irene will pop in in the morning to see that y'all are all set for breakfast."

"We're not five," Royal muttered with a wicked smile.

Marcel eyed him suspiciously.

Laughing, Easton settled onto the couch beside Royal. "Yes, we'll be fine, Nonc."

Looking around the compartment, Marcel patted his pockets. "I think I got everything."

As he opened the door, Marcel added, "I wasn't sure what time y'all would be in tonight, so I took Spartacus over to Callie's."

Both Easton and Royal groaned in unison.

"Last time she dogsat, she fed him so much junk, he was shitting every ten minutes."

Frowning, Marcel pointed at Royal. "I've told you about watching your language."

Amusement darkened Royal's eyes. "But I'm not lying."

"No, no you're not," Marcel conceded, glancing at his watch. "But it's too late to go get him now. You know Callie goes to bed early. We'll just have to deal with it, be it as it may." He scanned the room a final time. "Okay, *c'est tout*. Call if you need anything." He exited.

Shaking his head, Easton cast Royal a wry smile. "He acts like we're going to write on the walls in crayons or break into his liquor cabinet."

Royal shrugged, stood, and shuffled to the refrigerator. "Want a brew?"

"Sure, but none of that lite crap. It makes me burp too much."

He opened the door, rested his elbow on the top, bent, peered inside, and snickered silently to himself. For the amount of beer on the bottom shelf, one would think they were a bunch of lushes. Maybe they were, but it had nothing to do with the quantity of alcohol in the fridge. Marcel was teaching himself how to use a grocery app for curbside pickup and had insisted that he hadn't needed any assistance.

"Doggone, the groceries sure are high in this town," the elder had complained. It wasn't until the order arrived that any of them realized that Marcel had clicked Submit four times, quadrupling every item. Not wanting the hassle—and what Royal suspected to be out of embarrassment—Marcel had opted not to pursue a return.

Royal reached over the lite and retrieved two drafts. He handed one to Easton and flopped back down on the couch.

"So, when did you start hanging out with tweenies?"

Royal twisted the cap off his bottle, his eyes widening. "You noticed it too?"

"Well, duh. He was sitting at the table. How was I supposed to miss a whole kid?"

"I meant his age. He says he's fifteen."

Easton blinked twice. "No way! Ten, tops."

"Wow. I gave him twelve. I think Gerald instructed him to lie about it."

"*Co faire?*"

"Because he's a dick."

"You're going to have to give me more than that."

"He's got him working the stables, and I don't mean a couple of chores. You know policy states everyone needs to be at least fifteen to work any part of this tour unless it's selling merch. Plus, Gerald leaves him unsupervised."

"In all fairness, we got left alone at that age too."

"Not for longer than twenty minutes at a stretch, and never at night or in a strange town. Pixie sticks, we're grown and Marcel still has people checking in on us. We make a living riding thousand-pound animals that could snap us in half, and he doesn't trust us with a datdurn waffle iron. Heaven forbid we use his George Foreman grill."

Easton smirked. "Checking on *you*, and you did set the curtains on fire."

"Oh, bite me. That toaster was whack." He took a slow swig of beer, lifted his long legs, and propped his booted feet on a footstool, crossing them at the ankles. "All these years, I never would have pegged Gerald to be this type of guy."

"People change, Roy."

"Overnight?"

"Who said it was overnight? Some changes are gradual, so subtle that you never notice until one day, they're bitch-slapping you in the face."

"Eh." Royal shrugged, unconvinced.

"Or maybe you never really knew him."

"You think that's possible? To be around someone for years and not know them?"

"Sure. Why do you think divorces happen?"

"Uh, because people grow apart."

"Sometimes," Easton agreed, nodding. "Other times, it may be they found each other before they found themselves."

"*Quoi?* Unpack that."

"It's like some ancient person—Aristotle, Lao Tzu, Chef Boyardee—said. You can't know others until you know yourself. If you don't know what you want, you can't communicate that to others, and others can't give you what they don't know about. Maybe Gerald has never shown you the real Gerald because he doesn't know who that is."

"So, you're saying Gerald treats his child like shit because he doesn't know any better, and therefore, the rest of the world doesn't know either. I call horseshit. Any parent should know that their children want to be loved."

"Relationships are complicated. Bad parents can still love their kids. Junkies know drugs destroy their life, yet they still take them. Plus, you're mixing apples and oranges. Your question was how you couldn't know about Gerald's parenting, not how Gerald treats his son."

"Same thing."

"No, it isn't.

"Yes, it is."

"People see what they want to see."

"Where'd you hear that?"

"I read it on the back of a cereal box."

Royal lowered his beer from his lips. "Say what?"

"I heard it from Dr. Truvy during one of those psychiatric sessions they mandated I attend to determine if my prefrontal cortex was firing enough for me to ride."

Royal snorted. "Who of us isn't misfiring up there, with a twinge of megalomania?"

"That's what I said, but that's not the point. If we walk into a hospital and see someone in a white lab coat and scrubs, we'll probably assume that person is a doctor. That may or may not be true. It could be someone who works in a scientific lab, a nail tech, or even someone who just needs a jacket to keep warm. The person didn't lie because we made assumptions without asking the proper questions. Any mistakes in judgment would be on us for not doing our due diligence. That person didn't make us think what we thought. Sure, it could be an intentional mislead, or it could be the person throwing on the first coat he found without giving it a second thought. At the end of the day, it is our responsibility to seek the truth. We don't get to act like victims if we fail to do our part. You never asked Gerald what kind of parent he was."

"But—"

"You didn't know because you didn't ask. He's likely always treated his kid the same. Why are you suddenly interested?"

"I'm not." Royal stroked his finger along the chilled glass bottle, its coolness beginning to parallel the dropping temperature of his blood as his nerves tensed. "I mean, I'm not going to let a kid go around hungry. Duchess always said it's kinder to shoot a dog in the head than allow it to starve to death. I can't shoot a kid." He smiled equally as charismatic as it was self-deprecating.

"You couldn't shoot a dog either."

"I merely feel sorry for him, you know. And it sucks that no one has done or said anything. I mean, someone else must know. I can't be the only one."

Easton relaxed into the worn cushions of the sofa and considered a moment before responding. "Well, you could try reporting Gerald, but what will come of that? I'm sure promoters aren't paying Jerry. So, there's no real evidence of him working. He'll look like a son earning an allowance. Without visible scars or a confession, the police probably won't intervene. And with us moving every other day, by the time the ink dries on CPS papers, we will have been in six other states."

Like it or not, Easton made valid points. "You're right. Moreover, putting that kind of information out there without irrefutable proof fuels the fire for picketers to drag us even more and accuse all of us of child trafficking or some shit. We're damned if we do and damned if we don't."

"At least now he has us looking out for him."

"Us?"

"We both know you're going to be watching out for him now, and I'm not going to let you do it alone. So, yeah—us."

Royal tilted his bottle and clinked it against Easton's. "Cheers."

"Cheers."

This was the type of evening Royal enjoyed—chilling with his homeboy. Though they had spent many hours in the past on this sofa and others shooting the shit, it felt both familiar and new simultaneously. Rolling his head back against the rear of the couch, he studied Easton's profile as Easton removed his hat and hung it on the hook above their heads without looking up, a testimony to how many times he'd performed the simple act. In the cool glow of the sconce-style wall LED lights, his hair appeared more copper than the mahogany Royal knew it to be. He'd neglected cutting it for several weeks, and now his natural waves were becoming evident. He swept his hand through it, giving it more volume where it had been pressed flat from his hat and creating a messy look that took others hours to perfect.

The light also toyed with the color of Easton's

eyes—a solar burst of hues that both reflected and amplified light—framed by dark lashes. The explosion of gold surrounding his pupils overpowered the cornflower blue of his irises. Science called the condition central heterochromia. Royal called it beautiful.

Easton raised his beer, and Royal tracked the bottle until it reached his companion's lips. In response, Royal's lips parted slightly as Easton tipped the bottle and closed his lips around the rim. *Peas, beans, and cabbage greens!* His eyes snagged and lingered on the bob of Easton's Adam's apple as he swallowed. Barely, Royal managed to suppress a gasp but was powerless against the breath stalling like an unbroken mule in his chest.

"You know," Easton said softly, "you never explained your issue with Maddox."

Well, fuck! "Not that again."

"He seems nice. All he wants is a friend."

Horse pucky! "Uh-huh."

Easton stared at him evenly. "It isn't like you to not give someone a chance. Well, it is, but it's also not. Usually, you would have come around by now for a fellow rider."

"I wouldn't trust him if his tongue was stamped and signed by a notary and six Supreme Court justices, all right? Frankly, I'd rather hold hands with the devil. His spirit animal is probably a roach—one of those big, burly flying ones—and he's as shady as the fine print on an extended warranty."

"Why, Roy? Why don't you trust him?"

Royal sighed, a portentous feeling mounting in him causing him to be uneasy. "You're really pushing this, aren't you?"

"Why are you getting defensive?"

"I'm not." He was.

"If you think something's not right about him, don't you think you should tell me so I can look out for it too?"

Dammit, don't be logical. "No," Royal retorted a tad too sharply.

"No?" Easton's brows arched, and he turned to face Royal, his eyes burning holes into Royal's soul.

"I don't want to talk about it."

"Are you serious right now? You're supposed to have my back."

"I do. You should trust me."

"You want to discuss trust, and you don't trust me enough to tell me?"

Ah, merde!

"I... I...." Royal pressed his lips together so tightly that they lost color. This had become a chess match of words, and in his mind, he could map out the next moves. He'd affirm that he indeed had his friend's back, and Easton would argue that withholding his concerns wasn't having his back. And back and forth they would tango, the dance floor shrinking with each move until his king was captured. Hell, he was mixing metaphors of chess and ballroom dancing, which demonstrated just how fucked he was. "He seems oily enough to pour on a salad."

"That's not fair."

"What do you know about this guy?" he asked in desperation. "He popped up out of nowhere. So, you want to hang out with him without knowing anything?"

"That's kinda how it works, Roy. You get to know people by spending time with them. It's how you form friendships."

"He wants to be more than your friend," Royal blurted before his brain caught up with his tongue.

Fuck! What we have here is a January 30 King Charles I situation. Checkmate!

CHAPTER 17

EASTON

What did he just say?

Easton's eyes widened to the size of his mémère's knockoff Ming dynasty saucers that she'd won at church bingo, and his mouth twisted ruefully as uncertainty infused his brain. Unsure if he was more baffled or angry, he sat speechless and stumped, his stare focused on Royal and refusing to allow him to look away. Oh, he'd heard Royal's words plain as day. Royal hadn't stuttered or mumbled or spoken some forgotten foreign language. His speech quality had been of normal rate, volume, and clarity, yet Easton couldn't force the words to make sense. The sentence hung suspended in his brain. The definition of each word seemed out of context in relation to each other and his comprehension of the syntax scrambled.

Make it make sense.

All was quiet except for the hum of the RV generator and the whispering breeze circulating from an oscillating box fan. Because he couldn't continue to sit here looking and feeling stupefied in the strained silence, Easton slowly placed his beer in the sofa cupholder and rubbed his sweaty palms on the front of his jeans, thankful to have a task to occupy his hands and mask some of his apprehension. His lips trembled as he parted them to speak, knowing he was teetering on a potentially dangerous subject. The glint in Royal's eyes spoke volumes.

"What do you mean?"

"*Ce n'est rien*," Royal mumbled.

Oh no, you're not getting off that easy.

"No, nothing is nothing, but what you said is *definitely* something. Nothing is the chitchat you make in line or at the Piggly Wiggly or Shell pump," Easton rebuked, verbally slicing through Royal's denial with all the swiftness and precision of a neurosurgeon's scalpel. His head tilted at a defiant angle. "You wouldn't have said what you said while bagging Funyuns and hoagie buns or squeegeeing off your windshield. Speak your mind, Royal. *Ne pas as la langue dans sa poche.*"

"Fine," Royal sputtered. "I meant he's into you."

Easton's eyebrows shot up, his mixing emotions warming the blues of his irises. "Into me?"

"*Oui*, Easton, into you as in hooking up."

Easton snort-laughed. He would have accused Royal of being drunk, only he hadn't had that much. "Get out."

"I'm serious. You don't see it because you're oblivious to those kinds of things, especially since it's a guy."

Puffing out his chest, Easton's spine stiffened as he considered how he should interpret the statement. "I think that's an insult." He paused another second. "*Oui*, it is. I do pay attention. And what do you mean, especially because he's a guy? What difference does that make?"

Royal choked—on what, Easton didn't know.

"You don't mind?"

"Why would I mind?"

"Because it's...." Royal scooped both hands through his hair, his brow knitting. "It's...."

"*Oui?*"

"You... just...." He didn't seem to be able to complete the sentence. However, the parade of emotions flickering in his eyes indicated that he had plenty to say.

Just say it.

A faint hint of panic flashed across Royal's face, and his pulse thumped visibly in the hollow of his throat.

Royal panicked? Speechless? What the hell is happening here?

Easton leaned back against the couch, his shoulders sagging with awareness and disheartenment. This wasn't how he'd expected to come out. Well, he hadn't exactly. He hadn't said the actual words, but the implications were there. One could assume. Royal could assume. So, had he come out? In any case, Easton hadn't expected Royal to be all open-arms "welcome home, prodigal son," but the scene in his head always played out vastly different than what was before him currently. Narrow-minded anger and yelling, he anticipated, not recoiling in the-plague-has-come-to-visit horror. Royal's expression seemed a hybrid between wanting to sprout Icarus's wings and taking flight as if he were haring off before a leper, but there was something—an emotion Easton couldn't decipher—skulking behind the horror. It looked to be a different kind of terror. It looked like... anguish—the kind that comes after being deeply hurt. Like the horror experience after tripping but before thudding to the ground. Easton grappled to make it make sense.

Royal cleared his throat and spoke softly. "Do you... want him to like you, East?"

Easton considered for a moment, contemplated his responses in this uncharted territory. "Does it matter?"

Royal's jaw tensed. "That's not a denial."

No, it wasn't. The tension in the room rose another notch.

"I already told you. *If* it's true, it doesn't bother me." For a lack of knowing what to do, he released a slow breath and shoved his fingers through his hair, scraping his scalp. "But obviously it bothers you."

"It does."

And there he had it. Finally, his best friend had uttered the beginning words of condemnation.

Might as well get it all out now that we've started down this path. There's no need to continue the masquerade when we both know what's loitering behind the mask. Speak the truth and shame the devil.

"Why, Royal?"

"He's competition."

"Saint Peter on a scooter! Everyone here is competition. Would it be better if he were a vendor or a stock hand?"

"Not *your* competition. *My* competition."

Quoi?

Royal's arrogant streak was no secret, but his dismissing Easton was all-the-way new and nothing that Easton appreciated.

"Listen, you may be in the lead now, but I'm not out of it. I stand just as much a chance of winning as you do."

"Not that competition."

Blinking twice, Easton rubbed his hand across his forehead. "Huh?"

"I don't want to compete with him for you."

Easton tipped his head back and laughed at the preposterousness. "Seriously? Royal, you're my best friend. No one's ever taking your place."

"And if I wanted more?"

"More?" The word ricocheted aimlessly in his mind. And when it didn't take on a new definition as he possibly (and ludicrously) expected it would, he stared wide-eyed and stupefied at his comrade—mouth agape, face ashen, and forehead wrinkled.

More? He can't mean more as in more *more.* He gnawed the inside of his cheek. *Can he?*

"Uh.... Okay?"

Who said that? Who says that?

Royal scooted back with an uneasy gleam in his eye. "Listen, I didn't mean to make you feel weird. I'm sorry."

Sorry? What the whole hell is he sorry about? Fuck yeah is more like it—that was if Royal was saying what Easton thought and hoped he was saying.

He searched for the words, but none came. There was only one way.

Don't, his brain warned, but his body was already in motion. With zero warning and fueled by impulse, Easton's palm slinked around Royal's neck, pulling him forward until their lips converged. Goose bumps sprinkled the length of his spinal cord and knotted at the nape of his neck as the cobwebs and realization began clearing. He was the patient one. The quiet one.

The passive one. Yet he'd all but lugged his best friend into his lap. This had been such a *Royal* move. But Royal hadn't initiated it, had he? He hadn't extended an invitation. Easton wasn't sorry. He should be. He may have regrets, but he wasn't sorry. He'd stepped out. Like climbing onto a bull, he didn't always know how it would end, but he rode the bucking beast as if he would win. However, what he'd done now had been infinitely more dangerous. He could be destroying his friendship. Yep, in hindsight, he should have given this more thought.

Retreat.

His mind sifted through the two dozen reasons why this was a bad idea, but his body didn't stop, wouldn't stop. He expected to be met with a shove, punch, or elbow, but instead, Royal immediately opened to him and accepted the tongue that he shoved inside his mouth. Easton pressed his body against Royal's until he heard him moan. Months of pent-up tension exploded and incited him to persist. Encouraged by Royal's nonresistance, Easton slid his other hand across Royal's hip.

CHAPTER 18
ROYAL

And the rocket's red glare, the bombs bursting in air....

Holy shitbuckets! I'm lip-locked with Easton. I'm. Kissing. Easton. Have I died?

Easton's tongue swept across Royal's bottom lip.

I don't care if I have. This... is... amazing.

Royal parted his lips to take a moment... take a breath... take *something*. Hell, he didn't know why he parted his lips. Perhaps it was instinct, that primal part of human nature that emerges when it's tapped. Whatever the reasoning, it allowed Easton the opportunity to slide his tongue inside Royal's mouth, and he took full advantage.

Advantage? No. Royal was willing. More than willing.

After all this time of knowing Easton and wondering, Royal now had answers—or, at least, one answer. His mind sifted through too many thoughts to count. Many questions would surely need answering later. And consequences to be paid. But not now. For now, he wanted to remain lost in the sweet sensation of Easton's greedy kisses and the feel of his firm, demanding lips that stole his breath and lit him up from the inside out with electric sparks. He tasted like beer and undeniable male sexiness and nowhere resembled the softness of a woman. How odd. How different. Yet it felt natural. Natural but not normal. No, this wasn't *normal* by any means between friends.

What is happening right now?

Royal's mind struggled to wrap around the reality. However, currently, he didn't give a damn whether it was real or if he'd been whisked into *The Twilight Zone*. He'd deal with that later. At present, he wanted to enjoy the feel of his best friend's tongue coiling around his and lifting him to some magical place where he floated in exultation. Fuck if it wasn't real. All he needed was....

It stopped.

Easton moved away, his eyes glazed with a hazy lust.

"Y-You...," Royal stuttered, his voice hoarse and breathy. He touched his tingling lips with the tips of his fingers.

Easton nodded. "Yeah, you did too."

Yes, he had, hadn't he? He should be elated. He *was* elated. Ecstatic, in fact. Over the moon. His best friend had kissed him. So, what was his problem?

His best friend had kissed him.

Fantasy—a far-fetched, inconceivable, or impractical mental image created in response to a psychological need. Oh, did Royal ever have a host of needs. But fantasies were fantasies for a reason, and Easton had now jerked Royal's fantasy into a confusing reality.

"Um...." *Pull it together.*

A bang on the door jolted Royal, and he bolted to his feet, unsure if his shaky legs would hold.

"East? Roy? Y'all in there?" Wade's voice came from the other side of the door. "Anyone home?"

"Yeah," Easton answered, rising. "Coming." Two steps later, he swung the door open. "What's up?"

How is he so calm?

"That damn Henley locked me out," Wade huffed, stepping inside and hauling a tank the size of a carry-on duffel. "I ran over to Dalton's, and when I came back, he was gone. My phone and everything's inside. I saw your lights on and hoped to use one of your cells and hang out until Henley returns."

No!

"Sure, no problem," Easton replied, moving to the fridge. "Want a beer while you wait?"

Excuse me. Want a beer? What in the Godzilla-versus-Ghidorah catacomb do you mean, he can stay? We have the small matter of your tongue being rammed down my throat to discuss.

"Yeah, a beer would be great," Wade responded. "It's as hot as Satan's asshole on the summer solstice in the rig."

Easton handed Wade a beer. "Your air not working?"

"Yeah, must have quit sometime this afternoon while we were out." He tapped the tank. "It's why I went to Dalton's, to borrow his air compressor to clean the fins."

"At night?" Easton questioned, raising a brow. "In the dark?"

"You try spending five minutes in that Dasht-e Lut without air. Being shut up all day, it's like an Easy Bake Oven."

"Which is it?" Royal asked, finding his voice. "A desert or a kid's toy?"

"Both." Wade made himself comfortable in a chair. "I figure that's why Henley left. I told him I'd only be gone for a minute, but the hose wasn't with the compressor. It took forever to find it." He took a swig of beer before continuing. "I would have gone back to Dalton's to wait, but when I arrived, his face had been all ruddy, and Henriette's hair had been wild and sticking every which way. I figured I'd interrupted something."

You're interrupting something here too.

"What were you two doing?"

Something in Wade's voice made Royal uneasy. Or perhaps it was paranoia and more wackiness of the day that made him question their visitor's tone.

None of your damn business.

"Um... talking?" Royal's face turned what he was certain was meant by the phrase *a whiter shade of pale*, and he examined his voice. He sounded guilty, like a child who'd been caught swiping his finger in the icing of a cake intended for guests.

Wade's face twisted. "You asking me?"

"No," Easton replied. "He's avoiding saying that we had a disagreement, but it's forgotten now."

Royal grunted under his breath. *Who the hell forgot? How could he?*

"About what?" Wade persisted, a leery gleam glowing in his eyes.

Chuckling softly, Easton sat on the sofa bench and crossed his legs. "You think Royal needs anything specific to be disagreeable about?"

Wade nodded in more acknowledgment than agreement. "True dat."

"*Parfois, tu montes sur mes nerfs,*" Royal growled, leaning against the counter and aiming his gaze at his best friend.

Raising his beer, Easton tipped it toward Royal. "Possibly, but I'm still your bro. Yeah?"

"*Oui.*"

Easton was right—to an extent. No matter how much he got on Royal's nerves, they were still bros. But had they crossed the line to be more? Sure, it was just a kiss, but what a fucking kiss. And it was... well, a *kiss*. Sorry, nowhere in Royal's handbook did bros kiss—at least not the way Easton had kissed him. Wade needed to get the fuck out. Maybe he would feel differently later, but at present, Royal couldn't care less if he roasted like a pig in a pit in his camper.

No, that wasn't true. Royal did care about Wade's well-being and comfort. He didn't seriously want him to be hog-roasted. It would be a waste of firewood, as Wade didn't have enough meat on his bones to roast. But Royal did wish he'd chosen another door to knock on. He needed to leave so Royal could talk to Easton.

Wade tapped his finger against his longneck bottle. "Must have been some disagreement to have Roy's cheeks pinked."

Sheesh! Not your business.

Royal took a deep gulp of beer to swallow down his frustration and shifted his gaze to a blank spot on the wall to calm himself. He couldn't look into Easton's eyes—not after what had transpired.

Stop freaking out and calm yourself.

But I'm not imagining it. Wade knows something's up.

Throw him off the scent.

"It's hot in here," Royal rebutted.

"Feels good to me," Wade countered.

"That's because you've been lugging that ten-pound baby around outside." Royal gestured to the air compressor. "Anything would feel good to you." He drained his beer and retrieved another from the refrigerator. *Draw him off more.* "Where do you think Henley got off to?"

"No telling."

Royal dug into his pocket, retrieved his phone, and extended it to Wade. "Well, as East said, hang out as long as you need. Marcel, Upton, and Cody are on a road trip, so there's plenty of room for you to crash here if you need to."

Wade accepted the phone and texted his missing companion. Without looking up, he asked, "A road trip this time of night?"

"Upton's made off with his bull rope and needs a replacement," Easton informed him with a sigh.

"But how—"

Royal shook his head and interrupted Wade. "We don't ask questions." *And you shouldn't either, dammit.* "Do you want to play spades while you wait?" *Cards are safe.*

Wade twisted his face again. "You can't play with three people."

"Sure, you can," Easton corrected. "Just throw out the clover deuce."

Royal moved to the counter and retrieved a deck of

cards from a drawer. "No need," he stated, holding up the box. "New deck. We got jokers."

"Okay," Wade agreed, returning the cell to Royal.

"Cutthroat it is, then," Royal added as he opened a hideaway table.

Royal couldn't remember the age he was when he'd learned how to play spades, although he was certain it was long before he should have been taught any adult card games. But he remembered the *where*. On a dim porch overlooking the bayou and lit by the subtle glow from an inside lamp next to a window with lace panels, he'd sat crisscross applesauce, chewing fruity gum. It was that night that he'd been introduced to the corruption of cards by a group of older boys working on the ranch for extra money to pay for bull-riding lessons.

"This could lead to gambling," Easton had whispered beside him.

"What's life without a gamble?" Royal had responded.

They were boys then. Now, as men, did Royal feel the same? Did he want to gamble with their friendship? He sighed. Maybe. Then again, as his mother always said, fate interrupts most mistakes to allow destiny to fall where it may. He'd never understood what she meant until now, when some awareness was beseeching him. Maybe Wade's arrival had been a good thing—the fate to interrupt on behalf of destiny.

"Are we playing or what?"

Wade's voice returned Royal to the present. Both Wade and Easton had sat at the table and were staring at him, waiting for him to take a seat as well.

"Yep." He slid into the vacant seat and unwrapped the cards. "I'll deal."

Even in a game of chance, there existed a certain degree of control.

CHAPTER 19

EASTON

*W*ADE! *O*F ALL PEOPLE TO SHOW UP. *W*HY COULDN'T *Henley have stayed his ass at the camper until Wade returned?*

Easton stared at his cards and tried not to frown. His highest card was a nine of diamonds and not a single spade in sight. No way he wasn't drowning—in more ways than one. Royal kept diverting his eyes to avoid looking at him. Easton couldn't blame him, though. He had said things to make the situation weird. But dammit, couldn't he say these things to Royal, his best friend? Perhaps some lines were meant to be crossed.

"Board," he bid as if he had a choice. He'd have to be strategic and try to win small, unexpected hands.

Whatever had made him think going all philosophical and confessing his feelings to Royal was a good idea? Well, besides the fact that Royal was a confidant and Easton thought he could say anything to him. No. He'd *hoped* he could. Deep down he knew it likely would go the way it was currently leaning. He had no choice but to accept it. He'd opened his mouth and set it all in motion. He couldn't wave a magic wand and undo it. The truth setting one free was utter bullshit. The truth had assigned possibly a death sentence to his longest and dearest friendship. His head spun, whipping any coherency from his thoughts. The muscles in his stomach wadded like boiled uncleaned chitterlings, and he thought he might puke. He felt himself smothering as if a pillow was crushed against his face, stealing his breath and weighing down his lungs. He placed a card on the table and promptly lost the hand. No, not smothering. He was drowning. *Blub, blub, blub.*

EASTON HAD HAD TO BID BLIND THREE CONSECUTIVE TIMES to get back into the game. But not only had he risen from the ashes of a negative score, he'd somehow managed to win. All it had taken was one hand to turn things around in his favor—proof that comebacks and redemptions were possible. Of course, he already knew that, but tonight, it seemed to take on a different life. He enjoyed ending his nights on a high note—winning at cards, Wade sulking from losing as he returned to his camper, kissing Royal.

Sliding beneath the sheet, he glanced at the digital clock on the shelf that Marcel refused to declutter. Some days, it ran fast, and other days slow. Rarely was it correct. Easton suspected today was a slow day because that was how it felt—laborious and fucking weird. The odd part was, he couldn't decide which he wanted—for the day to be over and done so he could forget about what happened or for time to stand still and allow him to remain fresh in the moment of having the taste of Royal's lips on his. The beer hadn't washed it away, and he hadn't brushed his teeth before crawling into bed. He doubted one night of skipping oral hygiene would lead to a mouthful of cavities, but if it did, so be it. It was worth it.

He secured the window curtain shut, adjusted the wall reading light, and tugged on the privacy curtain as he did every night he slept in the RV. However, the privacy curtain had been fickle the past week, getting stuck on the rod at the halfway point. Sighing, Easton was in no mood to fiddle with it and allowed it to remain open. On most nights, whether it was open or closed was irrelevant once the lights were out. It was so dark that it was a struggle to see two steps ahead. But every now and then, he needed to take care of *personal business* and appreciated the added concealment.

Although he'd traveled with the same companions for years and they all knew what each one of them got up to, he didn't fancy them—especially his uncle—knowing when he was watching porn or jerking off—even if he'd done both with Royal in the past. Tonight, he would need to do some *relieving*. He'd been rocking a semi for the past twenty minutes, and no way would he be able to sleep with that going on. He'd tried conjuring some mundane mood-killing images to suppress his horniness, and it would work for a few minutes before he'd sprung back to life. But the sure-fire way to put it to rest was to T.C.O.B.

To prepare, he fished out a box of tissues and tube of lube from the under-bed storage, tucked the contra-band under his pillow, and shimmied out of his boxers to avoid rustling about once Royal had situated himself in the top bunk. It was difficult enough to rub one out undetected without rummaging to gather supplies in the dark.

Royal exited the bathroom and stood at the foot of Easton's bed beside the ladder for the upper bunk.

"*T'es bien?*"

"*Oui.*"

"You don't look okay. You look troubled."

"I'm fine, Roy. Just thinking about home."

"What about it?"

"I'm trying to remember why I decided to move."

"You said you were tired of the bayou stench."

"Lots of smells go into making that stench."

Royal's brow bunched. "*Quoi?*"

"It's more than the water. It's the trees, foliage, and marsh. The mud and animals. Decay and rot. Animal excrement."

"Okay, you could have stopped at foliage."

"It's true, and you know it. There's a lot of death in those bayous—creatures, plants, fish...."

"A lot of life there too." Royal leaned against the bedpost. "I don't know where you're going with all of this—"

"We became blood brothers on one of the banks. Remember?"

Smiling, Royal nodded. "How could I forget? You cried like a baby."

"You nearly severed my finger."

"*Pish!* A scratch."

"A scratch that required six stitches."

Royal's smile widened. "You always focus on the technicalities."

"If I did that, I would have snitched on you. Instead, I convinced everyone that I got a fishhook stuck and ripped it out. Had to get a tetanus shot, and that shit burned." He rubbed the scar of said incident. "I never told anyone, Royal. There are some things only between us."

Royal eased onto the mattress, his lower back against Easton's legs, and he took Easton's hand in his. "*Oui,*" he agreed, rubbing the faded injury.

Easton startled at the contact.

How can a hand rough with callouses be so smooth against my skin?

For a moment, he stared at their connected hands. *What comes next?* He felt compelled to speak, but he couldn't conjure the words of anything to say. Something needed to be said.

Royal shifted. Or maybe it was he who had shifted. He was uncertain, but no doubt, they were closer—invading each other's personal space. Although he'd been this close to Royal before, this felt decidedly different. His body surged with energy, and he could detect something similar radiating from Royal. Did he dare take the bold initiative to kiss him again? No. Why? Because Royal leaned forward and pressed his lips to Easton's—a light graze that initiated a flame in Easton's lips, cheeks, chest, and groin. Powerful stuff. Like kryptonite infused with oxycodone—surreal yet earthy. Intoxicating.

Kee-yaw, he tastes good. He smells good. More. I need more. Aseteur!

Melting into the languid kiss, Easton's fingers found the hem of Royal's T-shirt and brushed across the warm skin before sneaking them beneath the waistband of Royal's sleep pants.

Royal jerked away, panting.

"Oh, G-God, I'm...," Easton stammered, scrambling to hoist up the sheet from where it had drifted down. Kissing was one thing. Going for the cookies was quite another. *"Je suis désolé."*

Liar.

He wasn't sorry, although he probably should be. "I didn't mean—"

Another lie.

He did mean it, and Royal called him on it.

"Bullshit." Royal clutched Easton's biceps and tugged him back.

"But I—"

Royal heaved Easton forward and crushed their mouths together. Their tongues greedily roved in demanding exploration. Royal's stubble scratched against Easton's skin as he skimmed his mouth down to his Adam's apple, tattooed clavicle, and dark nipple.

A strangled gurgle tore from Easton's throat.

"You can't take it back," Royal growled, yanking the twisted sheet from between them, revealing Easton's gleaming cock. "Look how hard you are." Rubbing Easton's full length, Royal curled his grip over the crown. "How long you've made me wait for this."

"Made you wait?"

"Stop talking. All those years of teasing."

"I've never—"

"Fine," Royal snapped, hooking his thumbs in the

band of his PJs and guiding them down below his deep V. He placed his knees on either side of Easton's legs and rocked back onto his heels. Lightly tugging a fistful of Easton's hair, Royal hauled Easton up from a lying position into a seated one and then pushed down his head. "I said to stop talking," he repeated.

Oh!

Easton received the message and bent forward to Royal's crotch where his erection bobbed within a nest of neatly trimmed dark hair, flush against his abdomen and almost reaching his navel. He drank in the splendor of Royal's mostly nude body.

Why aren't I hesitating? I should be hesitating.

Because this is what you want? This is Royal, and he's asking. No, telling. He wants this.

Massaging the shining head in circles with his fingers, Easton then flicked his tongue across the top, lapping up the trickle of clear fluid leaking from the slit. Royal's response sounded half panicked, and Easton smirked.

That's what you get for being such a Dom.

Before he overanalyzed the situation, Easton drew the rigid shaft fully into his mouth and sucked firmly but slowly. He allowed himself to sink into enjoying the act and all the throaty sounds and grunts Royal emitted.

"That's so good," Royal cooed, winding his fist tighter in Easton's hair. "You've done this before?"

Easton pulled off with a pop and looked up, his eyes wide at the jealousy in Royal's voice. "No. Don't you think I would have told you?"

Royal tilted his head in consideration. *"Je ne sais pas.* You've never mentioned wanting to kiss me."

"And how was I supposed to say that to my best friend?"

"Because I *am* your best friend, and you should be able to say anything to me."

True.

Easton nodded. Royal knew every insignificant detail about him, such as his secret love of comic books and phobia of worms. Technically, it wouldn't classify as a *DSM* definition of a phobia, but they weirded him out all the same.

"I'm sorry."

Royal's lips curled into a lustful smile. "That's okay. You're about to make it up to me." He pushed at Easton's head, and Easton resumed his position, allowing Royal to bury himself in his mouth.

Even if Easton didn't want to do this—which he did—his body involuntarily moved. He wasn't certain what to do and had no developed plan, no strategic technique. He did, however, know what he'd seen on videos—who said cable TV wasn't educational?—and he knew what he liked done to him by a woman. Before climbing on his first bull, he'd observed other riders and imitated them when it had been his turn.

That had worked out rather well, and he had nothing to lose now by using that same method of imitation. He considered how this could be messy and potentially embarrassing, but his brain had already decided there was no retreating.

While cupping Royal's balls in one hand and fisting the shaft in the other, Easton wound his tongue around the head in drawn-out spirals. He paid special attention to licking the delicate underside before hollowing his cheeks out for suction. Repeatedly, he moved up and down, trailing his tongue along the dorsal vein and pulling more firmly each time but never coming off the crown until Royal hissed and pushed him away again.

"Wait!"

At first, Easton thought that in his clumsiness, he'd hurt him. However, the desperate gleam in Royal's eyes told another story.

"I need a minute," Royal managed to grit out with a ragged breath.

Easton didn't want to wait, but he did because, above all else, he wanted to satisfy Royal. By satisfying Royal, he'd ultimately be gratifying himself. He licked his lips.

Royal grinned. "You like sucking my cock, then?"

"Very much." Easton's cheeks reddened at the confession.

"And you're sure you've never done this?"

"*Quoi?*" Easton's eyes widened with disbelief. Was Royal accusing him of something? "No, I haven't. I'm sure I would remember if I had."

Extending his hand, Royal stroked Easton's jaw and ran his thumb across his bottom lip. "It's only because you're incredibly good at it. If you're sucking me off this good now, I can't wait to see what you do after you've had some practice."

Practice? Wait.

That sounded as if Royal intended for them to do this again. Assuredly, Easton had no problem with that, but boy, what a bold assumption.

Royal's hand traced down Easton's chin to his throat, chest, and abdomen and rested on his hipbone. "Let's get you into this game, shall we?"

Oh, we certainly shall.

Easton could only nod as Royal took hold of him and squeezed his eager dick. He had to be mindful, though, because one taut jerk and he was a goner. It would be over before he began. But then again, that would be okay because Royal had all but promised him a next time, hadn't he?

Royal straightened from his slouched-shoulder Hero Pose straddling Easton's legs and pulled Easton from his forward seated position onto his knees so they were chest to chest.

"This," Royal whispered, "I hope you enjoy too." He spit in his hand.

"Wait." Reaching beneath the pillow, Easton retrieved the bottle of lube, opened it, and sheathed their cocks with a generous dollop.

"I see you had plans." Royal smirked, slinking his arms behind Easton's back and clutching his shoulders. Their lower bodies aligned so that their leaking shafts glided against each other. He pressed forward and up, grinding against him, moving his hips in a quickening rhythm. With each gyration, more beads of precum smeared down their lengths. The movement furiously built friction.

Easton was caught off guard when his breath suddenly hitched, and it felt as if a bolt of lightning had struck him. He had no control over his body as it stiffened and convulsed with pleasure. There was no preventing the climax that overtook him, and sparks flew behind his eyelids. A sizzling rapture mounted in his stomach and pinged down into each of his toes. His orgasm exploded out of him, the first spurt hitting Royal's chin and the second his pec. Easton lost count of how many and where they landed after that.

"Holy fuckatoids," Easton puffed, gazing up at Royal through dilated pupils. "I didn't mean to go so soon, but... I didn't even get to—"

"Shh!" Royal placed his index finger over Easton's lips as he eased him back onto the mattress. "When a bull hits the gate coming out the chute, the rider has an option for a re-ride. We have all night to do whatever we want."

The promise and lust in Royal's eyes caused Easton to squirm. Never in Easton's life had he experienced passion as desperately intense as this, and like a greedy child, he licked his lips, eager for more.

I'm your huckleberry. Giddy up!

CHAPTER 20

ROYAL

Never play Russian roulette with a loaded gun. But if the gun isn't loaded, is it Russian roulette? Royal knew fooling around with Easton was playing a dangerous game, yet he couldn't stop himself from pulling that trigger. *Bang!* Of course, some would argue that the game is merely another channel to get an adrenaline fix. True, Easton caused his blood to pump, but this was more than that.

He studied Easton, whose face was glowing with post-orgasm bliss. Royal couldn't recall ever seeing his roll dog look this sexy, and the urge to devour grew in him. Leaning forward, he captured Easton's lips and licked into his mouth, pressing his body into Easton's until he moaned powerlessly in surrender. This pleased Royal, and his body thrummed with need.

"Lay back and enjoy the show," Royal ordered. He

pushed Easton gently onto the pillow and repositioned himself to straddle his friend's lap. "This," he
said, dragging his palm agonizingly slowly down the
trail of dark hair from his navel to his neatly trimmed
pubes and then cupping his heavy balls, "is all for you.
Everything building in here will be on you shortly."
With his free hand, he swiped an X on Easton's chest.
"Right here."

Easton's lips parted and his spent cock twitched,
but he emitted no sound.

With a groan, Royal stroked his dick from base to
tip and rolled his palm over the crest, smearing lube
down his thick shaft. The touch felt good, but Easton's
expression combining a mixture of yearning and
concentration was what set Royal ablaze. In response,
his hips surged forward as he began to fuck his hand in
earnest, and his breathing became shallow.

"I want to taste you," Easton whispered.

Royal slowed his fisting. "Okay, but only a little
bit."

Like a child being rewarded, Easton grinned,
licking his lips, and leaned forward. By "little bit,"
Royal had intended a swipe of the tongue. However,
Easton engulfed him, suckling the tender flesh
beneath the rim before taking as much as he could.

"Dammit, East." Royal attempted to pull back to
no avail.

Easton only leaned forward and slurped greedily,

his tongue swirling in dizzying patterns and splotches of color burning on his cheeks. Royal quickly realized that he'd lost control of the situation and was at Easton's mercy. He shuddered and fought hard not to close his eyes.

"That's so good. So good," he gasped through sporadic breaths.

"*Mm.*" Easton skimmed his mouth down and sucked on Royal's balls.

Royal grabbed a slat of the overhead bunk and held on for dear life, his knuckles losing color. He'd had blow jobs before, but Easton's mouth was like an industrial shop vac. And the visual was indescribable. "You're not going to be satisfied until I.... Oh!"

Royal's testicles drew up tight, and his back arched. He was done for. Slamming his eyes shut, he gave in to his climax, and long ropes of cum shot from him and...

Holy shit! Into Easton's mouth. He's swallowing. And he's not stopping. He's... he's... he's milking me dry.

He'd had some—not many—women swallow him, but none like this. Easton seemed to relish it.

He's killing me.

Finally, Royal's softening dick could take no more, and he pushed his hungry lover off.

"Easton, please."

Biting his bottom lip, Royal watched in disbelief as Easton's Adam's apple bobbed one final time before he lay back. Royal collapsed beside him and released a long, exhausted breath, unable to do anything but lie there as a satiated lassitude coursed through him as if he'd been collared with a somnum sachet.

Easton propped himself on his elbows. "Is this Royal Guérin tossing in the towel after the first go-round?"

"You know better than that, but I am going to have to catch my breath." He wiped the sweat from his forehead with his arm. "Where'd you learn to give head like that?"

"Instinct, I guess." Easton rolled onto his side to allow both of their bodies to fit more comfortably into the compact space. "How'd you know what to do the first time you ate out a girl?"

Royal snorted. "I was so drunk, they told me that's what I did."

"They?"

"Twins. It was a night."

"Mm." Easton rolled in his lips and sagged onto the pillow.

"What's that mean?"

He shrugged.

"Don't blow me off." Royal's lips twitched. "I mean, you can *blow* me but not blow me."

"I guess I'm wondering, how does this work?"

"How does what work?"

"This." Easton wagged his finger between them.

"You. Me. Women. I mean, what was this for you? Something to pass the time?"

"No, but...."

"But what?"

"I thought maybe it was for you."

"So, what? You were pacifying me?"

"No."

Why did he sound offended?

"What's the problem?"

Easton scooted up and sat erect. "I want you to shoot straight with me."

"Okay." Royal straightened as well.

"Earlier, you indicated that you would be interested in more than being friends. What did you mean?"

Ah shit! Not a conversation Royal wanted to have. "Friends with benefits?" No, that wasn't right, and Royal regretted it the instant the words slipped out of his mouth. Easton meant more to him than that. But he couldn't come out and admit that he was in love with him either. How would that work? First, they were in bed. He'd been taught never to say those three words before, during, or shortly after an orgasm. Second, life was spinning a little too fast for his liking.

"Huh." Easton lowered himself back on the mattress.

"East, what do you want me to say? It's not like...."

"Like what, Roy? Say it."

"You know what we do for a living. We can't tell anyone."

"So, I'm your dirty little secret?"

"*Quoi?* You want to tell people? You want to take that risk?"

Easton bit his lower lip and shrugged. "No."

"Then what? What do you want?"

"*Je ne sais pas.*" Easton lowered his eyes and hunched his shoulders. "But I know it includes being with you. Like this."

When Royal was four years old, he swallowed a penny. Even at that age, he'd known pennies weren't edible, and swallowing one was something he shouldn't do. He was even aware of some—not all—of the negative consequences, such as choking or death. Granted, he hadn't known the ins and outs of bowel obstruction or zinc poisoning, but he'd known the outcome could be something horrific. He'd swallowed it anyway. It hadn't been a dare or an accident. He'd knowingly engaged in an incredibly foolish and dangerous act. Now, twenty years later, he found himself having swallowed a penny of a different sort. The first penny ended in a pile of shit. Would this new one end the same?

He pondered Easton's question of being a dirty secret and scratched his evening growth. His swallowing the penny hadn't been a secret. According to his mother, he'd gagged, clenched his throat, and experienced trouble breathing—kind of similar to how Easton had sucked him off. Royal didn't remember doing any of what his mother claimed. However, he did remember looking at the X-ray and the doctor giving him a cherry lollipop—a reward for naughty behavior. Easton had rewarded him, too, hadn't he?

The difference between his past actions and current behavior was that he had no desire to swallow another penny, but he had every yearning to get Easton in his mouth.

"Don't worry," he finally responded. "We'll figure it out."

He hoped that was true.

CHAPTER 21
EASTON

The sound of a key turning in the dead bolt had Easton shooting straight up in bed and fear piercing his soul. How he'd heard the lock was anyone's guess. He slept like the dead.

"Roy…," he began but stopped, realizing he was alone in bed. He smoothed his palm over the sheet beside him and found it cool. Had it all been a dream? Had last night never happened?

A sharp pain fired from left to right in his head. Surely, he wasn't hungover. He didn't recall having that much to drink and certainly not enough to cause a blackout.

Think. Think.

But did he want to *think* about it? Because there was a lot to unpack if he opened that Pandora's suitcase. It was reminiscent of an old Katy Perry song. He'd kissed a boy and liked it.

Oh, snap, crackle, and pop! What did I do?

Fantasizing about it was one thing. Engaging in it was quite another.

A tangle of emotions rippled through him as reality began to take root. He'd hooked up with Royal—his fucking best friend. How did that even happen? Well, he knew how. But why had it happened? He knew that answer too. Hell in a handbasket, what the fuck was his problem? Who in his right mind hopped in the sack with his ride-or-die, especially when that ride-or-die was the hottest ticket on the circuit? Had he hit his head again? Was this the aftermath of his concussion?

Naw, he couldn't wimp out that way. He hadn't been drunk. He didn't have a TBI. He'd known full well what he was doing. He'd wanted Royal. And holy catnip! From the current boner between his thighs just from thinking about the previous night, he wanted him again. Unlike Katy, Easton had more than *liked* it. He'd relished it.

But wait. Why was he Kirking out now? He'd known last night what the implications of hooking up with Royal were—had known, been warned against, and chosen not to listen. In fact, he'd been the one who had instigated... initiated... insisted. He couldn't very well cry foul now. Well, he could, but it would make him a first-class hypocrite. It had been what he wanted. Besides, when had he begun seriously second-guessing his decisions? That was a dangerous flaw for a bull rider. Hell no! One made a decision and stuck to it. There was no time for wishy-washy back-and-forth. That would get a person killed—or worse.

Okay.

He needed to get his wits about him. Last night hadn't been a dream. He was sure of it now, because not only was the memory amazing, but he also smelled like sex. But Royal wasn't in his bed, and from the coolness of the sheets, he'd probably been gone for some time.

Someone was coming inside the camper. No. They had already entered, and there was a ruckus. He heard footsteps and people talking.

"Dad-blasted idiots!" the voice boomed.

Marcel. He'd returned.

"You'd think they'd know better."

Upton.

"Those self-righteous nincompoops are so concerned with making their point that common sense evades them. Seat belts on motorcycles are more rational."

Easton swung his legs over the side of the bed and hoisted on a pair of boxers. Peering around his privacy curtain, he called down the hallway, "What's going on?"

"What're you still doing in bed?" Marcel responded.

Marcel always expected everyone up with the sun, and usually Easton was. However, Royal had worn him out last night. "I don't have to be anywhere until seven thirty," Easton grunted, pulling on a T-shirt and standing up.

"I meant," Marcel continued, "why weren't you helping put out the fire?"

"Fire?" Easton's features contorted. "What fire?"

"The stock—" Marcel slapped his hands on his hips, narrowed his eyes, and raised his brow in the way he always did when he was about to lay into Easton. "Boy, what in tarnation did you get up to last night?"

"Um, nothing. I was tired."

"Tired my blooming bunion! You been in my rum again?"

"Fine," Easton huffed. "I may have had a drop or two. Now, are you going to tell me about this fire or not?"

"Watch your sass, boy. You're not too old for me to bend you over my knee yet."

"Yes, sir. Sorry."

"'Em blasted protesting fools broke into the stock pens. Call themselves going to free the animals—at least that's the story they're telling."

"Instead, they knocked over a of table chemicals

that splashed into a portable propane forge that hadn't fully cooled." Upton brought his hands together and then quickly spread them in a rounding motion. "And *kaplow*! It sounded like a cannon. We heard it as we were pulling in. Couldn't hardly see anything, though, because of all the smoke. People were running around like crazy trying to get the livestock out. We saw Royal and figured you were somewhere running amuck in the mayhem."

"Royal was there?"

Why didn't he wake me?

Upton cocked his head. "You mean you didn't hear anything?"

Easton shook his head. "Nothing. Was anyone hurt?"

Marcel grunted. "A couple of the idiots who broke in were taken to the local ER for smoke inhalation."

"Serves them right," Upton added.

"No, no," Marcel replied, shaking his head. "We don't wish ill on anyone no matter how stupid they are. They belong to someone too. It just beats all that they claim we abuse the animals, while they're the ones who dang near killed every last one of them. And I'll tell you something else," Marcel said, wagging his finger. "They sure weren't reading us for filth when we were dragging their sorry butts out of harm's way. But I don't expect people like that to stay grateful for long.

They'll figure some way to twist it and have it be our fault."

"How would that even be possible?" Easton asked.

"You'd be surprised how people like that can perverse-engineer facts. They've years of practice of standing on false morals and rewriting narratives. It reminds me of my first wife. She was like that. We never had an argument that she didn't play *victim*. And she never apologized for anything." Marcel shook his head. "No, she'd just turn on the tears, and everyone would feel sorry for her. Then they'd come after me for being the bad guy. Granted, I made my share of mistakes during the marriage, and I can own up to that. But I was far less guilty than I'm credited."

Easton resisted the urge to exchange glances with his cousin—who likely was thinking the same thing—and studied his uncle instead. Although Easton had been in grammar school at that time, he recalled thinking something wasn't quite right with his ex-aunt. She'd given off a doleful energy, even on the happiest of occasions—perpetually pouty and forlorn and rarely smiling. He'd frequently wondered why, but it wasn't something any of the family ever discussed—at least not in front of the kids. He'd often pondered if her mood was the culprit of the split but had never asked. However, since Marcel had brought it up, Easton didn't see the harm in asking now.

"Is that why the two of you divorced?"

"Mainly." Marcel nodded. "It was four days before Christmas. I'd been doing some roping at a lot of small-town events to scrounge up some extra cash for the holidays. Quentin wanted an expensive gaming system, and Zoe had asked for a new bike. I get home, and there's this new fancy-schmancy couch sitting in my living room."

"How could you tell?" Upton remarked. "I remember all your furniture being covered in plastic. Even the floor had those vinyl runners."

Easton nodded in agreement.

"She had peculiar ways, that's for sure. It should have been my first clue."

Intrigued, Easton asked, "So, what happened with the Christmas gifts?"

"The money I'd left with her, she'd blown on this overpriced hunk of stuffed fabric. She'd bought Quentin some dollar-store magic kit and Zoe a cheap rag doll. Well, I blew my top. I mean, there I was, breaking my back, and she was out blowing every dime I made. The kids hear us from the other room arguing and run in. Next thing I know, Quentin—he couldn't have been more than eight—is hitting at my legs screaming to stop being mean to his mother."

"Wow." Easton couldn't imagine ever striking his uncle.

"I wish I could say I was a better man, but I'm not, and I wasn't. I yanked his little tail up right fast. Ain't no kid going to tell me how to run my house. Her brother lived next door, and he comes crashing in, talking about take my hands off his sister when I hadn't touched one single hair on her head. And I snapped right then and there. I thought to myself, 'I don't have to take this.' So, I walked out."

A wave of shock washed over Easton, not only because he'd never heard this story before but also because he'd never known Marcel to walk away from anything. It wasn't in their family's blood to quit.

"So, you just washed your hands of them?" Easton asked hesitantly. "I mean, I get why you wouldn't have anything to do with Noreen, but Quentin and Zoe?"

Marcel shrugged. "That wasn't my doing."

"Quentin said you never tried to contact him after the divorce," Upton interjected.

"That's true. At first, I was hurt and didn't want to. Later, when I came to my senses, I asked, but Noreen said no."

"Couldn't you have asked the courts for visitation?" Easton prodded.

"What good would that have done? I had no legal rights."

"What do you mean? Fathers have rights," Easton persisted.

"If I was their father, yes."

Easton's jaw dropped. "*Quoi?*"

"Quentin was a little over two and Zoe barely six

months when Noreen and I met. I raised them as my own. But each time she and I would get into it, or I'd get onto the kids about something, she'd throw it in my face how I wasn't their real dad. Plus, she was teaching them not to respect me. Quentin running up on me like that was only the beginning."

"D-D-Do they know?" Upton stuttered, his face pale.

"I doubt she's said anything to them—all the more for her to play the victim of me having abandoned her than owning the fact she hooked up with a strung-out meth head who was forcing her to turn tricks and is now serving thirty to life for an armed robbery and second-degree murder."

Blinking hard, Easton attempted to collect himself. "Shut your mouth! What you say?"

"You boys are both old enough now to know and appreciate the truth. But sometimes things don't get said because there's no reason to say them. I could have taken that secret to my grave, and who would it have hurt? And I suspect them hating me is a lot less worse than them knowing who their real kin is."

"So...." Easton scratched his chin. "You're saying secrets are okay?"

"What I'm saying is, sometimes it's nobody's business."

"Huh." Easton nodded.

CHAPTER 22

ROYAL

Sighing, Royal flumped down onto a bale of straw and scrubbed his hands across his face. What a morning it had been. His intentions when he'd crawled out of Easton's bed had been to sneak to the bakery he'd seen in town and surprise his new lover with a warm pastry. Instead, no sooner than he'd made it to the end of the campers, he'd heard what sounded like a gunshot. It was followed by a flash, and he'd seen an orange glow in the distance.

His feet moved before his mind thought twice about running toward the direction of frantic shouts and frenzied "Old MacDonald" sounds. The closer he'd gotten to the turmoil, the more the air had thickened with a vexing stench of what Royal could only describe as rotten cabbage and skunk funk. From there, all was a blur. His body had moved on autopilot as he sailed blindly through the smoke—hastily grabbing animals, grasping equipment, and even snatching one of the passed-out dumbasses off the ground who later was determined to be the cause.

Now that the situation had calmed, the gravity of what had occurred slammed into his spirit. His eyes stung. His nostrils stung. His skin was covered in soot. He smelled as if he'd been dredged off the bottom of a bayou floor and looked like someone found curled up at 3:00 a.m. in a Waffle House parking lot after a weekend bender. But his mother always said miracles happened every day. He supposed today was one of those days.

In all of his time on the rodeo, he'd never seen or heard of an incident of salicylic acid exploding. How had it even gotten close to an open flame? And why was there an open flame in the holding pen anyway? *Had* there been an open flame? The more he thought about it, the less it made sense. If he didn't know any better, he'd say the incident was sabotage—arson. However, the cluster of protesting Tweedle Dee and Tweedle Dum bandits didn't seem smart enough to have pulled off anything so sophisticated. It appeared more like dumb luck—or, dare he say, a curse.

As much as he attempted to consciously suppress the thought, it kept rising to the basin of his cognizance and demanding attention. Goose bumps prickled his skin. That stream of thought led nowhere good. Shaking his head again, he drew another deep breath. As horrible as this ordeal had been, he couldn't let the morning events settle into his mood. He had important things to tend to today, and he'd already begun by tempting fate.

At the fire, he'd seen Marcel, Upton, and Cody. They'd returned from their trip ahead of schedule. A few minutes earlier sans explosion, and he might be having quite a different morning experience. All he needed was those three walking in and discovering Easton and him tangled together in nakedness. He didn't want to imagine that conversation, and thankfully, he didn't have to, especially since he and Easton hadn't had the awkward *morning after* talk. He hated those types of discussions. They ranked right up there in the top three with the parental birds-and-bees chat and a friend's poor hygiene confrontation. And honestly, he hadn't only wanted donuts when he'd left this morning. He'd wanted some time to take in what had transpired.

He wanted to be cool with what had happened, and for the most part, he was. After all, Easton had initiated it. Royal hadn't pressured or tricked him into the decision. No one had been drunk—well, not *that* drunk. And Easton had seemed confident in his choice.

That gave Royal comfort. But what came next? What were they? Friends? Friends with benefits? Just a semi-drunken hookup? And if Easton wanted something more—something in the range of the R-word—what then? Royal didn't do relationships. They were messy, especially on the road, yet he thought he might want one with Easton because, well, Easton was different. Easton meant something to him. He always had and always would. There was so much—

The sound of shuffling footsteps and sniffling drew Royal from his ping-ponging thoughts. He looked up to see Jerry lugging a bag of sawdust almost his equivalent in body weight.

"Hey," Royal called. "Grab a sit-down."

"I can't. I have to take this—"

"It can wait." He patted the straw beside him. "Sit."

Jerry hesitated but dropped the sack, slumped onto the hay, and swiped at his face with his forearm.

"What's with the glum mug? Everyone made it out intact."

A muscle in the boy's face twitched. "My dad said it's my fault for leaving the salicylic acid and copper sulfate too close to the forge."

"Horseshit!" Royal spat before he thought better of it. "Is Gerald out of his fucking mind?"

Jerry's eyes grew wide.

"Listen, it was the fault of the assholes who had no business being there. They knocked it over... or threw it in. Who knows?"

"Yeah, but if I hadn't left it there—"

"Don't even finish that sentence. How many times have you put those chemicals where they were?"

Jerry bit his bottom lip as he paused to consider the question. "Every night?"

"Right. And how many cities have we visited so far?"

"About fourteen," Jerry hedged.

"Correct," Royal agreed, nodding. "How many days is that?"

"Umm...." Jerry rolled in his lips as he silently calculated. "Forty?"

Not great at math, huh?

"Forty-six," Royal corrected. "For forty-six days, those chemicals have been stored in the same place in the same method. The only thing that made this morning any different was intruders. This isn't on you. Do you hear me?"

Jerry nodded unconvincedly.

Damn Gerald and his bullshit.

Royal stood and stretched. "C'mon," he ordered, jerking his head. "We'll drop that off wherever it needs to go, and then you can help me get ready for a television segment that I'm doing."

"But—"

"No buts. This morning has been shot to shit, and I need someone to help me get back on schedule." He didn't, but if saying so prevented Jerry from being degraded and worked like a workhorse, then so be it. "I'm going to be late as is for this bullshittery I'm scheduled to do. I'd tell Wade to fill in, but with all those LED studio lights, close-ups in HD will highlight his capped teeth and make him look like the shoddy dupe of Dracula. This is a morning show. Can't be scaring the kids this early."

The youth giggled, and Royal hoisted the sack over his shoulder. "Where to?"

Jerry puckered his lips to protest but decided against it. "They set up makeshift pens in an old byre. Over there." He pointed.

"*Allons.*"

THE MORE PRESSED POWDER WAS DABBED ONTO ROYAL'S forehead, the more profusely he sweated beneath the overhead studio lights. The embroidered logo jacket didn't help matters any. He could tell by the makeup artist's heavy sighs that she was becoming perturbed by his need for multiple reapplications before filming began.

"Aw, don't you look adorable," Upton teased,

tipping back his hat and propping himself against a high stool.

"Fuc—"

"Royal!" Marcel snapped and folded his arms across his chest.

"We're not live," Royal muttered under his breath. "They can edit me out."

Snickering, Upton continued. "Ooh, you're in trouble now."

Easton nudged Royal with his elbow. "Ignore him. You can slap him later."

"Promise?"

"All right, boys," a studio person whose name and title Royal had already forgotten said. "Just relax. We'd like to get this segment in one take."

"Good luck with that," Royal mumbled and strummed his fingers on the counter.

Easton's brows arched. "You okay? Usually, it's me who's fidgeting around at these sorts of things. I know the morning was a lot."

"More like a whole tree."

"Exactly, which is why I'm asking if you're okay."

"I'm fine."

"You sure? You're seriously edgy. Cody said you were in the thick of it before the firefighters arrived."

"Yeah, we all were. It's no big deal."

"But it is. You're a hero."

"Naw, everyone just did what needed to be done."

"Roy, you carried a man out."

"Only because he was in my way and his roly-poly ass was too fat for me to step over."

"And performed CPR."

Royal shook his head. "I hit him in the chest a few times."

"Stop it. Quit being modest. You saved a man's life."

"You don't know that. He may have been fine without me. Besides, the paramedics did all the real work when they got there."

"Yeah, sure. I don't know why you can't accept credit for what you did."

"It's nothing anyone else wouldn't have done. I just happened to get there first. Doing what you're supposed to never requires you to win any medals... unless you're sitting on a bovine." He traced a design on a potholder with his index finger. "I don't under-stand why more people can't simply do the right thing."

The lines in Easton's forehead bunched. "Who are we talking about?"

"Gerald. You know he...." Royal shook his head. "Ugh! I don't want to talk about it."

Two women wearing clothes too fancy for anyone doing anything in a kitchen joined Royal and Easton at the counter. Royal had forgotten their names but knew they were the hosts... hostesses... or whatever the stars of the daytime show were called. One of them—the one wearing the violet pantsuit and mauve lipstick—smiled broadly at him. She'd hinted that they go out for lunch after taping and slipped him a business card with her private number scribbled on the back. He had no intention of calling—mainly because he had no idea where that card was now—but he smiled back at her. She was a good—okay, maybe not *good*, but convenient—distraction from the tornado of thoughts churning in his head.

"Ready to crack some eggs?" she asked.

"Always," he responded.

He felt Easton inch closer to him, and the woman's eyes narrowed.

Oh shit! This could get awkward.

Beads of sweat gathered at his hairline.

"Get ready," someone from the side of the set called. "In three, two, one, action."

"And we're back," the other woman, who was wearing a Barbie pink dress so tight that if she sneezed, it would grant viewers a sneak peek of her snack pack, said. "Here to help us prepare a traditional hobo breakfast are Golden Star Buckle winners Easton Faucheaux and Royal Guérin, two real-life cowboys who will be riding in the Championship Stampede Showcase this week at the Asphodel Fields Arena. They'll be rustling up a genuine, rustic cowboy breakfast consisting of buttery pancakes slathered with lingonberry and kumquat jam, peach sticky buns, molten-hot duck-fat hash browns, gold star sausage, and eggs."

Gold star sausage? Quoi?

Royal darted a questioning stare at Easton, who looked equally as baffled. He leaned toward Easton slightly and whispered, "What the hell is she talking about? We've both poked the kitty?"

Easton rolled in his lips and snorted, suppressing a laugh.

"This hearty meal using plump, stuffed sausages and loads of spices will fill you until you're stuffed and completely satisfied," Violet Woman chimed in.

"Damn. Might as well have said hot and horny." Royal murmured.

Easton rolled his lips in farther but snorted louder.

"Cut!" a male voice yelled. "Gentlemen, I know you're both excited, but I need you to maintain your composure."

"Look who he's calling gentlemen," Upton catcalled.

"*Brasse mon tchu.*"

"Dat swannit, Royal! I'm about to take a switch to you."

"*Quoi?*" Royal asked, looking at Marcel innocently. "I didn't say it in English."

"They have closed caption on them so-called

smartie TVs—loaded up with the artificial intelligence."

Royal's eyes widened, and he turned to face Easton fully. "*The* artificial intelligence. What the fuck does someone who says *smartie TV* know about AI?"

Easton let loose the laugh he'd been struggling to suppress, causing Royal to laugh as well.

CHAPTER 23

EASTON

"Royal, I'm told you're a master in the kitchen," Willy-Wonka-violet pantsuit said, batting her lashes.

If she flaps those batwings any faster, she's going to have liftoff right out of this bat cave. Back off.

Easton grunted. "Who told that lie? Anything you cook has the pleasant taste of sawdust."

Slapping his hands on his hips, Royal huffed. "I know *you're* not calling anyone out. The only thing you've ever stirred is drama, and even that wasn't that good."

"At least I don't burn water."

"Oh, that's what we're doing? You want to throw down? Okay. Let's see what you got." He pulled a bowl of eggs closer to him and looked at the hostesses. "How do we make a hoe boy breakfast?"

"Cut!"

Easton pointed at Royal. "This one's on you."

"What I do?"

"It's hobo. Not hoe boy, nut."

Royal flashed his signature smile, his sensual, plump lips quirking at one side. "You sure about that?"

Easton would have responded. He wanted to clap back, but he was spellbound, his eyes transfixed on Royal's lush lips like they shouldn't have been. He also knew he should look away. Others were watching, and this was a job. Where was his professionalism? Well, to be fair, he had been instructed earlier to show personality, and Royal had plenty of that. He was simply following his cohort's lead. Well, not so much following as being comfortable being himself with Royal at his side. Royal always made it easy for him to let his guard down.

"Let's pick up where we left off. Take three," the director ordered.

"We're going to get started with a nice hot pan," the Purple People Eater stated, sidling up next to Royal and flashing a perfect row of what were probably veneers. "Get it nice and hot."

The insinuation in her tone wasn't lost on Easton, and he shot her a cool, polite smile.

Take a shower.

Royal adjusted the temperature control on the stove accordingly.

"Now we're going to crack the egg," she continued.

"Be careful not to break the yolk." She demonstrated using a spoon to skillfully separate the yolk from the white.

Royal attempted to mimic, but his egg plopped into the pan, shell and all.

"Shi—" He caught the explicative on the verge of tumbling from his lips and quickly self-corrected. "Shish kabob!"

"No, like this," Violet Beaucoquette cooed, intervening by handing Royal another egg and placing her hands over his.

All hands on deck? Why is she touching him? There's no need for her to touch him.

A bitter taste clogged Easton's throat as he attempted to swallow his exasperation. A not-so-jolly green monster suddenly reared its prickly head and squatted squarely on his shoulder. He hadn't anticipated having to witness some backlot, generic morning show Al Roker rip-off chick eye-fuck his best friend over a saucepan sizzling with sacrificed chicken embryos—not that there was anything unusual about a woman getting wet for Royal. What woman with one eye, half a milligram of estrogen, and a nonpartisan libido wouldn't be turned on by the pure maleness that oozed from every pore of Royal's bronze skin? Easton saw this kind of thing all the time. But today…. Today was the day after, and he was in no mood for Wonka Woman to be fondling his man.

His man?

Whoa!

His thoughts had flown all the way left, and Easton had to think about that. He needed to think about a lot. Royal had always been his boi. He'd even been his man but never his *man*. One night and—

Get it together. Keep things copacetic.

Easton picked up an egg and cracked it—at least, that had been his intention. He *tapped* the egg on the side of the skillet, and it—a double yolk—exploded like an oil-filled pressure cooker with obstructed vents over high heat. Yolk splashed across the stove, over his hands, and onto his cohosts. It made no sense that an object so small could make such a huge mess.

That's not normal. Is it?

A twinge of apprehension bubbled in his gut.

Then again, what about this day has been normal thus far?

Pink Panther squealed as if unexpectedly stuck by a needle.

"Good stars!" Grapevine yelped, her eyes spitting anger.

"Yippy yo-yo!" Easton stared at the disaster. "These chickens on steroids or something?"

"Cut!"

"How in the addition, subtraction, subfracation, trigonometry, geometry, combinatorics, differential, multiverse, new-world math did you manage this poultry-zygote baptism?" Royal questioned, swiping yolk from his cheek.

Easton brandished an expression that was somewhere between stupefaction and chagrin. "*Il n'ya pas de quoi,*" he answered with a speculative chuckle and shrug.

"No one thanks you," Royal replied to Easton's *you're welcome.* His lips twitched. "Although it is fitting for you to have egg on your face after all your bold smack." He gestured at the egg dripping from Easton's chin.

"Oh, you're *cracking* me up."

"*Omelet* that lame joke slide."

"Enough, you two," Marcel griped.

"C'mon, Nonc. Cut 'em some slack. You know they're *eggs-tra* special."

Marcel cut a daunting glare and pointed his finger at Upton. "You stay out of this." Shaking his head, Marcel approached Easton. "Let me look at that jacket. Lawd, I hope none of that mess got on the logo. You're being paid to show that."

Easton accepted a towel from one of the stagehands and took it as an opportunity to position himself between Royal and the talking blueberry. "It's fine," he assured Marcel. "Just *egg-cellent.*"

Royal squinted into the glare of the key light and snickered.

Marcel shook his head. "Y'all are the reason I drink."

"I thought it was a throwback from your days of protesting prohibition," Royal teased.

"Move!" Placing a hand on Royal's shoulder, Marcel lightly shoved him out of the way to inspect Easton's jacket. "This is precisely why I warned Balor not to have the two of you do this together. Y'all act like five-year-olds. I swear, it's taking every milligram of Valium pumping through my veins right now to keep me from hog-tying and whipping all of y'all," Marcel muttered, spinning Easton around. "It seems okay."

"I told you it was," Easton confirmed.

"Listen," Marcel sighed, "I know this has been a chaotic morning, but can we please get this done so we can get back on schedule? I need you to settle down." He turned his stare to Royal. "You too. You're both antsy. And you...." He faced Easton again. "You need to smile and stop looking at the host like you want to shove her in the oven."

Push her in the oven. Why didn't I think of that? No, no, no. She'd never fit.

Besides, he wasn't sure if it was a real oven or just a television prop. It would be a shame to rack up real charges over something fake. It was the equivalent of robbing a bank with a plastic gun. The sentence was the same.

Easton gulped. If his face was giving all that, his uncle would surely begin to pick up on other things, and that spelled trouble. He needed to downplay it and fast.

Green monster, slink back to your cave.

He planted on a carefully bland expression.

"I don't know squat about cooking. Plus, these lights are, like, a thousand degrees. You could fry me crispier than a bad tan instead of them buy-one-get-one-free egg grenades."

"I know, I know," Marcel agreed. "But we have to sell harder at some of these smaller venues, especially now with the fire being a headline story. Who knows how the media will spin it? They'll be paying extra-close attention to everything we do now. If they try to highlight the fire as some kind of negligence on our part, it's vindication for the protesters that we don't have the best interest of our stock at heart. That, in turn, will spook sponsors to back out, which could shut us down. We're in a political climate, and that air can choke us all."

Easton's grimace increased.

Great. Super. Can't wait.

The thought of snooping media peeking in his window was just the cherry atop everything else.

"This here is good, wholesome publicity," Marcel continued. "Viewers will gobble this up—that is, if you can manage not to assassinate anyone else with more eggs."

Lifting his cap, Easton rushed his fingers through his hair. "I'll try, but I didn't do anything unusual with the last one."

"Maybe the pan was faulty," Upton suggested.

Royal snorted. "You idiot. How can a pan be faulty?"

"The same as your face," Upton retorted.

In rebuttal, Royal flipped Upton the bird.

"Royal!" Marcel snapped.

"*Quoi?* I didn't say anything at all this time."

"I'd take this belt off and give you a good swatting if I didn't think my breeches would fall down around my ankles."

"Wouldn't that be a sight? If this airs on PBS, the kiddies can learn about long johns," Cody commented.

Marcel spun toward Cody. "I'll put you over my knee too."

"I don't see what the fuss is," Royal muttered. "Production is going to frankenbyte it the same way they do reality television anyway."

"All right, let's get ready for another take," the director called from the side.

Yes, Easton could use a do-over—a digression to prevent Marcel from becoming suspicious and a front to mask his own irritation at his "clingy-girlfriend" behavior toward Royal that would have any warm-blooded male hightailing it to the deepest depths of leave-me-the-hell-alone woods. A discovery by Marcel certainly would make everything weird. Additionally, Easton needed to quickly master a convincing enough act for the world to buy into the toxic masculinity stereotype he was expected to allude to. Straightening his jacket, he rolled back his shoulders and faced the hostesses.

Get to work.

His focus needed to be bull riding—or the actions that would get him back atop a bull. And that meant jumping through the hurdles of PR mumbo jumbo. He could only accomplish that by being levelheaded, and being levelheaded meant accepting hard facts. First, not only had Royal not made any promises about where this thing between them was headed, but he'd also never said anything about giving up women. And even if he did, it didn't mean women wouldn't hit on him anyway.

Second, sex was physical—the stimulation of body parts. Many things could be used for stimulation—hands, mouths, other body parts, clothing, toys....

Wait. Toys?

Easton blushed. What the hell did he know about toys?

Next!

Getting off had nothing to do with emotions. It was about having a good time. He'd had a good time.

Royal seemed to have had a good time. At least he'd sounded like he had, and his expression had looked sated. He'd not complained, and his words—unless he was lying—indicated that he was satisfied. But Royal never lied to him; therefore, Easton had no reason to believe he'd started now. No, they both had had a good time. Mission accomplished.

Third, Marcel's point was valid. Rodeoing was a political sore spot for everyone from animal activists to politicians grasping for a cause to fatten their platforms to bored attention-seekers with nothing more interesting to engage themselves in. They all came out in droves when the rodeos were in town. Easton could respect the ones who legitimately misunderstood the workings of a rodeo and sincerely desired to protect the animals. However, all the others could go jump into a cauldron of lava. Part of Easton's job was to stave off negativity whenever possible. How could he earn a paycheck if no one filled the stands and if no one attended to purchase from sponsors and vendors? Actors promoted their upcoming movies as part of their contracts. Athletes did the same by giving interviews, wearing patch quilt originals zipped up to their bottom row of teeth while beneath a furnace of artificial solar flares, and making appearances on cheesy cooking shows where the hostess made goo-goo eyes at his—

Oops!

There he went again. Anyway.... All of this was part of the job—his job. It wasn't just mounting an animal for eight seconds, and as a professional, he shouldn't have to remind himself of that constantly.

Fourth, and maybe most importantly, even if Easton didn't want to participate in this colossal shit show, he had more people to think about than himself—beginning with Royal, the man who would walk through fire with him—*for* him—without asking. If Easton fucked up, it could potentially fuck up the bag for his coworkers, who he considered friends—no, family. He couldn't do that to Royal even if he wanted to. Thus, there were no other thoughts to be thought. With that said, he needed to get down to business.

He nodded at the crew. "Let's get cooking."

CHAPTER 24

ROYAL

"Up next is one of those guys fans love to watch because he makes riding bulls look as easy as sipping fine wine on Saturday night under a blanket of stars with your honey. I'm talking about none other than fan favorite, Royal Guérin. Not only has he been strong all season, putting up consistent numbers against fierce competitors, but he's been doing so on some of the highest-ranked bulls. He's not messing around out there. Tonight, he's climbing on the twenty-two-hundred-pound Atomic Sonic, a bull only in its first season but that has shown everyone why it's here with these veteran bulls. This bull isn't one you can clutch your pearls on. It has height, power, and some gnarly spins.

"Now we see Royal in the chute, getting set and wrapping his rope just the way he likes it. That's the thing about these cowboys. They all have their own method, and they won't leave the chute until they're satisfied. He's readjusting now, shifting up to move away from the flank, and that's important. He doesn't want to be back there because it makes it hard to get around the bull, and on a bull like this, not making little adjustments early can lead to huge mistakes later. When that gate opens, things are bound to get wild. He gives the nod, and here we go.

"Oh, look at that. Atomic Sonic explodes from the gate straight into a jump, and look at how high that bull is off the ground. This bull means business, but so does the cowboy atop. Royal's setting his hips and riding the momentum of the kick back to the front. And there's what we're talking about—one of those nasty spins, but Royal's right there with it, shifting his hips into the inside of the spin and transferring his weight to his right leg. Whoa, and another big jump. Atomic Sonic must think this is a catapulting event, because it's aiming to cast Royal off to the moon. Royal is slung forward but quickly recovers. And this is where we see the skills of the rider. Royal isn't guessing what he needs to do. He knows exactly where he needs to be on that bull and the intensity he needs to use to get there. Make no mistake, there is nothing random about what Royal's doing. He knows how to find the rhythm of a bull, and that's the key to staying on. Most riders would have been in the dirt by now. Big bucks. Big spins. And that's going to do it.

"Now watch this dismount. Royal's going to wait until the bullfighters straighten that bull out a bit before yanking *off his wrap. There we see him undone, and now he's going to jump off to the left. He lands on his feet while keeping low to the ground, and Atomic Sonic kicks right over his head. Beautiful execution here tonight by Royal Guérin, and this crowd is loving it. Forty-eight and a half for Atomic Sonic and a solid forty-six for Royal for a total of 94.5."*

Marcel slapped Royal on the shoulder. "Good ride."

"Shit, boy! You need some oxygen? Looked like that bovine was trying to buck you to the tippy top of Machu Picchu," Upton yelled, laughing and punching Royal.

Royal grinned back. "For a moment there, I thought he may have. He slapped down, and all I had was a mouthful of dust and an eyeful of horn. I thought I was on the ground until it went back up again." He looked around. "Where's East?"

"He walked over to the judging booth to see what's happening with his bull," Marcel responded. "Something was going on with its eyes. The vet thinks it may be irritation from this morning's smoke. A couple are going to have to sit this one out, which means some riders now are being assigned different bulls."

Royal's expression turned to concern. "I thought all of that had been decided earlier."

"It was until it wasn't," Marcel replied.

"But the vet checked them out and gave them all the all clear," Royal continued protesting.

"Now, Roy, you know how these things go."

"Yeah." He sighed. He did know. It wasn't unusual to have a switch, but something about this didn't sit right with him. He glanced at the judge's booth, where Easton gave him a double thumbs-up and flashed a goofy grin. "Maybe I should go up there and see what's going on."

"No," Marcel corrected. "What you're going to do is get over there and give that ring announcer a statement. Easton's a big boy. He can handle his own business."

Royal's frown deepened—not because he thought Marcel was wrong, but, rather, he disliked having his excuse stripped away. Generally, Royal enjoyed being in front of the cameras after a stellar ride, but currently, he wasn't feeling it.

"Stop pouting and get over there," Marcel stated, giving Royal a light nudge.

"I wasn't pouting."

Upton chuckled. "Dude, if your bottom lip dropped any lower, it would blend in with the carpet."

"There's no dang carpet in here," Royal uttered as he marched off to the ring reporter. "And what do they want me to say that's different than any other time? It's the same questions with the same answer. *'How does it feel?' 'Well, I stayed my ass on.'*"

"Boy, what is wrong with you? You just completed

the most impressive ride of the night, and you're acting like a petulant child."

Cody snickered. "You know Roy don't know about adulting and big boy breeches."

"And you don't understand English and subject-verb agreement, but you can kiss—"

"Royal, go!" Marcel ordered.

Royal grunted and headed toward the interviewer. "Yeah, yeah, I'm going."

Easton

"IT'S COMING DOWN TO THE WIRE. TONIGHT HAS BEEN THE stiffest competition all season. These cowboys are all looking to make it to the championship, and they know the only way to do that is to give it their all and take the fight to the bull. At this level, one small mistake can cost every-thing. With tonight's scores, Easton Faucheaux is on the bubble and now finds himself in a must-ride situation. He understands this as he prepares to climb aboard Onyx Alpha—a bull he rode last week and struggled to make the requisite eight. Let's see if tonight will be any different.

"The chute opens. Onyx Alpha spins hard to the right, almost folding itself in half, and that has Easton laid back farther than he wants. And wow! Look at that bull buck. The height of the Eiffel Tower on that one."

This fucking bull, Easton thought, wrestling to get back to the middle of Onyx Alpha's back. How had he managed to pull this bull twice in a row? Well, he hadn't, technically. His bull had been pulled out of the lineup last minute. Last freaking minute. It didn't get hurt in the chute. No accident had occurred in the holding pen. Nope. All of a sudden, it developed smoke inhalation from this morning.

Come on!

Onyx Alpha wasn't even supposed to be in the rotation. Its name should have been scratched off the list with a crayon. Rode bulls were allowed at least two weeks to rest between events. So, how had Onyx Alpha gotten into the mix? It made no damn sense no matter which way Easton pretzel-twisted it.

No matter now, though. It had been put into the mix, and East had drawn the short straw. He couldn't ponder the why and how while straddling a mobile billboard of fuck around and find out. He had to make it through the next seven and a half seconds without looking like *Who let him in?* and *What fool is this?* and this bovine's bitch. But staying on wouldn't be enough. He needed showmanship to earn the high points and stay in this compettition. And that wasn't going to happen with his hand about to pop out of his rope and him barely hanging on by his fingertips.

"Good God Almighty!"

"You continue to beseech prevarication, you derisory stooge."

Easton knew that sound... that voice... that unnatural.... He'd heard it before. He looked downward, where a swirling violet cloud of dust was forming into...

"No!" He worked his hand beneath his wrap and hoisted himself forward. A strong smell of infection, excrement, and rot filled his nostrils. Bile rose to the base of his throat and lodged there, refusing to proceed upward or to retreat in reverse.

Onyx Alpha's hooves propelled clay and minuscule specks of gravel into the air. What resembled dismembered limbs and curdled entrails emerged from the arena floor in mangled heaps.

Seven seconds.

"Jesus, help me. *Notre Père, qui est aux cieux, que ton nom soit sanctifié—*"

"Your prayers cannot help you. Nothing can."

Onyx Alpha whipped left, and Easton's head flung back with a piercing pain that streaked from his neck to his sternum and snaked around to his lower back. Easton exuded a new sheen of sweat, and his skin prickled with goose bumps at the realization that his legs were numb.

Do I hear singing?

The scratchy whispers of a lullaby rang in his ears —so soft, yet screaming.

"Hush, little one. Go deep down into the hole beneath the willow root. Shred the flesh and ram sawdust into vessels after bucking out of the chute. Snap the neck and pulverize the bones to ash for spectators' delight. Surrender now and accept one's plight."

Six seconds.

Was he up? Down? Still on? Easton scrambled to get his bearings. He couldn't afford to panic no matter what he was imagining. Now, if never at any other time, he had to maintain his cool or else…

I'm going to die.

"Yes, you are," came the cackled response.

Five seconds.

"Bastard!" Clenching his teeth, Easton lurched forward as Onyx Alpha lunged into a bull death spin. Easton's vision filled with the curve of thick horns, and his body stopped mere centimeters from contact. He felt himself slipping, his center of gravity off.

It's over.

"Hang on, East! You got this."

Royal.

Royal's voice flooded his ears. But how was that possible? How could he hear Royal over the crowd? Over Onyx Alpha's stomps and grunts? Over whatever the fuck that was rising from the bowels of hell and speaking to him? He heard Royal above it all.

Four seconds.

He didn't have shit, but if Royal believed in him, he'd hang on.

He tugged on the rope again, righting himself—or repositioning to a less awkward position, at least. Hell, he didn't know. Between the industrial overhead lights blinding him and a dirt floor that had turned into a minefield of cadavers, he was disoriented and ensnarled in a briar patch of metaphysical weeds. He could have been upside down and dragging behind the bull's ass for all he knew, except he doubted it. The crowd wasn't loud enough. If he were being dragged, the place would have been shaking like the Roman Colosseum as the crowd demanded a macabre coup de grâce.

Stomp, stomp, stomp.

Up and down, Easton danced with the bovine beast. Dust swirled like a tornado around its hooves. A more distinct shape had formed, and an emaciated hand extended toward his foot.

"Get away! Don't touch me!"

"Come home, Easton," the eerie figure replied.

Home. That was where Easton wanted to be. Home with Royal by his side and not this bullshit.

Three.

Although Georgia had been good to him and had been better for his training and career, he missed Louisiana. He and Royal could build a cabin overlooking the bayou and spend their days ranching and raising horses.

Two.

If not horses, gators. There were plenty of those ancient dinosaurs swimming about. They could do bayou tours or open a gator farm. But no. Royal loved the rodeo. He'd never leave, not even for him. Easton's heart sank at the latter thought, and a hard thud stole his breath. He was off the bull and rolling. Creatures crawled after him, gaining speed.

"You are mine, Easton Faucheaux. You belong to me."

Something sticky pressed against his neck—like small, gummy needles sinking into his throat.

Then everything went black.

CHAPTER 25

ROYAL

"EAST!"

Dear God, please be all right.

Royal's heart lurched in his chest as he kneeled beside his best friend, who hadn't moved since being slung from the bull. The rise and fall of his chest indicated life but not much more. "East, talk to me."

This wasn't how it was supposed to be. Sure, they took risks. Sure, shit happened. But this…. No. Absolutely not.

Royal clenched his teeth, feeling helpless and cognizant of his every move. He reached to stroke Easton's cheek but quickly redirected his hand to touch Easton's shoulder in a way that couldn't be mistaken—not even by the most homophobic alpha male's scrutiny—for anything more than brotherly affection. All eyes were on them. The spectators. The cameras. The promoters and sponsors. He wanted to do more, say more, but he knew better. Now wasn't the time for missteps.

Easton's eyes fluttered open. "Did I make it?"

"Well, shit, if that's not the first thing you ask." Upton chuckled with little humor.

Marcel shot Upton a glare before refocusing on Easton. "Are you okay, son?"

"I feel... weird. My legs.... I couldn't feel them, but now, they're tingling. That thing came at me."

Upton's expression twisted. "What thing?"

"That—"

"That son-of-a-bitch bull," Royal interrupted. "What do you think?"

Easton stared up at Royal, and Royal stared back with a warning glare.

"Can you stand, or do we need to call for a stretcher?" Marcel asked.

"No stretcher," Easton objected. "Help me up."

"Not a problem." Royal hooked Easton's arm around his neck and hoisted him to his feet.

Easton swooned, threatening to collapse.

"You okay?"

"*Oui*, just need to get my bearings."

Swiftly, Marcel draped his nephew's other arm around his shoulder. "Let's get you to the medic."

"I'm fine."

"Uh-huh," Royal grunted. "Tell me that when you can walk upright."

"I can," Easton protested. He jerked his arm to remove it from Royal's shoulder to prove his statement, but his friend's grip on his wrist was too firm to break.

"Hush, both of you." Marcel shook his head. "You two will be bickering on your deathbeds."

Ordinarily, Royal would have a smart comeback, but his thoughts were pinging in too many directions for him to say anything. Silently, he assisted Easton out of the rink amid the crowd's standing ovation howling from the bleachers. The cheers somehow seemed different now—not necessarily for a job well done but, rather, for a near-death experience. Many cowboys died in the arena or as a result thereof. That was acceptable for others and even for himself but not for his friend. Royal couldn't be happy. He couldn't cheer. All he could do was feel relief.

NINETY-ONE POINT SEVEN. *DAMN!* HEARING THE SCORE announced over the loudspeaker brought Royal no joy. Just a half second less and his peace of mind would have been restored. Instead, the half second struck him with misery. It wasn't because he feared competition. No, he thrived in the face of being challenged. Rather, that damn score kept Easton in the running to win. It meant he would be riding again, and again in harm's way.

Frowning, Royal propped his feet on a crate as the medic examined Easton at the medical station. He'd grown up around ranching and rodeo. However, he suspected he was about six before he understood the seriousness of bull riding. He'd been shopping with his mother in a rural lifestyle store for greenhouse supplies when Shaw Verglas, a rodeo veteran, slowly hobbled into the store. As he moved down the aisles, he'd clutched his buggy like a walker. His boots scraped against the floor as he shuffled more than stepped. His hands trembled as he removed items from the shelves. Up close, he seemed nothing like the vibrant, sprightly ball of spitfire from the arena. Even his voice didn't have that much boom.

"What's wrong with him, Duchess?" Royal had asked, tugging his mother's hem.

"It's the life of a cowboy, Petit."

Royal had witnessed Shaw ride many times and had been there the night he'd gotten stepped on by a monster beast named Bubblegum Machine—wittily named due to riders not being able to predict how the bull would behave. But Shaw had gotten up that night and walked out of the ring with the assistance of the bullfighters. He'd smiled and waved at the crowd before exiting. Aside from a limp, he'd looked healthy and strong. However, the man in the store looked fragile, haggard, and broken with his beard scruffy, cheeks sunken, and eyes dulled. That had been the day Royal learned a difference existed between showtime under the bright arena lights and reality.

Watching Easton be examined was reality.

"I doubt you'll take my advice," the medic said, removing his stethoscope from around his neck and shoving it into a medical bag. "I think you should schedule an MRI."

"For what?" Easton snorted.

"Because you took a nasty fall, and your legs going numb isn't ever a good sign."

"But I'm fine now."

Royal rolled his eyes. He could tell his friend was anything but fine, but what was the point of arguing? Easton wouldn't change his mind, and he'd feel betrayed if Royal argued otherwise. After all, Royal was the one person who was always supposed to have his back—even if he bitterly disagreed. His only option was to wait until they were alone and try to talk some sense into him. Thus, as long as they were in public, he would present a united front.

"You're wasting your breath talking to that hard-head. He thinks we're in gymnastics where somersaulting off a vault and sticking a landing is just part of the score—not that he could have broken his neck." That had sounded more supportive in his head than coming out of his mouth. "Besides, his head is hard as rocks. You can't hurt nothing there, and you sure as shit can't knock any sense into it."

"If you're not going to say anything helpful," Marcel snapped, "then sit there and be quiet."

Easton grinned at his friend, and Royal acknowledged it with a small nod.

"Lawd, I hope your mama wasn't watching tonight," Marcel muttered, shaking his head.

The medic leaned back and pushed up his glasses. "If you're not going to go for a scan, at least take it easy for a couple of days."

"He will," Marcel interjected. "The next event isn't for three weeks, and I'll horse-tie him to a bed if I need."

Royal snickered. "That's a bit kinky, wouldn't you say?"

"Roy!" Marcel spat. "I'm warning you."

Easton chuckled. "I promise to take it easy, Doc."

Marcel nodded. "We'll be leaving tonight for Tifton."

"I'm not going to Tifton."

"*Quoi?*" Royal and Marcel inquired in unison.

"I want to go home... to Maringouin."

Without skipping a beat, Royal replied, "I'll take you in the truck."

"No need," Marcel replied. "We can all go in the RV. I have to drop Upton off in Opelousas anyway. What's one more stop? Besides, it'll be nice to spend some time with family."

CHAPTER 26
EASTON

"Are you sure?" Marcel asked.

"For the umpteenth time, *oui*," Royal replied. "Go have fun."

"But you're the one who should be celebrating your first-place win."

"And I will… with a can of ravioli and glass of Callie's sweet tea."

"Are you positive you're okay? You've had a hard day too." Concern laced Marcel's voice.

"Perfectly exceptional. Listen, Easton will probably sleep all night from the painkillers, and I just want to…." He sighed. "If I'm going to drive the first leg back to Maringouin, I probably need to hit the hay early too."

"Well, if you're sure."

"Yep, and take that knucklehead with you."

"You can kiss my hairy—" Upton began but stopped when Marcel pinched his bicep. "*Ow!* Nonc, that hurt. Now I'm going to have a bruise."

"Come on here, boy," Marcel ordered. "I'm not dealing with your foul mouth all night."

Easton listened to the RV door close as he continued to stare up into the darkness of his bunk. He hadn't taken the painkillers. Oddly, he wasn't in pain. He had been, but then....

Even if he had been in pain, he doubted that he would have taken them. Recently, he'd been prescribed too many, and addiction was no stranger on the rodeo circuit. The ugly truth shrouded in the medicine cabinet was that many of the riders were strung out on oxy and fentanyl. Although people liked to delude themselves because it maintained their sparkly comfort-zone insistence that all is pretty in the world, the sport billed as family-friendly and bursting with funnel cakes and chocolate-chip and nut-sprinkled caramel apples had all sorts of seedy rougarous lurking in the corners. No one ever set a goal to become a junkie, but less strong over-the-counter painkillers didn't skim the torture their bodies felt. And if the circuit medic who handed out prescriptions like breath mints failed to write a legit one, riders never had to wander far to find a seller. However, it wasn't just the riders. It also was the bullfighters and the stock contractors. It trickled down from there to spouses who needed to dull the emotional pain of watching loved ones suffer and slowly spiral down a pit of drug use—easier to join them than attempt to reform them. But that wasn't why Easton hadn't taken the meds.

Drugs not only evaporated his pain, but they also stripped him of his ability to think clearly. He'd seen something out there again tonight, and no one—including himself—was going to convince him that drugs were clouding his thoughts. Something strange had happened—had been happening.

The curtain was yanked back, and light flooded in from the compact walk space.

"I know you're not sleeping," Royal stated, leaning against the bunk post and flashing a photo-acceptable smile. "I saw you cheek those pills."

"You see too much," Easton answered, squinting against the light. "Royal—"

"You know you're going to wake up feeling like shit in the morning."

Yeah, just like he knew Royal had intentionally interrupted him to avoid having the conversation Easton wanted to have.

"You think I won't be able to handle it?"

"Oh, I know you *can* handle it. But why should you have to when there's another way?"

"You power through pain."

"But I've also not been bumped around as much as you have been lately."

Easton smiled. "Gloating?"

"Of course not." Royal grinned back in return. "But maybe I will tomorrow."

"Nice win tonight. You were damn near perfect."

Royal snorted. "What do you mean, *near*? I was phenomenal."

"Geez, it never gets old with you."

But I want to get old with you. I want to get naked with you.

"Why Maringouin?" Royal asked.

"I got a hankering for sac-a-lait."

Royal arched his brow. "Who's going to bait your hook?"

"Screw you," Easton rebutted with his best effort to sound offended. "We were ten, and I only asked you once."

"Hm." Royal tilted his head toward the floor and then peered up at his friend through his dark lashes. "Seems hitting your head has altered your memory, as in diminished your ability to count."

Squirming, Easton settled back on his pillow. No, he hadn't forgotten. Bloodworms weirded him out, and the mere thought of touching one made his skin itch like a dog infected with mange. So, yes, much to his chagrin, he'd had Royal do the honor of baiting his hook. Who knew he would need an NRA—non-reminder agreement?

"Actually, there's a guy on Rue Vol who sells—"

"Flipping hell, we're going to jail over some damn crappie."

Easton snorted. "When was the last time anyone was prosecuted over five pounds of fish?"

"Indeed." Royal flopped onto the end of the mattress by Easton's feet. A moment of silence passed. "Now, do you want to tell me why you *really* want to go to Maringouin?"

Easton knew he would get nothing past his best friend. "*Je ne sais pas.* I just feel like I need to be there.... Regroup. Mawmaw always claimed us Faucheaux draw energy to align our chakras from the bayous."

"Chakras?"

"*Oui*, it's the—"

"I know what it is, but I'm surprised that you do."

"Why?"

Royal hunched his shoulders. "It's not exactly everyday conversation in our circle."

"Well, I learned about it a long time ago to protect my *ka*."

"Wh-What?"

"*Ka.* It's—"

Royal threw up his hand, his cheeks splotching red and spine stiffening. "*Arrêté.* Stop."

Baffled, Easton swallowed the rest of his sentence.

What in the world?

Easton studied his companion, who looked as if his gall bladder had ruptured.

"Yeah. Okay." Easton rarely saw Royal freak out, but there was no mistaking the expression of absolute horror on his ride-or-die's face.

Do something. Say something. Fix this.

"It's, um... been a while since I visited my mom. I tell her I'm okay on the phone, but she likes to lay eyes on me every now and then to see for herself. You know how it is."

"*Oui.*" Royal nodded.

Silence.

Geez, this is awkward. Fucking weird. What is he thinking? Talk to me, dammit.

"Royal...."

"I'm going to fix that ravioli now." He stood.

"*D'accord.*"

***

Royal

ROYAL PRESSED THE TIMER ON THE MICROWAVE AND THEN stared up at the dome light on the ceiling. He recalled the Knight Bus scene in the *Harry Potter* movie when the titular character observed the chandelier from the *Titanic*—at least Royal had always associated the light fixture with the doomed ship—ominously swaying as the bus jetted through the streets of London. The RV was parked and in no danger of sinking, but Royal felt the dread, angst, and helplessness of being flung around as he imagined the passengers on both the bus and ship had. His heart told him he should be able to have a discussion with Easton about.... About what, exactly? That was where he got stuck. His mind wouldn't permit him to turn that curve, not even with the man he shared everything with. It was more emotional baggage being stockpiled, and one day— sooner than later—Royal would need to conduct a deep clean of that storage shed. He didn't want his silence to become a wedge between him and Easton.

Perhaps going to Maringouin would be a good thing. Not likely, but at least Easton wouldn't be getting on any bulls. The part of Royal worried about that could relax momentarily.

"You going to take that out?"

Easton's question dragged Royal back to reality. "*Quoi?*"

Nodding at the beeping microwave, Easton added, "I thought you were hungry."

"Yeah.... Um.... What are you doing out of bed?"

"Same as you."

Royal opened an overhead cabinet and removed two bowls. "I would have brought it to you."

Easton frowned. "I'm not an invalid."

"No one said you were," Royal responded, collecting the baking dish from the microwave and then spooning pasta into the bowls. "These look small to be double stuffed."

Easton moved into Royal's personal space but remained silent. They were inches apart. All Royal needed to do was turn his head, and their lips would have been on each other. But Royal didn't turn. He froze, staring at the steam drifting from the food. Well, the majority of him froze, with the exception of his dick that bounced to attention.

Fuck!

The timing wasn't at all appropriate or convenient. It was as if he was twelve all over again and springing a boner at the slightest breeze. Except this wasn't some random northeast wind that deprived him of bodily control. Not only that, but a thousand and one other things were happening. His dick should have been in time-out. But no. It was having its own party, creating an all kinds of fucked-up situation.

Silently, he counted to ten and released a long, sluggish breath. Easton hadn't moved. Royal hadn't expected him to. Slowly, he turned, and their mouths lightly grazed each other. Royal's insides ignited like a furnace, his pulse beating erratically. Instant combustion.

"I've waited for this all day," Easton whispered,

positioning his hand at Royal's waist and urging up his T-shirt until his fingertips skimmed bare flesh.

"We shouldn't...." The words faded from Royal's lips. Why bother protesting when he wanted the same thing and was humming with sensations? "We have to be quick. Marcel and Upton could return at any minute."

"They'll be gone for most of the night," Easton rebutted, nibbling on Royal's bottom lip.

Royal took a step away. "East, this isn't safe for either of us. We can't afford to not be careful."

"*Je sais. Je ne suis pas bête.*"

"When have I ever called you stupid?"

"Never," he agreed with a shy smile. "But your actions—"

"Actions?" Royal observed genuine hurt in his best friend's eyes and reclosed the distance between them. Pressing their rock-hard bodies together, he toyed with the soft curls at Easton's nape before kissing the tender flesh below his ear. Meanwhile, he grasped Easton's right hand and coaxed it to his bulging crotch. "Because I worry?"

"No, be—"

The doorknob rattled, and both Royal and Easton jumped back just as Marcel entered with Balor Adder trailing. "I ran into...." His eyes darted between the two men. "Y'all look guilty."

"Unless you have court records and videotape

evidence, I unanimously plead the fifth." Royal shoved a bowl of pasta toward Easton, being sure to use a towel as a potholder to shield his swelling situation. "And the sixth, seventh, and eighth for good measure." He settled his gaze on Balor.

The lines in Marcel's forehead bunched together. "You have more than a twinge of crazy going on upstairs in that noggin. As I was saying, I ran into Balor as I was about to hop in the truck, and he had a brilliant idea that he wants to run by y'all."

"Well, if it's more work, it can keep running." Royal stabbed a ravioli with his fork and crammed it into his mouth.

Marcel crossed his arms and eyed Royal's bowl. "You were serious about fixing ravioli, weren't you?"

"I don't joke about food. Now...." He moseyed to the table and sat. "What is this *brilliant* idea?"

"You tell 'em," Marcel instructed the promoter.

Balor cleared his throat and smiled in the way that let Royal know he would dislike whatever followed, especially since he was pitching directly to him and not his agent. Marcel kept Royal on schedule and his crew tight, but he didn't talk money.

"People these days enjoy the personal aspect of entertainment—the behind-the-scenes, if you will."

Royal's lips curled downward. He could smell where this was headed. "Uh-uh."

Balor threw up his hand. "Now, hold on a minute before judging, and hear me out."

Easton moved to sit beside Royal at the compact table. Royal gathered his friend hadn't put two and two together yet.

"You wouldn't have to do anything other than be yourselves and go about your usual day. Filming crews have learned how to be noninvasive, and—"

"Filming crew?" asked Easton.

Ding, ding, ding. He got it.

"You mean to have people follow us around?"

Balor shuffled. "Only for part of the day. Once the cameras are set up—"

"Set up where?" Easton questioned, slowing chewing.

"They put them in various places, but you'll forget they're there."

Easton's fork clanked loudly against his dish. "I'm not having cameras installed in my mama's house. No way. You can't be serious." He glanced at Royal.

"I already said no," Royal responded, shoveling more food into his mouth.

"Now, listen, boys. This is a good opportunity for everyone," Balor continued. "This franchise could use some positive publicity, and both of you are on the leaderboard. Several of the other guys have already agreed. For example, a crew is going to film Maddox Pyrite ranching bison in Arizona."

"Monkey see, monkey do."

"Roy, mind your manners," Marcel warned.

"We're going home to rest." Royal jerked his head toward Easton. "He needs to rest. How are we supposed to do that with cameras constantly in our faces?"

Leaning forward, Easton propped his elbows on the table. "We only have three weeks. Doesn't it take time to arrange something like this?"

"The cameras can be set up in less than twenty-four hours. With your go-ahead, everything can be installed before you arrive. I'll get you set up with personal cams for vlogging, and if Marcel agrees, we can get cams in the RV before you leave."

Easton sat back again. "I think I've lost my appetite."

"I know what you're thinking."

"No, you don't."

"Roy!"

"He doesn't." Royal stiffened. "Neither of you do. You're asking us to put our lives on display for public consumption and sacrifice every bit of our privacy. We won't be able to fart without the world hearing."

"That would be edited out," Balor replied.

Shaking his head, Royal wasn't buying it. Despite his public profession, he resented the conclusion drawn by some that his profession translated to his entire life being fair game, displayed to and dissected by others. Those types of people ignored the dichotomy within him.

"We both know that isn't true. I'm no expert, but I know how these things work. Film gets spliced together any old kind of way to make a contrived storyline for shits and kaboodles. Meanwhile, we get left looking like Bobo the Clown. Not that you would give us final approval, but we don't have the time to be in some editing hack room. We have a championship to focus on. Remember? Besides, cut footage always *leaks*. Once out there on the internet, it never goes away. One wrong word taken out of context and our careers are done." Royal shook his head again. "Trust and believe, I understand the assignment."

"And I take it you agree with him, Easton."

"I do."

Balor sighed. "Well, I'm sorry you both feel that way." He turned to Marcel. "I guess I'll be going."

Marcel smiled weakly and opened the door. "Let me talk to them alone, and I'll call you."

Shit. Here it comes.

"Sure." Balor glanced back at Royal and Easton. "You boys have a safe trip home."

The second the door closed behind him, Royal took the initiative before Marcel could. "This isn't a mistake, Marcel. I know we've all always believed in taking our pennies where we can get them, but this transcends business. We're talking about putting cameras in our houses. Our *homes*. Why are we expected to do that? Isn't it enough bloodlust what we put our bodies through in the arena, or do we also have to invite them into our beds too?"

Marcel snorted. "Let's not exaggerate you being shy about who you invite home. Half of the lower forty-eight's female population has taken a toss in that hot skillet of sin you call a bed."

A hearty laugh burst from Easton. "Good one, Nonc. I didn't think you had that in you."

Royal bounced a glare at Easton and grunted. "Whose side are you on?"

"Yours, but you have to admit, it was funny."

"Listen, Royal, I hear you. It's a big ask, but I do believe the pros outweigh the cons. This industry is struggling, and any positive light that can be cast on it is worth a little sacrifice. Everyone's giving a little."

"What if," Easton asked, strumming his fingers on the table, "we meet in the middle?"

"Middle? There's no middle."

"Hush, Roy. What did you have in mind, East?"

"Forgoing the house cams and film crew and let us do all of the vlogging."

Okay, so maybe there was a middle. Easton's strong point always had been acting as a peacemaker and negotiator, so it should have come as no surprise to Royal. He blew on a ravioli.

"That may be doable," Marcel agreed. "I'll call

Balor, and if he agrees, I'll have him send over contracts to the agents." He narrowed his gaze at Royal. "Don't play hardball with salary."

"I nev—" Royal began.

"And don't fix your mouth to lie. I know you. Balor has shared with me that he's willing to be more than generous."

Royal grunted, shoved pasta into his mouth, and chewed slowly. This wasn't an argument he'd win nor a discussion he wished to continue. He waited until Marcel left before speaking again.

"Now do you understand?" he asked, reclining in his seat.

"*Oui,*" Easton begrudgingly agreed, resting his chin on his fist. "But what are the odds that Balor Adder would have come here?"

"It's been a weird fucking day."

"The weirdest."

Royal's phone pinged. He withdrew it from his pocket and pinched the bridge of his nose as he read the message.

CHAPTER 27

EASTON

"Bad news?" Easton inquired.

"Depends. It's Jerry. He and Gerald are about to head out."

"You don't look happy."

"Well, no." Royal stiffened. "I mean, it could be a good thing. He gets to go home and be with *sa mère*."

"What's wrong being with his mother?"

"Nothing. It's just a long drive to make cooped up with an asshole."

Easton leaned against the counter, folded his arms across his chest, and studied his friend. The way Royal clenched his phone and bit his bottom lip gave Easton pause. He'd witnessed that expression too many times and heard the words not spoken. No doubt, his friend now teetered toward slipping into a dark place. Easton opened his mouth to speak but then reconsidered. Instead of confronting the obvious, Easton decided to change the subject temporarily. Honestly, he needed a distraction too. His own emotions were still ricocheting inside him from earlier.

"How about we get out of here for a bit?" Easton finally asked after taking a couple of swallows to find his voice. "We could go for a walk."

"You're supposed to be resting."

Yeah, right. Who can rest?

"The fresh air will do me some good."

Royal contemplated for a moment and then consented. "Earlier, I saw a pond on the edge of the fairgrounds. It looked peaceful."

"Lead the way."

***

After emerging from a veil of trees, Easton plopped down on the grassy, sunbaked ground and peered up at the stars beginning to peek out as tiny sparkles of silver and ivory against the pinky-orange evening sky. A steady chatter from grasshoppers and crickets replaced honking horns and rowdy voices at the caravan park. Closer to the water's edge, moss padded the ground. A faint breeze created small ripples in the pond and brought with it the sweet scent of honeysuckle. How Easton adored that fragrance. Royal's assessment had been correct. The place was peaceful. It reminded Easton of home. The location's seclusion didn't hurt either.

"*Gardez-donc*," he said, pointing. "Cygnus."

"Cygnus has always been the constellation to throw me for a loop. I've never understood how someone looked up and saw a swan and then convinced everyone else of the same."

"It kind of does, though. You have to use your imagination."

"I guess." Royal tilted his head. "You were always good at imagining things."

The corners of Easton's mouth turned downward, and a sickly twist crept into his gut. He didn't know how to take the statement. "And how does one decipher between imagination, perception, and wishful thinking?"

"The five senses. If you can touch it, taste it, smell it...."

"And if that's not to be trusted?"

"Well, there's always the existential thing of 'I think, therefore I am.'"

Sighing, Easton leaned back on his elbows. "Sometimes, I get tired of thinking—thinking of what to say and what not to say. Of what to feel or not feel. Of what others expect me to do and not do."

"Hey." Royal bumped Easton's knee with his. "You don't have to be anyone other than who you are or do anything that doesn't make you happy."

"Are you sure about that? Because that seems it's all I've been doing here lately." Disconcerted, he flattened his lips together and scowled down at his boots. "I'm not like you, Roy. It's hard to keep everything bottled up. I wish I had your talent to compartmentalize life instead of having everything coagulate into a sludgy gook. Makes me feel like I'm losing my mind, like I'm on *Blue's Clues* island and didn't get a damn letter."

"East...," Royal stated tenderly, using the crook of his finger to lift his companion's chin and bring their gazes back together.

The robust scent of juniper blended with alpine soap jarred Easton's realization that he was sprawled against the earth with Royal hovering inches above him. Mint-green eyes peered at him—stabbed at his soul and drained him of all thoughts. The eyes flickered a question. Or perhaps they mirrored his own. Regardless, the stare pinned him motionless to the ground despite scarcely feeling Royal's grip on his wrists.

"What are you going to do?" Easton asked, struggling to dislodge his voice from his throat. It trickled out barely audible.

"I'm...." Royal leaned forward, closer, his hot breath hitching slightly. "Debating."

"Well, if you're going to regurgitate the litany of reasons us fooling around is perilous, be aware that I don't care. So don't bother proselytizing."

"Aw." He decreased the space between them further. "Look at you making use of those college exam words. It just demonstrates how smart you are—that you should be making brainy decisions."

"Informed decisions are smart," Easton challenged, his gaze fixated on Royal's mouth and his pulse ticking in a throbbing tempo. Or was it something else that was throbbing?

"True dat."

"Then what are you debating?"

"If I should take what I want."

"You can't take what is freely given."

Royal acknowledged with a soft hum and paused, mesmerized—and then he fused their lips.

The kiss spilled through him, and Easton responded with a noise he'd never heard himself make. Funny how he'd been racking those up lately when it came to Royal. In reality, he'd developed a compendium of odd emissions and could open a museum of sonancy and acoustics. He'd be embarrassed if the heat coursing through his body from Royal's tongue hadn't been causing a comprehensibility lobotomy. However, he didn't care how he sounded as long as he could have this moment in which Royal's tongue tangled with his. And he'd meant what he'd said earlier. Royal could take nothing from him because he willingly surrendered. Easton would give this man whatever he asked and even what he didn't.

Royal moved, wedging his knee between Easton's legs and rubbing his thigh against Easton's entrapped budge.

Too many damn clothes.

"How will you sound if I do this?" Royal slid his hand down Easton's arm, splayed his palm on his chest, and flickered his fingers across his nipples.

Another noise tumbled out of Easton, low and lusty, and Royal cruised his mouth over to the hollow of Easton's throat, where he lavished attention on the sensitive flesh.

Easton began lowering his free hand, but Royal trapped it and hoisted it above his head to be pinned with Easton's other hand. Mentally, emotionally, and now physically, Easton was at Royal's mercy. Seconds later, he felt his shirt hem being tugged from his jeans, followed by the jerk of his belt. The sound of his zipper being undone drowned out the sound of chirping insects, and he stilled. Looking down, he watched his friend work his hand into the opening and beneath his cotton briefs. He sucked in a breath and bit his bottom lip as Royal took hold of him, curling his fingers around the thick, smooth length. Instinctively, East-on's hips jerked forward, craving friction.

"Get me off, Royal. Please," he added in a desperate plea.

"I will," he replied, sliding his hand down with a light squeeze. "I'll make you feel good."

"*Oui.*"

Easton's jeans scraped his body as they were pushed to his knees. And then...

Oh, God!

Royal's tongue pressed against his cockhead leaking with precum. Multiple lines trickled down his shaft and dripped onto a nest of pubic hair, and he watched Royal lap at them—short precision strokes—with his tongue.

Heaven.

Easton couldn't tear his gaze away from the view that was equally as gratifying as the tactile sensation. However, as much as he enjoyed it, he wanted...

"I want to taste you too."

He didn't have to ask twice. Royal hastily wiggled out of his shirt and unbuckled his belt. Easton leaned forward, but Royal pressed his palm to his shoulder.

"Lay back," Royal ordered, pushing down his denim and turning simultaneously. Once his jeans were to his ankles, he positioned his knees on either side of Easton's head.

"Oh," Easton responded, understanding the

assignment. Reaching up, he slid his hands to cup Royal's ass and sucked in his cock until it breached his throat. He savored the salty taste.

A strangled groan leaped from Royal's chest, delighting Easton.

Oui, that is what I want to hear.

"More, more. Eat. Feast on me," he mumbled around Royal's rigid dick.

Complying, Royal extended his legs back, leaned forward, and took Easton into his mouth again. Using only upper body strength, he balanced himself on his hands and toes. Slowly, he bent his elbows to lower himself and then pushed back up, pumping his thickness inside Easton's jaws. He repeated the movement once, twice—until Easton couldn't bother himself with counting.

Holy shit! He's push-up fucking my mouth and sucking me off at the same time. Fuck, that's hot!

Up and down. Slow. Methodical. Deliberate. Royal set the pace, controlled all movement. Easton marveled at Royal's triceps flexing and relaxing with every expertly executed push-up. He could give a Marine in basic training a run for his money. But Royal wasn't in basic training. He was giving and receiving a blow job.

Pleasure rose in Easton like a flood—drop by drop until the levee could hold no more. His voice went hazy, as did his vision, when the tension in his abdomen coiled. Light burst from behind his eyes, and his breath sputtered out fast and ragged. He had no time to give warning. His orgasm exploded from him in fiery jets down Royal's throat. As his body vibrated with the last wave, his own mouth was flooded with his lover's seed.

CHAPTER 28

ROYAL

Royal tumbled onto his back and waited for the earth to stop shaking. Drained and sated, he stared up at the stars. The bliss he currently felt must be how it felt to walk in heaven. Every pore in him resonated with ecstasy. But why was everything delectably delicious —deep-fried Twinkies, bacon, sunbathing, vaping— so unhealthy? Fucking one's best friend definitely fell into this category.

"That was incredible," Easton stated between jagged breaths. "I came so hard, I think I cracked a vertebra."

"Well, I think both of my nuts ruptured into my spleen."

"Let me check." Easton rolled onto his side and cupped Royal's softening dick in his hand. "They feel intact to me."

Royal swatted Easton's hand away. "Stop that before you stir something back up."

"Maybe I like stirring things up."

"You? Mr. Play By Every Rule?" Royal snorted. "I'm the reckless, irresponsible one, remember?"

Hitching up his underwear, Easton rolled onto his stomach. "I don't know why people say that about you."

"Maybe because it's true."

"True to who? Aside from Nonc, you're the most responsible person out here. You're always looking out for me, Upton, Cody, and even Wade."

"I'm d—"

"Don't deny it. You're now looking out for Jerry too. It's why you got so upset earlier."

"He's a kid, and I didn't get upset."

"Families have problems, Royal. They have to work through them. Maybe a lengthy car ride together is what they need."

Royal shrugged.

"Want to know what I think?"

"No, because you have that look like you're about to spout some bullshit."

"It's not bullshit, but I am going to give you a dose of reality. I think this entire situation with Jerry and Gerald has you thinking about your father."

"As I said... bullshit."

"Roy—"

"I don't want to talk about this."

"You don't have to talk. You can listen."

"I—"

"You have a big heart, Royal. Huge. And it's big enough for both a mother and a father. The fact that he hasn't reached out to you doesn't mean you shouldn't reach out to him. There may be plenty of reasons why he hasn't, and that's not me defending him. But someone always has to be brave enough to make the first move, and you're no chicken."

"But—"

"Jerry looks up to you."

"I never told him to do that."

"Doesn't matter. How do you ever expect him to get to the point of one day standing up to his father when you can't demonstrate that you've done the same?"

"The situations are completely different."

"Only because you're trying to convince yourself that they are. Not only are you not a chicken, you're also not a hypocrite."

"But Duchess—"

"*Ta mère* will understand."

Royal detested when Easton made logical arguments. Sighing, he nodded. He knew when he'd lost the battle, and he didn't feel like putting up an argument when his bare ass was on the ground in the middle of a field and his underwear around his ankles. "Okay."

"Okay? You'll reach out?"

"*Oui.* One call, but that's it."

"One is all it takes." Easton planted a soft kiss on Royal's lips and replaced his hand on Royal's crotch. "Let's play some more."

Despite being spent, his cock twitched, not completely depleted.

"What game did you have in mind?"

"How about I suck you off again?"

"You could, but...." Royal rolled onto his side and pushed Easton onto his back. Being impatient, he jerked at Easton's briefs, ripping and leaving them to dangle on one hip.

"Damn, Roy."

"Spread 'em." He sucked on two of his fingers and then stroked Easton's taint.

"Oh." Obeying, Easton bent his knees and allowed his legs to fall open wide.

"You ever play down here?"

Easton shook his head. "No."

"Never?"

A bright pink bloomed in Easton's cheeks. "No."

Royal slid his slick fingers to Easton's hole and traced it. "Why not?"

"*Je ne sais pas.* Have you?"

"No, I've never played with your ass before."

"You know what I mean."

A playful smirk curled Royal's lip. "*Peut-être un petit peu.*"

"A little? What's that mean?"

"It means I may have been a little curious." Had it been anyone other than Easton asking, Royal would have never admitted it without being tortured—and even with suffering brutalizing punishment, a confession was doubtful. He moved his fingers in a teasing circle. "Maybe inserted a finger or two."

Easton's mouth dropped open. "And you never told me this?"

"Why would I tell you?"

"Because... because...." He shook his head as if attempting to clear it. "Just because. I'm your best friend. We tell each other everything."

Royal's smirk widened. "Well, I'm telling you now."

"Are you going to put your fingers in me?"

"Do you want me to?"

Please, please, please say yes.

"*Oui.*"

Thank you, merci.

He slid his fingers down but halted at the sound of his phone buzzing. However, it wasn't only his phone buzzing. Easton's was as well. He glanced to where his phone had slipped from his back pocket and lay abandoned on the ground.

Shit! Marcel.

Seeing the name caused his dick to go soft instantly. Reluctantly, he sat erect and retrieved his phone to read the text.

"It's Nonc," Easton stated.

"I see."

"He's back at the RV and wants to know where we are."

Dammit.

More playing would have to be put on hold. "I can't wait," he griped, hoisting up his pants and underwear, "to get back to Maringouin and away from —" He was going to say people, but that wasn't accurate. He'd agreed to vlog.

Fuck!

A PROMISE IS A PROMISE.

Royal stared at the ceiling, lulled by the choppy white noise of Upton's fan, and pondered the stranger things in life—although he doubted things could get stranger than his day already had been.

Here's to hoping.

Easton had been his only highlight and scrap of normalcy—as always. In a perfect world, Royal would have bounded from his bunk and crawled beneath the sheets with him. It took every ounce of self-restraint not to, but he knew it wasn't possible with Marcel and Upton a few feet away. Still, the temptation was real. He could use Easton's strong arms around him—his encouragement and strength. Despite most people considering him to be the strong one, they couldn't have been further from the truth. He siphoned his tenacity from Easton.

He should have been asleep, but it had been hours of dozing off and on in fitful sleep and bizarre dreams. As it happened, he'd nearly rolled over the rail and out of the bunk. That would have been a story to have to explain. His body averred that he was exhausted, but his mind...

Ugh!

His thoughts were in overdrive, as if energy was boundless. They could give The Flash a run for his money. Sleeping was pointless.

Might as well get up.

He didn't move. Instead, he thought about Jerry, who he'd texted shortly after returning to the RV. Reportedly, so far, so good. Gerald hadn't been acting a complete ass. Maybe Easton was right, and they only needed time to work things out. But then again, it was hard to be a dick behind the wheel and focus on the road. And speaking of...

Shit.

Royal hopped from his bunk, threw on a pair of jeans and a T-shirt, grabbed his phone, and headed to the cab. After plopping down in the captain's chair, he opened the curtain and drew his right knee to his chest, resting his foot on the seat as he observed the faint morning glow at the horizon. *Peaceful.* The sun would be up soon—or soon enough.

What time is it?

He glanced at his watch. Converting the time, he concluded that it was close to 9:00 a.m. where Ignacio Araujo was, and his mind reverted to his previous thought.

A promise is a promise.

He searched for an excuse, came up blank, and studied the time again.

Not too early. Damn.

He sighed.

Okay.

Scrolling through his phone contact list, he stopped at a number he'd had secretly stashed there for years. Maybe it wouldn't work. Maybe it had changed. Maybe it was disconnected. Maybe it wasn't. Maybe, maybe, maybe.

Unsulfured molasses fuck.

His finger hovered over the Dial button for several seconds before pressing. He didn't want to do this.

I should hang up. I'm going to hang up.

"*Olá?*"

At the sound of the voice on the opposite end of

the line, Royal's voice lodged in his throat like a boulder.

"*Olá?*" the male voice repeated.

"Um... *oui*.... *Olá*... um...."

Calm yourself. Breathe in. Let out.

Royal took a deep breath. "I'm trying to reach Senhor Ignacio Araujo."

"*Sim*. This is Ignacio."

Shit! What now? What do I do?

"My name is, um... Royal Guérin. I'm Salethia's son. Salethia Guérin."

There was a brief pause before the man responded. "*Sim*." His voice changed.

Royal recognized the change. It was one of, well... recognition. Recall.

This is madness. Hang up.

But then what? Why bother calling only to hang up?

Idiot! Why did I call? I shouldn't have called.

"Um," he began again. "She informed me that you're my father. But," he quickly added, not allowing time for a response, "it's okay if you want to deny it. I'm accustomed to your absence, and it's fine."

"I see."

"You don't have to be concerned with me wanting anything from you. I'm too old for child support, and I don't need a kidney or any other vital organ. I just.... I...." His voice trailed off, and he stared out the front windshield again. "I'm sorry. I shouldn't have called."

"It's okay, Royal. It's good to hear from you."

A small amount of tension in Royal's shoulders eased. "Yeah?"

"I've been hoping you'd reach out."

"Why wait for me? You could have."

"These things are complicated, though they don't seem so much so now. I was young. Stupid. Scared. When I finally discovered some sense, I didn't want to be a disruption."

"Why would you think that?"

"You were doing so well... in school... bull riding... winning championships."

Royal's breath caught. "You know I've won championships?"

"*Sim.* I've followed your career."

Gripping the steering wheel for anything to hold onto to reassure himself that he was still grounded, he clutched it tightly. "You've followed my career?"

"*Sim.* I've seen you ride."

"You've watched me on TV?"

Dammit, Royal, pull it together. Say something other than sounding like a fucking parrot.

"*Sim.* And in person."

Do what?

Royal nearly tumbled from his seat. "I... I... I gotta go," he blurted abruptly.

"Call again," Royal heard as he disconnected with trembling fingers.

What the absolute fuck?

"Roy?"

Royal's head snapped up from staring at the phone to see Easton standing in the cab's entry.

Easton's brows bunched. "You okay?"

"*Oui, oui.*" Royal slid his foot onto the floor and straightened in the seat. "About to get us on the road."

"You look shook."

"Naw, it's nothing. *Ce n'est rien.*"

"You don't sound like it's nothing." He placed his hand on Royal's shoulder.

The warmth of his friend's touch gave him comfort. Grasping Easton's hand in his own, he flipped it over and lightly kissed his palm. "*Merci.*"

"What for?"

"For always being there."

The frown lines on Easton's face deepened. "Roy, what is it?"

Sounds of shuffling drifted from the rear of the RV.

Royal shrugged and displayed a reticent smile. "I'll tell you about it later. How about putting on some coffee?"

"Okay. Sure." Easton's response lacked confidence.

Turning back toward the dashboard, Royal cranked the engine.

CHAPTER 29
EASTON

"*Eh bien, c'est ça*," Marcel huffed, setting his phone on the counter.

"What's it, Nonc?" Easton asked, stuffing the last of his dirty clothes into his laundry bag.

"That was Balor on the phone. He said the fire marshal has concluded his investigation and determined the cause to be accidental."

"*Quoi?*" Easton, Royal, and Upton asked in unison.

"How can that be?" Easton continued. "It hasn't even been twenty-four hours."

"What kind of shoddy Inspector Gadget sleuthing could he have done?" Royal inquired.

"The only one anyone needs," Marcel replied, leaning against the counter. "It's only the preliminary report, but Balor doesn't anticipate anything changing."

"So, it's over?" Royal shoved his hands into his pockets. "The sons of bitches just get to get away with it?"

"Afraid so."

"Can't Balor and the other promoters appeal, ask for a second opinion, or something?" Upton inquired.

"I suppose, but they're not."

"I don't get it, Nonc," Easton griped. "Why wouldn't they put up more of a fuss?"

"My guess is to avoid any delay in the tour. If it's arson, the insurance isn't going to pay until everyone associated with the rodeo has been cleared. That means diving into every crevice and crease and whereabouts and getting-uppings of each person. I'm sure there are plenty of cowboys who'd rather not explain what they were getting up to when the fire started."

"But they know protesters broke in," Royal continued to dispute.

"What they know, Roy, is that people were there— lots of people. They can claim they saw the smoke and rushed to help, the same as you. They can claim that someone arranged it all to frame them to cover for an inside job."

Royal snorted. "That's ridiculous."

"Ridiculous or not, the point is, they can say anything. And once one begins venturing down that crooked road, he can't stop until reaching an end. There are a lot more people who could have reason to sabotage the circuit than the ones carrying picket signs—owed vendors, disgruntled stock hands, drunk cowboys, delinquent teens, in-debt breeders... and the list goes on. All of those people have to be ruled out. This way is easier."

Easton cinched closed his laundry duffel and made a face. "It just doesn't seem right." He glanced at Royal, who was replacing the air freshener beneath the sink.

Marcel pinched tobacco from a tin, stuffed it between his cheek and gum, and snapped the lid back onto the tin. "All right. I want all three of you boys to listen to me and listen good. I know this tour has been grueling for each of y'all, but now isn't the time to lose focus. You can't concern yourselves with this. Let the promotors handle it the way they see fit. Understood?"

"*Oui*," the three answered in unison.

"Now...." He straightened. "Upton, you take out the trash while I top off the water in the tank before we get back on the road."

Easton waited until Marcel and Upton exited the RV before speaking again. "You think protesters will leave us alone now?"

Shrugging, Royal patted the border collie brushing against his legs. "For a while, perhaps, but they're like a grade-school bully. One day, they enter your life and stick around without much of a reason. Then they move or you move. Either way, they vanish as quickly as they appeared—sometimes sans explanation. The reason doesn't matter. You may never see them again as long as you live. Or you may see them at your twenty-fifth class reunion. Or they may take a job managing the local grocery and you see them every day. You just don't know, but you can't waste your time wondering and feeling like it's a loose end. It's like the Maya Angelou quote. If someone with the inside knowledge tells you something, believe him."

"I don't think that's the quote."

"Close enough. If Marcel says that's the end of it, that's the end of it." He pointed at Easton's bulging duffel bag. "Unlike your laundry. Dude, when was the last time you got intimate with a washing machine?"

Easton chuckled. "Leave me alone. I've been busy."

Grunting, Royal turned and walked toward the rear of the RV. "Not with winning."

"Oh, screw you."

Royal glanced over his shoulder, wiggled his eyebrows, and flashed a wicked smile. "You'll have to wait. I'm going to grab some shut-eye. Wake me when we cross the state line."

Home sweet home.

Easton climbed the hill and sped past a tall balding cypress with its charred bark split on one side like a banana peel. *Lightning.* He swerved left to avoid a large limb with a splintered end on the ground partially hidden by water and thick foliage, but his back tire clipped the edge. The rear end of the four-wheeler bounced high before slamming back down. Water and mud splattered onto his face, prompting a hearty chuckle. He missed home. These woods. The bayous. The...

Ew! Rodent disposal unit.

That he didn't miss. Although he wasn't close enough to be certain—but closer than he desired—it looked like a western ribbon. Nonvenomous but still a hell no in his book.

Goosing it, he veered the ATV right, plowing over another downed branch. The quad tilted. Leaning to shift his weight to prevent overturning, he missed seeing a low-hanging limb. The quad landed with a callous jolt at the same time as his shoulder made brutal contact with the limb. He jerked, snatching the wheel, and the four-wheeler began skidding sideways down the ravine.

"Crap!"

Up ahead, Royal screeched his four-wheeler to a halt, his smile slipping from his face.

Easing off the throttle slightly to maintain a steady speed, Easton yanked at the handlebar, hoping to turn his direction downhill. However, the nose pitched up.

Game over.

Easton released the handlebar and was slung to the ground as the four-wheeler began tumbling down the incline to the bayou. He slid a couple more feet before coming to a stop in a patch of spider lilies.

"East!" Royal cried, sprinting toward his friend.

"I'm good, except for maybe a hunk of clay-doh now modeled up my ass," Easton answered, rolling from his stomach to a sitting position and catching his breath. "And my quad may now be salvage yard savvy."

"Fuck the quad." Royal kneeled and snatched Easton forward by the shirt. "The important part is, you didn't knock all your damn teeth out." Lightly, he grazed his lips across Easton's once, twice before gradually sinking into the tender kiss.

"Mm." A warmth of sensuously delicious emotions spilled through him, swelling his heart with love, tenderness, and joy. A raw gleam of heat glimmered in his eyes. "You're only saying that because you don't want to help push it up this steep-ass hill."

"*Oui*, that's true too." Royal snickered.

"I knew it!" a male voice growled low and steely.

Both Easton and Royal swiveled to see Wade standing beside Royal's four-wheeler.

"I knew the two of you were a couple of depraved, disgusting sickos," Wade continued, his eyes gleaming lasers of venom and malice that cut through Easton like a serrated dagger. "The pervert vibes have been looming around y'all for years."

Homophobia activated.

Easton sat paralyzed, unable to speak or respond in any way as he focused on Wade and his scowl of utter repulsion. Never in his life had he ever had anyone look at him with such revulsion, judgment, and animosity. Even animal rights activists had never regarded him with as much loathing and condemnation. Yet here Wade was, doing just that—a man he'd grown up with and considered family. But in an instant, all of that had vanished. He could tell by Wade's expression that he was dead to him.

"Wade, listen—"

"No, don't tell me to listen, Royal. I'm not one of your little media groupies who you can wheel some bullshit excuse at. You're a fucking fag. I know it, and —" He held up the digital camera Royal had attached to the grill of his ATV to film footage for the vlog they'd agreed to do. "—now the entire world will know too."

"Hold on." Royal stood, his knuckles blanching from his clenched fists. "You can't show whatever's on that camera to anyone."

"Oh, can't I?"

"It'll destroy our careers. You know that."

"So? Not my problem."

"Is that how you want to win? By default, when the Association kicks us out and blackballs us?

Because that's what will happen. Are you that desperate?"

"This has nothing to do with desperation or a fucking championship and everything to do with y'all being fa—"

"Fine! I heard you the first time," Royal rebutted. "I'll give you whatever you. Money. Endorsement. Drop out. Grovel at your feet. Name it, but leave Easton out of it."

"Oh, he's all the way in this. Or are you in him?" Wade shifted his weight. "Who sticks who? Is he the bitch, or are you?"

"Enough!" Marcel snapped, emerging from the path obscured by trees.

"But they were—"

"I don't give a good goshdarn what they were doing. It's their business. Gimme that," he demanded, snatching the digital camera from Wade. "Now git on home and open your mouth to no one. *Comprendez-vous?*"

"Yes, sir," Wade sulked.

"Your mama, rest her soul, would be so ashamed of you right now. These boys are your family."

Wade shook his head. "I'm not kin to that."

"Stop this nonsense. These boys helped take you in when you had nothing. If not for them, you'd still be sleeping in that burned-out abandoned train depot. But they fed you. Clothed you. Bought your gear with their allowance, and never once told anyone. They'd never throw that in your face. Now here you are, stealing off Royal's quad, acting all highfalutin as if they owe you something. You've got some nerve judging them when they never once judged you."

Wade hung his head.

"*Mais là*," Marcel further chastised. "Skedaddle."

Deflated, Wade trotted up the hill.

"And you two." Marcel spat, his frown lines deepening. "Disappointing."

"I can explain," Royal began.

"There's nothing to explain. If I've said it once, I've said it a thousand times. You don't get on those blasted rolling mudslingers without wearing a helmet. Y'all not gonna be satisfied until someone gets their skull cracked wide open. Both of y'all know better. Y'all git on back. I better not see y'all going more than five miles per hour."

"Yes, sir," Royal responded.

Turning, Marcel shook his head, laid the camera on the four-wheeler's seat, and grumbled, "A man can't even fish in peace around here anymore. These used to be decent woods where you could placidly feed a body to the gators and mosey on your way. Now y'all whooping and hollering out here like it's a Saturday-night 'Cotton-Eyed Joe' brawl at a juke joint with bad clam chowder. And East," he called over his shoulder, "there's calamine lotion and Benadryl in the bathroom cabinet for when you decide to stop waddling in that poison oak."

Easton glanced down to indeed see the itchy vines mingled among the spider lilies.

Shit!

He hopped to his feet.

Royal waited until Marcel disappeared back into the trees before turning his attention to Easton. "You okay?"

"*Oui*," Easton answered, finding his voice for the first time since Wade's appearance.

"I'm sorry."

"What for? It's not your fault Wade is Wade." Easton swiped his arm across his forehead to dry the sweat but smeared mud instead. "Think he'll tell anyone?"

"Naw. If so, I'll have to kick his ass, but I think Marcel will keep him in line."

"Who would have thunk Nonc would be cool with this?"

"Sometimes, I think there's a lot more to that ol' man than we know." Royal looked to where Easton's ATV had landed. "Well, let's go examine the damage."

Easton nodded and started down the ravine. On the surface, he seemingly had pulled it together. However, his insides still quaked with the magnitude of a 9.0 earthquake. His initial reaction to Wade discovering them and subsequent threats of having his sexuality wagged around like soiled linen for avid eyes to gawk at had been horror followed by anger. But now, he just felt sad—sad that a friend could turn so easily and that the world hadn't progressed. Of course, Easton had known a lot of intolerance and hate existed in the world. But there was knowing and *knowing*. There was being aware and experiencing. This hit on such a different level, and it hurt—bad. More than he ever imagined it could.

He watched Royal make his way ahead of him down the incline.

"Watch your step," Royal advised. "I spotted a poison extension cord before you spun out."

"*Oui*, I saw, but I think it was harmless. Garter."

"Dude, get your eyes checked. That was a fucking copperhead."

That was Royal—always looking out for him, coming to his defense, and seeing what he was oblivious to. Easton managed a tiny smile.

CHAPTER 30

ROYAL

Such a phony!

Royal plastered on his most convincing poker face because he wasn't certain about anything he'd said regarding Wade. And he sure as hell wasn't in control of his emotions that had more bounce than Tigger. They were all over the place. On one hand, he wanted to ram his fist into Wade's smug face. How could Wade say the things that he had? Especially to Easton, who'd never harm a fly. Royal could take it. He was used to people looking at him as if he were shit and didn't deserve life—as if he were less than human. It was something a person of color got used to but was never comfortable with. It always stung, but Royal could handle it. He had no choice. Duchess had raised him to have alligator skin. He would never understand why the world was so full of hate, but he accepted it.

Besides, he was the rowdy one—the one with the big mouth who stole spotlights. Not Easton. Royal might stick his nose in others' business because he could be nosy that way sometimes. He wasn't immune to a tasty tidbit of juicy gossip now and again. But that wasn't Easton. No, he'd walk away without listening and say nothing. So, if Wade felt compelled to blast anyone, Royal felt it should be him. Wade had no reason to go after Easton. Yet...

Wade had a big mouth that grew exponentially bigger after guzzling whatever was on tap and a volatile temper. A couple of pilsners and he wouldn't give a ripping, flipping, whipping toot about a single word Marcel had said. Nevertheless, Royal had to convince Easton, who had looked as if he might pass slam out, that he believed it. It wasn't fair to saddle his best friend with doubt and worry. Easton had enough going on in his life without adding Wade's bullshit to the mix. Then again, so did Wade.

Royal attempted to put himself in Wade's shoes. Would he have been shocked about what he'd witnessed? Sure. Although... Wade had indicated that he'd had his suspicions. So, maybe he wasn't shocked. But what right did he have to be angry—because he seemed furious. It didn't concern him. This was a man who whipped out his pecker and pissed in sinks and who posted his ex's American Express number on Craigslist after learning she had cheated on him.

Surely, his delicate sensibilities couldn't have been offended.

True, he was—as they all were—influenced by a toxic homophobic environment. Yet, for Royal, this didn't seem to explain enough. Wade was his friend—as Marcel had said, they were like family. How would being family not be enough to show a sliver of compassion or tolerance? But Wade had threatened them. He'd held up that camera and said he would expose Easton. Yes, the threat also included exposing Royal, but he could half understand that part. After all, he begrudgingly had to admit that he did behave like an ass sometimes. But Easton was nothing but good to people—his heart pure gold. It was the quality that made him special. So, how could Wade disregard that so easily? If anyone should be ticked, it should be Easton. His heart truly ached.

Fuck!

Royal recalled when his grandpapi passed away. This felt like that, except all the stages of grief had been molded into one and were oscillating for dominance. Currently, fury was winning, and rage coursed through him. If he could have, he would have shaken every tooth loose in Wade's mouth. However, that wasn't something he could do for Easton's sake. He couldn't afford to do anything that would set Wade off and unleash his viciousness on Easton. All he could do was pray that Marcel's words had had enough impact to keep Wade silent. Only time would tell, and time had a way of unsatisfyingly stretching out. Thus, he couldn't focus on it and had to accept not knowing.

"It doesn't look too bad," Royal stated, inspecting the four-wheeler that had landed on its side. It was built to be sturdy—to withstand plowing through thickets and woods. He had to be equally as sturdy.

Sell it. Make him buy the act.

He pushed the ATV upright and pressed the starter. The four-wheeler sputtered but cranked.

"I think we're going to be okay here," he stated, attempting to convince himself about more than the four-wheeler.

***

"Petit, darling, I wish I'd known you were coming home earlier, and I wouldn't have agreed to go on this girls' trip," Royal's mother complained, arranging wax paper in a Tupperware bowl.

Royal leaned against the kitchen counter, thumbs stuck into the front pockets of his denim. Thick with the aromas of cinnamon and sugar, he soaked in the scents of freshly baked pastries cooling.

"Duchess, don't dare change your plans on account of me."

"But it's just a play, and probably not even a good one. There'll be others."

"Nonsense. It has rave reviews. You've waited months for these tickets and jumped through triple hoops of volcanic fire to get them." He inched closer to a plate of beignets. "Besides, you should get out with friends more."

"I'd rather spend the time with you. I don't get to see you hardly enough."

"It's not like you'll be gone for five to seven business days. I'll be here when you return tomorrow."

"Smarty." Her velvet voice suited her regal demeanor. She patted Royal on his arm as she passed him to collect another storage container from the overhead cabinet, her clean scent of shampoo and soap mixing with the baking aromas. "It feels rude leaving you here alone."

While his mother's back was turned, Royal pinched off a chunk of beignet and crammed it into his mouth. "I'll invite Easton over to watch a kaiju movie and become a taco connoisseur."

Pivoting, his mother frowned. "Splendid. Not only am I abandoning my child, I'll be the reason Lisette is deprived of hers."

"Well, maybe I'll head over there."

His mother scoffed. "And intrude on their family time?"

"You know she's probably wondering where I am right now."

"That's true. You two have always been two for the price of one wholesale. Didn't even need a coupon."

Royal chuckled and watched his mother resume packing the pastries. She had her ebony hair scooped in a tidy bun and held by several vintage clips. More silver strands streaked her hair than the last time he'd visited. However, instead of aging her, it made her look more refined and elegant. Such a genteel-looking woman with delicate bone structure yet deceptively strong. He didn't doubt she could wrestle a polar bear if she had to and win. Marveling at her beauty, he mused with pride.

Poor bear.

Then the smile faded, and his eyes grew serious.

"Duchess, I need to tell you something."

"That y'all finally confessed your feelings for each other?"

Royal's jaw dropped, and his heart embedded itself someplace between his rib cage and his esophagus. "*Quoi?*"

Oh my lanta. How the hell...? That hadn't been what he was going to say—not even close.

"No."

Holy shit? Did I just come out to ma mère?

"Well, don't you think it's about time y'all did?"

Speechless. Wide-eyed, he stared at his mother. She glanced at him as she scurried around the kitchen.

"Petit, you're as pale as a bar of Ivory soap, which

is quite the trick considering your coloring. Oh, that reminds me. I need to put dishwashing liquid on the grocery list." She strolled to the refrigerator and added the item to a piece of paper held by magnets.

He still had no words.

"Royal, baby, I'm going to need you to blink twice if you're okay."

Silence.

"Do I need to grab the defibrillator?"

Nothing ever got past his mother with her weirdly intuitive hawk instincts. How had he thought she wouldn't have known? But that was exactly what he'd thought.

Stupid.

"How are we even having this discussion?"

"*Whew*, you're still with me." His mother exaggerated a sigh of relief. "That's a good thing. I haven't checked the batteries in that thingamajig since I bought it years ago. I have no idea if they still have juice. Instead of giving a jolt, it may only tickle. Wouldn't that have been something? The good news is, they relocated the fire station. It's closer now. Still probably won't do us any good this far out, but it gives you about a 20 percent chance instead of 10 that they'll make it here before you voyage to meet Saint Peter. That's double. Plus, they'd already be here when I'd have to explain your demise to Easton, so he'd have even better odds."

Throwing up his hands, Royal shook his head like a shaggy pooch receiving a bath. His cheeks burned, and he felt his armpits growing damp.

"Oh, dear. Is it still supposed to be a secret? I can go back to pretending not to know." Although her voice was filled with concern, Royal detected a smidgen of humor.

"Did Marcel say something?"

"He finally figured it out, did he? Well, it's about time. If it doesn't have four legs, that man's about as obtuse as the tires on that rotting, beat-up jalopy in his garage, like he's some shade-tree mechanic. Bless his heart."

Is this my life right now?

"Wh-Wh-What?"

"Oh, it doesn't matter." She closed the lid on the container and gave him her full attention. "So, if that wasn't what you wanted to tell me, what was?"

"I called Ignacio," he blurted.

Now his mother's eyes dimmed as if she'd been informed of a nuclear holocaust. No. Wounded by one. "Oh."

Dammit!

That was not how he wanted to tell her—just bellowing it out like a blue-light special over an intercom with no preamble. What the hell was his problem? The hurt he saw bunched in her eyes made him feel like dogshit. No, worse. Like the specks on dogshit. If he could take it back, he would, but he couldn't.

"I wanted to—"

"You're a grown man. You don't have to explain yourself to me."

"Duchess, please. I want to. *S'il vous plaît.*"

His mother emitted a reluctant sigh and nodded. "All right."

"You've always given me everything I've ever needed. I couldn't ask for more, yet it's always felt weird that there is a person who I share half my DNA with walking around in the world, and I've never spoken to him. Maybe that's what's been pushing me. Chalk it up to innate-slash-genetic curiosity."

"What did he say when you spoke with him?"

"Not much, but I didn't give him much of a chance. I can't explain why I did it, but I needed you to know that I did."

"*D'accord.* Now I do."

"Please don't be cross with me."

Her lips curled enough to be considered a smile. "If I'm not cross with you for risking your life every week, how can I be cross about this?"

Closing the short distance between them, Royal threw his arms around her and drew her in close.

"But you pinching off the beignets I baked for the girls is another thing. You're grounded."

"Aw, shucks! Does this mean I have to sneak out of

my window again? Cos climbing over those yucca bushes is a bitch."

"Like they've ever been a deterrent. You ripped up plenty of perfectly good jeans doing so. I'd be a thousandaire today if I'd bought stock in denim patches."

Royal's grin broadened. *God, I love this woman.*

CHAPTER 31

EASTON

Easton wanted to be alone, to sulk and bask in misery without the disruption of toxic positivity. The world sucked—at least for the moment. Well, maybe not the entire world, but Wade did. But Wade wasn't alone in his douchebaggedness. He hadn't invented bigotry and hate. He'd been taught them, which meant there were others who felt the same. It couldn't be denied despite how much Easton wanted to bury his head in the sand and pretend all was still good.

Easton had witnessed an ugliness that he never wanted to glimpse again, and remaining shut away in his childhood room surrounded by shelves of his model airplanes and plastic dinosaurs where all was safe provided that possibility. However, it was Thursday in the Faucheaux household, and Thursday meant pinochle night with the Broussards, his parents' closest friends.

Unmistakably, Easton liked the Broussards, but ever since he began walking, Delmar Broussard had been trying to marry him off to her eldest daughter, Rana. Even if he'd been physically attracted to her—which he wasn't—he wouldn't have connected with her on any other level. Sure, Rana was sweet, but she had, in his opinion, a fucked-up attitude about dating and love. She'd made it clear on more than one occasion her intention to marry for stability and possibly learn to love the poor slob she'd hitched herself to sometime after that—as if love was an afterthought and an emotion that could be manufactured. Although Easton's credit score was well above 700, he didn't desire a partner with whom he'd have to submit a PowerPoint presentation of his financial portfolio and 401(k). He wanted someone to love him for him, to accept him for who he was as he was. Someone like Royal. Royal would never ask to see his credit score. Of course, Royal already knew that information; but if he didn't and had asked, Easton would have no qualms disclosing. But that all was beside the point.

Royal was the reason Easton had dragged his sulky ass out of bed thirty seconds after receiving a text inviting him to dinner and a movie. So, there he was, standing in Salethia's gleaming kitchen, watching as Royal removed the hot cast iron skillet from the oven and plopped it onto a silicon trivet. Easton's mouth watered at the smell of the Cajun crab dip. He could always count on Salethia leaving them something tasty to chow on while she was away. Tonight was no different. And his own mother hadn't been a slouch either. She never sent him empty-handed and had made a plate of blackened crawfish remoulade and muffuletta deviled eggs. He'd picked up the six-pack of double-dry Ghost in the Machine courtesy of a quick pit stop at the Piggly Wiggly.

"Where are the chips?" Easton inquired, licking his lips.

"To hell with chips. Duchess baked baguettes this morning. I already sliced them and put them in a basket on the coffee table in the den."

"Oh, *key awau*! We get the good stuff."

"Did you expect anything less?"

"No." He hadn't. The two of them had the best mothers on the planet. "Huh," he muttered.

"*Quoi?*"

"*Ce n'est rien.*" Easton shook his head, indicating his thought was nothing of importance. But it wasn't *nothing*. It was very much *something*.

Since the Wade incident, Easton hadn't been able to shake the reality of what coming out would mean and how it would affect his career. He'd thought he'd known, but it hadn't been until he'd seen Wade's expression and heard his disgust that the message resonated at a level of consciousness that couldn't be denied. The fear of being caught again and being exposed was overwhelming. On the rodeo circuit, reputations could be ruined on the skimpiest hearsay. So, how could he be around Royal day in and day out and not think about or crave what they had experienced? And he didn't mean only the sexual stuff. He hadn't dreamed it possible, but he and Royal had grown closer over the last several weeks. And the truth was, Easton could envision himself with Royal. Try as he might, he couldn't forget or ignore what had transpired between them. And there lay the fucking problem.

If he couldn't forget, he would need to avoid it. He would have to put distance—physically and emotionally—between them. But that also would mean Easton would have to avoid Salethia. And his own mother would pitch all nine innings of a conniption if Royal stopped coming around when he was in town. He was like another son. In truth, Easton sometimes questioned if his family liked Royal more than him. So, the "Huh" he'd uttered was the realization that every part of his life was entwined with Royal's. Royal was his destiny, yet this yucky world was scraping its social righteousness claws against the blackboard and screeching condemnation from a *morality* pulpit. He sighed. Why did it have to be that way?

The *why* didn't matter. He'd just have to do it—

pull back and stomp down his emotions the way he shoved away any fear of climbing on a bull.

I can do this.

"Grab some paper towels, will ya?" Royal asked, stacking food on a wooden serving tray to carry it to the den.

"Sure, no problem." He walked to the pantry to get a roll of Bounty.

Tell him.

"Um... Roy...."

Returning to the kitchen, Easton found himself alone. He shut off the light and made his way down the long hall to the den off the split level where Royal was settling onto the couch. Easton placed the paper towels on the table and sat next to Royal.

"Any preferences?" Royal pulled up the guide on the TV and began scrolling.

"No crying or singing movies. And nothing that is going to make my brain hurt." He read the screen. "What about that one?"

"Uh-uh. It's about a son searching for his father, and I ain't got it to do tonight."

"Well, you know my feelings on the subject. I think you should contact him."

Royal clicked the description of an action movie about an underwater locomotive.

"I already have."

Easton froze midway through selecting a deviled egg.

"*Quoi? Quand?*"

"Before we left."

"And you're just now telling me?" Easton didn't give Royal a chance to respond. "What happened?"

"It was brief and didn't go anywhere, but he did say I should call again. He claims he's been following my career." Royal shook his head. "I didn't tell Duchess that part. I think that would have sent her over the edge for real."

"Whoa, whoa, whoa. You told your mother?"

"More like screamed it at her. I opened my mouth, and it spewed like projectile vomit. It was a complete shit show. It only happened cos she caught me off guard when she asked if we'd gone all chick-mode and did a deep dive into our emotional understanding, attachment, and attraction to each other."

Although seated, Easton's legs gave way, and he nearly slipped off the sofa.

Da fuck?

"She did what?"

"I thought Marcel had said something, but he hadn't. She figured it out. You know how she is. And you know who else knows if she knows."

My mother.

"Oh. My. God." Easton slumped back on the couch. "Mama hasn't said a word."

"She's probably not going to cos you live farther from the fire department."

"*Quoi?*" Easton felt his eyeballs drying, they were so wide.

"Never mind. Let's just watch a movie."

"Yeah," he agreed, his voice shaky and questioning as his mind continued processing. The only reason he agreed to drop the subject was because Royal's expression indicated that not only was he done but he was *done* done. "Okay. You pick."

How the fuck did things just get more complicated? How?

THE MOVIE ENDED, BUT EASTON COULDN'T HAVE ANSWERED a single question about it. First, the acting had been so egregiously atrocious that he hadn't been able to focus on the plot. Second, his thoughts were still scattered like breadcrumbs eaten by forest critters to Timbuktu and back. But mainly, it was due to the man seated beside him who smelled like desire but was on the *Romeo and Juliet* forbidden-love list. He understood why they couldn't be *together*. Hell, Royal had been the one to explain it to Easton. What Royal wouldn't understand was why Easton needed physical space between them. After all, for the majority of their lives, they rarely went a day without seeing each other.

For his sanity, Easton needed to keep away. Royal had a real chance at winning this year, and if what they'd been doing seeped into the media's grubby, stumpy fingers... it would be Wade times infinity. Simply enforcing boundaries wouldn't work—not when they practically lived together. It would be like a divorced couple cohabitating. Was it possible? Sure. Would the temptation to fall into old habits and patterns be tremendous? Did Uncle Sam tax the shit off the top of his check? Hell yeah! It would be hard, but...

I have to do this.

"Royal," he began slowly, "I've been thinking."

"Well, that's your first mistake."

"Asshole," Easton muttered, nudging him with his elbow.

"Always."

"I'm dropping out of the competition."

"*Quoi?*" Royal sat erect from his relaxed position and stared at his best friend. "Come again?"

"You heard me."

"*Mais pourquoi, sha?* You've worked like hell to get back in this thing. Why would you toss it all now? Is it because of Wade?"

"No. Yes. I mean.... It's everything, Roy. How do you expect us to pretend that we didn't happen or trust that we won't get caught again?" He waved his hands frantically. "People are catching on. Your mother. My mother. Who's next? What if it's Balor or one of the sponsors? Then what? You lose it all? You can't when you're so close to winning. I won't let you."

Royal's eyebrow quirked. "Let me?"

Fuck! Them's fighting words. He's going to make a big deal.

"You can't stop me from dropping out," he quickly added to stave off the impending protest Royal was gearing up to make.

"No, but I can call Miss RobiLeigh and have her birch-whip the shit out of you."

Easton's face twisted at the mention of his mawmaw. "You wouldn't dare."

"Oh, I would, and she'd come with heels blazing. That old birch in the south corner of your backyard always made for nice, flexible switches."

"That would be pure mean."

"Well, stop talking crazy and it won't happen. I know you're freaked out about—" Royal shrugged. "—well, everything. But this isn't the way, East. Trust me; it isn't. If anyone quits, it'll be me."

Easton snorted so deeply, his nostrils stung. "And I'm the one talking crazy? You quitting is beyond crazy. It's...." He searched for a word, but only one came to mind. "Idiotic."

Royal's jaw dropped. "Did you call me an idiot?"

"No, but what you're proposing is." Easton slumped back and stretched his arm across the rear of the couch, resting his hand on the pillow behind his host. "I don't know what to do." Closing his eyes, he whispered. "I'm scared, Roy."

Royal responded, but the words didn't register with Easton. All he felt was Royal's mouth hot and hungry on his own and his body being snatched against Royal's chest. Or maybe he'd tugged Royal to him. He didn't know nor care. His thoughts muddled as he sank into the delight of Royal's teeth nipping over his throat. His eager body arched at both the torturing and pleasing sensation of his best friend's—his lover's—lips and tongue gliding across his flesh. Each sweep of Royal's tongue hijacked Easton's breath before he could draw it. For an instant, fear rose in him at the realization that he'd never needed anyone or anything so desperately. Then as soon as the fear materialized, it vanished. This felt right. Royal felt right.

"I need to fuck you," Royal murmured, his voice husky with desire and eyes clouded with something almost savage.

Both excitement and panic churned in Easton's belly. Royal's dick was fucking ginormous, and Easton couldn't formulate the math of how it would fit inside his ass—not with algebra, trigonometry, geometry, or pseudomathematics.

"I want that, but—"

Royal shushed him, seeming to have read his

thoughts, and snaked his index finger into Easton's mouth. "I've never hurt you and never given you a reason to distrust me."

Easton nodded. "I know."

"Then if you want me, too, tell me."

"*Je fais.*"

"Good." Royal rose from the sofa and extended his hand.

Easton accepted, allowing Royal to lead him to his bedroom. Linear lights in the built-in shelving unit illuminated the area with a soft pale-blue glow. Trophies and photos lined the rows of shelves, and models of planets and moons still dangled from the ceiling. A glass curio tucked under a window covered with dark drapes displayed a collection of Funko Pops! also highlighted with linear lights. Not much had changed in the room since they were teens. The familiarity offered comfort but not a granule of the comfort of Royal's embrace.

Within minutes, their clothes were in scattered piles on the floor, and Royal sauntered to where his unpacked duffel bag was resting on a chair. After a moment of rummaging, he returned with a condom and lube, pushed Easton onto the mattress, and crawled across him.

"You show less fear on those bulls."

Easton's brows knitted. "I don't care about those bulls. But you... I don't want to ruin us."

"If I can stand you cooking chitterlings and your rot gut after eating grillade a la chique all these years, I don't think I'm going anywhere. Now let Daddy work."

With his thigh, Royal knocked open Easton's legs and drizzled the lubricant across his taint. He gave it a few seconds before working it into Easton's hole, starting with one finger.

Biting his bottom lip, Easton sucked in a deep breath.

"Relax," Royal cooed, inserting a second digit. He probed with quick, hard strokes until the muscles eased around them. Withdrawing his fingers, Royal smiled. "You're ready." After rolling a condom over the length of his swollen member and adding more lube, Royal positioned himself at Easton's entrance. "I'll go slow." He stationed his hand on Easton's hip and breached the sphincter.

"Oh my...." Easton's eyes fluttered shut.

Royal stilled. "No, look at me."

Obediently, Easton opened his eyes and stared at the face of his lover. Inwardly, he smirked at how quickly he'd become contented using that word to describe Royal.

"Kiss me going in," he mewled.

Royal leaned forward and captured Easton's mouth with a deep, savoring kiss as he pushed completely inside with one languid movement. Easton whimpered as inch by glorious inch filled him. Pausing just long enough for Easton to regain his breath—and possibly his sanity—Royal thrust.

Clamping Royal's shoulders, Easton quivered as surges of pleasure jolted from his core and through his limbs. As the pace quickened, Royal's fingers dug into Easton's hips. The sounds of the bed squeaking, Royal's balls slapping against Easton's ass, and the wet sucking sound of the lube filled the room. Easton's ragged pants grew louder with every movement. However, when Royal reached between Easton's legs and began fisting his cock, Easton's pants converted into little more than audible puffs. The thumping of his heart roared in his ears and threatened to tear through his chest with the next thrust, and Easton's back arched against the mattress as a jet of semen shot out of him and landed on the base of Royal's throat. His heels dug into the mattress as a sunburst of blinding pleasure sparked at the root of his spine. A second stream hit Royal's chest and dripped down. On Easton's third spurt, Royal slammed into him and bellowed as he released inside.

Royal rolled off and molded his body around Easton, where they lay coupled in silence until their breathing returned to normal.

Sighing with contentment, Easton snuggled beneath the sheet. The look of unbridled ecstasy gracing his face was unmistakable as he drifted from the gluttonous clouds of a mind-deliquescing orgasm. He relished the feel of Royal's warm breath fanning across his shoulders and the soft pulse of Royal's pecs against his back each time he took a breath. This was real. But what else was real?

"Royal," Easton murmured, cocooned in Royal's embrace.

"Huh?" he responded drowsily.

"You did see it, didn't you? In the arena? The boo hag? *J'suis pas fou de sa?*"

"No, you're not crazy."

"But you don't believe me." Easton's shoulders sagged into the mattress.

Royal sighed and intensified his hug on Easton. "I do."

"Then why have you dismissed me? Why won't you discuss it with me?"

"Because you shouldn't talk about such things."

"Why not? That boo hag almost—"

"It wasn't a boo hag. They only surface when you're asleep."

Easton's eyes grew wide, and he rose on his elbows. "You *did* see it."

"*Oui.*"

Easton waited. After Royal failed to continue, Easton probed. "What aren't you saying?"

Royal

Shit!

Royal winced. He'd known this moment was coming—dreaded it. However, he supposed he couldn't delay it any longer. Staring up at the model planets swaying slightly from the air conditioning, he was reminded that the universe was relentless in its demands and pointless to rebel against. Zeus swallowed his wife to prevent the birth of a child more powerful than him, and look how that turned out. It ended with the god being bashed in the head to relieve a debilitating migraine and a war goddess leaping out of the gaping wound. Royal wasn't a god and didn't need a hole in the head.

CHAPTER 32

EASTON

"You pricked your finger."

Easton's eyes flooded with questions. "*Quoi?*"

"Do you believe in fairy tales?"

He remained quiet for a moment, slack-jawed and debating whether Royal's question was serious or not. Now wasn't the time for jokes. He had neither the mood nor patience for one. However, studying Royal's expression, Easton concluded that Royal was indeed serious and waiting for an answer. But why was this a question? *Unless... he thinks ghosts are fairy tales.*

"Don't treat me like an imbecile."

"No, that's not what I'm doing. Hear me out. Remember the Grimms' tale involving a spinning wheel?"

"Which one? *Rumpelstiltskin* or *Sleeping Beauty?*"

"Actually, they're the same but over time have been divided into two."

"I don't know why I'm asking; but *pourquoi*?"

"To disguise the truth."

Tiring of the back-and-forth cloak-and-dagger conversation, Easton sighed. "What truth?"

"That evil exists."

Easton made a rueful cluck and raked his hands through his hair, leaving it sticking up in tufts. "Roy, those tales were invented to scare children into obeying."

"And are you obeying?"

"I'm not a child."

Royal's broad chest rose and fell with a labored breath. "I know I'm about to sound Joker-in-a-strait-jacket, pre-electric-shock, escape-from-Azkaban batshit crazy. I wouldn't even mention it, but we vowed no more secrets."

"I'm listening, and it's Arkham, not Azkaban."

"Same thing."

"Well, no, but continue."

"First, tell me how you remember the stories."

"Royal." Easton huffed in exasperation and felt a bit queasy about the direction of the conversation.

"Just indulge me this."

Easton gathered his thoughts and tried to envision his mother sitting on the side of his bed, reading to him from the thick, worn children's book that had been passed down in his family for generations. He'd preferred action stories with space cowboys, aliens, or superheroes, but every Wednesday night, his mother had insisted on reading him one of the classics.

"Well...." He cleared his throat, feeling a little silly. "Rumpelstiltskin was a fairy who spun straw into gold in exchange for tricking a mother into giving him her newborn, and a witch cursed Sleeping Beauty to fall asleep because Beauty's parents didn't send the witch an invite to a party or some petty shit like that."

"Eh, that's the watered-down talking-mouse version, consumable by most palates. But what if I told you the real version was about rape and cannibalism?"

"Get out!"

"Fo sure. Let's start by clarifying what you said. First, Boothang wasn't some silk-stocking princess. She was a miller's daughter. Second, Rumpelstiltskin was an imp. Know what that is?"

"It's like a mischievous elf or something."

"Or something, if put politely. It's a demon."

"Demon?"

"*Oui.* The name Rumpelstiltskin means a pole or post that supports a structure—like a supporting wall. As in, if it's removed, entire frameworks collapse. Second, it didn't trick the mother. They had a deal, and she wanted to renege. The demon made its terms clear from the onset—no subprime-balloon-mortgage fine print or invisible ink. Some versions like to tack that on to give the mother a pass for selling her baby on the black market, but that's not how the story goes."

"I'm going to need something stronger than beer," Easton muttered.

"As for Sleeping Beauty, a king—not a prince—came along and found her sleeping. And while she was partaking in her semi-coma snoozefest, he nutted in her without a raincoat, knocked her up, and boogied down the yellow brick warped road riddled with potholes."

"*Quoi?* No... just no." Easton shook his head. "Who includes that in a children's story?"

"*Mais, ce n'est pas pour les enfants, sha.* In the original, it reads that the king toted her to a bed—most likely king-size—and 'gathered the first fruits of love,' which everyone knows is medieval code for getting freaky-deaky."

"Yeah, right," Easton mocked. "Everyone knows that."

"Hey, I didn't write it. Your beef is with Jacob and Wilhelm and possibly Vespucci for his discovery of cocaine. Now, do you want to hear the rest?"

"Not particularly, but go ahead."

"She later gives birth to twins. This king in *Sleeping Beauty* is the same king with the same spinning wheel in *Rumpelstiltskin*. And this is where it gets disturbing."

"Oh, I think we crossed the disturbed threshold

ten minutes ago when we didn't take the left at Albuquerque."

"There's no mention of two babies in *Sleeping Beauty*. That's because your ol' boy Rump had already gobbled up one of the little munchkins for brunch with Rosina Leckermaul's leftover gingerbread."

"Who?"

"The *Hansel and Gretel* hag. Keep up."

"Is there any reason you're trying to wreck my childhood memories? Eating babies? Really, Roy? And how'd *Hansel and Gretel* get in this?"

"I'm only explaining. I mean, they end up eating the witch instead of the other way round as planned, but it's still cannibalism."

"They did not eat the witch." Easton struggled not to shudder.

"They shoved her in an oven."

"Doesn't mean they ate her. It makes them people-arsonists, I guess." *What the hell did I just say?* Easton shook his head at his own words. "I can't believe I'm having this conversation. What does any of this have to do with me riding bulls? None of this is making sense."

"It didn't to me either, at first—not until how blood curses work was explained to me."

"Blood curses? This keeps going from bad to worse."

"Let's rehash what happened."

"Please don't," Easton groaned.

Royal ignored his friend. "A witch cursed Sleeping Beauty for her parents' actions, but a king came along and cheated the witch out of her due by breaking the curse. In the meantime and in between time, the king saturates her with his baby batter—"

"Oh God!"

"Since we know this is the same king in *Rumpelstiltskin*, we can use our deductive reasoning to conclude that this woman is Sleeping Beauty. When Rumpelstiltskin consummated his end of the fucked-up antedated dark-web trafficking agreement with Sleeping Beauty, she wanted to renegotiate."

"Can we please use some different word choices here?"

"He said no and devoured one of her twins. Now, all of this started when Sleeping Beauty's parents slighted a witch named Maleficent by not allowing her to hang out with the cool kids and not recognizing that she was a boss bitch. The word *maleficent* literally means to produce evil. Thus, in actuality, this witch was another demon—or maybe even the same demon in a different form. I'm pretty sure they all hang out together in hell and have their own social network going."

Easton considered pointing out that the underworld probably didn't have Wi-Fi, but why bother?

"The king broke the spell, but after he got his rocks

off, he didn't stick around to see what happened next. So, Sleeping Beauty went back to her parents' house because where else was there for her to go? Her parents thought everything was all cool in the hood because she was awake. But she didn't arrive alone. She had double-yoke rug rats in the oven and didn't know the daddy."

"If I ever have kids, remind me never to allow you to tell them a bedtime story."

"I'm only relaying how the story goes."

"Just get on with it."

"Well, somebody had to feed the crumb-snatchers, and Grandpa, Sleeping Beauty's father, couldn't afford it on a miller's salary. Therefore, he concocted a scheme. He bragged to the greedy king that his daughter could spin straw into gold. This was a lie, but the king called the miller's bluff and ordered Sleeping Beauty to be locked up. He demanded that she spin his straw into gold or he would Anne Boleyn-ify her—because he was banking on it being a lie, and this was a proven way of avoiding paying child support—and alimony too. He'd taken lessons from Henny VIII."

"Seriously, Roy?"

"You act like he's some righteous dude. The guy didn't even floss, much less bathe more than once a month. Of course, you couldn't blame him. They didn't have running water back then, and all the moats were leech and *E. coli* vacation resorts. Still, you can tell a lot about a person by his hygiene."

Easton rolled his eyes—again. "Anyway...."

"*Anyway*, the point is that Sleeping Beauty made a deal with the devil, who consumed her baby. The sins of the parent will be passed to the child, and demons don't just vanish. They roam the earth, wheeling and dealing and collecting souls."

What the fuck?

At this point, Easton was 98 percent convinced his head would explode at any second.

"You just rattled off a slew of words the length of a holiness church sermon, and I'm still as clueless as peppermint on a hemorrhoid."

"Remember Cody's last ride?" Royal asked more rhetorically than directly.

"Sure. It was as nasty as they come. That bull nearly tore his shoulder off."

"Do you recall the name of the bull?"

"*Oui.* Rump...." The name died on Easton's lips as his stomach sank to his toes.

"Uh-huh. Rumpy, short for Rumpelstiltskin. And in Sioux Falls, what was the name of the bull you drew?"

"El Diablo."

"Sired by Rumpy, as is Onyx Alpha."

The hairs on Easton's neck stood up.

"Cody has said numerous times that he would sell his soul to ride," Royal continued.

"No, he wouldn't."

"*Mais oui*, he would, and he did, knowingly or not." Royal paused. "A blood debt must be paid, *sha*. It won't stop until it is. He's your cousin. That bull has tasted your blood and recognizes it. And since Cody is no longer riding, it must be you."

"What about Upton? I mean, I'm not willing anything on him, but he's been nicked a time or two."

"You and Upton are related on your mama's side but you and Cody on your papi's. The demon doesn't recognize Upton because Cody and Upton aren't blood kin to each other."

"But why now?"

"We've been places—in arenas—vortexes that spirits are drawn to. They sense your energy, your chakras. They're pulling at your *ka*."

Stunned and too rattled to make eye contact, Easton stared at the floor and massaged his throbbing temples. "How do you know all of this?"

"That's hard to explain too. *Ma grand-taunty* has always been able to... sense things. It's something that runs in my family. It can lay dormant or submerged until something triggers it, something threatening."

"*Arrêté*. I need a minute."

Easton sucked in a large gulp of air while he processed the tornado of thoughts whipping around his cerebral cortex. How could he believe this? How could he not? While it all sounded *A-Clockwork-*

Orange-meets-Alfred-Hitchcock bonkers, it made perfect sense.

"So, you've been... *sensing things*... since Topeka?"

"Actually, it began before then."

"How much before?"

"When Maddox showed up."

"Maddox?"

"He made me realize how much... how much I love you and want to protect you. I was scared he'd steal you away from me."

"Roy—"

"It was the witch—the fortune teller—who put all the pieces together for me." His eyes darkened seconds before his face followed suit. "Just as the demon recognized you, she recognized me as one of her own. Apparently, I have... abilities. I can not only sense spirits but have a visceral aptitude to repel them."

"Ah. That explains why I could hear you above the crowd and everything else. Why once you came near, the... demon disappeared. But why wouldn't you tell me this before now?"

"It's a bit hard to digest and more than a little insane."

"Oh, I'd say it's about as sane as having cursed bulls trying to off you to resolve a blood debt. I mean, that's not your normal, everyday matinee."

"Touché."

"So, what do I do, Royal? Stop riding? Give up my dream?"

"The witch gave me something—a spell."

"Spell? You mean like magic?"

"K-Kinda. It's more like having a deep connection with nature and the universe and being able to tap into them in a way most can't. It's using sacred words taught to man but now forgotten."

"How do you mean sacred?"

"Ever wonder how long Adam and ol' girl lived in the garden before being evicted?"

Oh, please, please, please don't go where I think you're going.

"Seven days?" Easton's response was more question than statement.

"Nope. That was the length of time it took for Creation. I meant how long they took up residency before mucking everything up. They had a direct line to the Big Man during those days. Imagine those conversations."

Yep, he went there.

Easton gasped. "You're saying...?"

"All I'm saying is, Adam and Evie knew things and passed it down. As with most generations, they didn't realize the importance of oral history and only half paid attention. If you don't use it, you lose it. But some people were paying attention. What you call magic is the original language of man needed to rule Earth."

"And the—" Easton hesitated saying the word. "—*witch* taught you this language—a spell?"

"*Oui*, although, more accurately, she used the word *incantation*. She thinks I'm powerful enough to cast it."

"But?"

"I don't know, East. It means I'll need to.... Fuck! We're talking occult shit—like full-out Brother Blood. Through the centuries, people have defiled it. Remember, Adam and Eve weren't only chitchatting it up with the Almighty. Don't forget that other squatter freeloading in the treehouse. If I get it wrong, who knows what will happen.... What could happen to you."

"I trust you."

"Well, I don't trust me."

"You said you loved me like a brother."

"No. *Ah, couyon,* you're so dense sometimes." Royal gently kissed the tip of Easton's nose. "I'm in love with you, *sha.*"

Warmth spread through Easton's cheeks, and his heart galloped in his chest. He took it all in, considered, and questioned if his hearing had deceived him.

He's in love with me.

Out of all the outrageous things he'd heard tonight, this was the most mind-blowing of them all —yet it was the one he wanted to believe the most. It filled him. Completed him. He didn't need anything else.

After a moment of thought, he replied, "That means you'd never do anything to harm me. So, I have faith in you. Cast the spell. End this madness."

Reluctantly, Royal nodded.

Easton repositioned and snuggled closer to his bed companion. "Oh, and Roy...."

"Huh?"

"*Et, je t'aime, aussi.*"

Smiling, Royal leaned forward and rested his forehead against Easton's.

CHAPTER 33

ROYAL

Royal glanced up at the star-glittering sky and tucked in his bottom lip. Fertile earth dented with a soft squish beneath his weight with each dutiful step he wove between splinters of light and shadow as if attempting to pass a field sobriety test. The serenity of the balmy night amplified the crush of grass, chorus of croaking frogs, cacophony of cicadas, shuffling of reeds, and splashes of creatures in the water that served as an ecological score. As he made his way through the trees with the tenacity and stealth of a death-row fugitive from Angola to an abandoned chapel on the outskirts of the bayou, every presynaptic and postsynaptic terminal in his brain rapidly fired a distress alarm. This was a bad idea—a *very* bad idea.

Royal didn't know why he'd agreed to this. Not true. He did know. It was because Easton had asked him, and he'd do anything for Easton. But this was beyond.... Was there even a word for what this was? Insanity barely scratched the surface of describing it.

What in all of God's green earth did Royal know about casting a spell? Hell, what did he know about witchcraft and psychic abilities? Okay, honestly, probably a little more than he'd let on. He'd been doing some reading over the past months. Okay, okay. If he had to come clean with himself, he could admit that he'd been *researching* for a couple of years, but only because he'd thought he'd seen something—a shadow—one night in a hotel hallway. It had floated past him and followed Cody into the lobby.

Initially, Royal hadn't been certain he'd seen anything. After all, he had tossed back a few beers that night and maybe—not that he'd admit anything—had taken a few puffs of pot. But then there had been a series of strange events—nothing specifically that Royal could describe other than a general weirdness. Then it all stopped without explanation until right before the event in Toledo. Things had been whack-a-doodle ever since.

How convenient it would have been to blame his vision on a bad trip of whacky weedy. However, after witnessing the hotel incident with Cody, Royal hadn't toyed around with any funny cigarettes again or divulged what he'd witnessed to anyone. He hadn't known what to make of it until the witch helped lay it all out for him. In a way, he wished she hadn't. Ignorance was bliss, as the saying went. Now here he was, about to...

What the fuck am *I doing?*

His stomach churned and nose hairs itched.

There has to be another way.

With each step, his mind skimmed a Rolodex of alternative solutions. However, his mental files kept coming up blank. Nothing. Empty.

Fuck!

Swearing wasn't helping, and he wasn't sure it even made him feel better, but it was better than nothing, he supposed. His soul not only quaked for what could happen to Easton if casting went south, but he also knew what it meant for him. There would be no turning back.

"Mage" was what the witch had called him. As much as he wanted to deny it—to run screaming away in that moment and denounce the witch as a liar—his heart told him it was true. Events from the past that hadn't made sense suddenly did. The unexplainable had an explanation. Thus, he'd remained, listened, and learned.

The witch had explained that while some abilities were innate, others were learned. Sometimes, a person born with innate abilities would force them to become inactive if suppressed long enough. But once acted upon, their presence would be solidified, and all of the supernatural world would know of his existence and feel free to interact with him. Basically, he was inscribing his name onto a ghoulish internet freeway and opening his life to…. He didn't want to think about it. He couldn't and welcomed denial as his constant companion.

The crumbling stone walls of the chapel nestled in a cluster of Spanish-moss-draped oak trees came into view. A portion of its slate roof next to the chimney was missing, and lush green vines stretched across the broken windows. It once had been part of a large sugarcane plantation that, due to its uniqueness, had fallen into ruin in the crossfire of the pending Civil War. The plantation had been owned and operated by *gens de couleur libres* and farmed without slave labor. As tension between the North and South mounted, Southern laws defining racial status muddled the line between *gens de couleur libres* and freed slaves and stripped the former of legal rights. What war and politics hadn't destroyed, time and Mother Nature had.

"We're here," Royal announced, shining his flashlight at what was once the bell headstock. They had arrived on the west side of the structure. "Watch your step," he instructed, protecting himself with the sign of the cross as he continued toward the chapel. Although obstructed by overgrowth, he knew there were more than a dozen coping graves of his maternal ancestors that hadn't been relocated.

"Now I see why you said we couldn't ride the four-wheelers. These trees are ridiculous."

"The rumor is that when the owners learned their land was going to be seized by the government, they burned all the crops and planted mimosas, sweetgum, and yellow poplar to make it arduous for anyone trying to farm it."

"Well played."

The two walked the remainder of the way to the chapel in silence. Once inside, they spread a quilt across the decaying floor and sat down. Royal removed a wrinkled and torn sheet of paper from his pocket and read the scrawled instructions of the witch.

"It says we're to light four candles."

"Okay." Easton dug into the backpack Royal had set on the ground and found a grill lighter and bundle of white candles bound by twine.

Royal pulled the backpack toward him. "While you do that, I'm to put mint, allspice, sage, ginger, cinnamon, cloves, basil, nutmeg, and pyrite into a bowl. *Pooyah-ee!*" His brows bunched. "Are we getting rid of a demon or baking bread pudding?"

Easton looked up from unbinding the candles and shrugged. "You're asking me? You're the one with the instructions. Didn't you read the list before we bought all this stuff?"

"Some of it," he abashedly admitted. "But when

you said you'd finish the list while I was in sporting goods, I didn't bother."

"Didn't you think you needed to know what you'd be working with? Suppose it said you needed a vestal virgin to sacrifice or something?"

"I guess I would have had to go with the *or something*, cos it's damn near impossible finding a virgin of any kind these days."

"True."

Silently, Royal cussed himself and retrieved the blue calcite bowl to add the spices. He'd pilfered the bowl from his mother, part of a mortar and pestle that she used to make chimichurri, hummus, and pesto. Fortunately, she had others, and hopefully, she wouldn't mind him swiping this one. But the spell had been specific about the materials required. He hadn't known what blue calcite was until he looked it up and saw that it resembled the mortar and pestle.

"Mm." Concern clouded Easton's eyes, and he hesitated before asking his follow-up question. "Do you think it's a hoax?"

"No." Royal shook his head. "If it is, I guess we'll find out. Keep going."

Seemingly satisfied with the answer, Easton nodded and returned to untying the candles.

Around the bowl, Royal positioned aventurine stones, three pennies, and Palo Santo sticks. No joke, the Palo Santo sticks had been a pain in the ass to find.

"Now what?" Easton asked.

"I light the sage smudge thingamajig, and then we hold hands."

Easton nodded.

"Close your eyes," Royal instructed, taking Easton's hands in his after he'd completed the instructions. He closed his eyes as well—partly to concentrate, because the witch said drawing from his *ka* would increase the likelihood of a successful casting, but mostly because he didn't want to witness anything that happened. He'd ripped that portion from the paper the witch had given him before leaving her tent. He hadn't wanted to chance anyone seeing it and then conjuring up some moronic idea to try it— the way he was now.

Royal carefully chanted the words he'd practiced and memorized of a forgotten language—not dead or abandoned like Latin but struck from memory at the Tower of Babel. He spoke slowly to articulate each word to the best of his ability, yet a degree of uncertainty regarding correctness could have partly contributed to his lagging rate.

He concluded the incantation.

"That's it?" Easton questioned. "It's done? Did it work?"

Royal had no clue and shrugged.

"Well, what now?"

As Royal parted his lips to answer, a rustling of

wind rattled the branches, and a new kind of silence ensued—a stillness, the kind felt minutes before a twister dropped. Even the sloshing of the bayou had ceased. A chill pimpled Royal's skin as a sense stronger than any he'd ever known overtook him. Slowly, he opened his eyes, expecting to find darkness, and gasped at the sight. A dense mist shrouded the entire heart pine floor, obscured visibility, and dampened the air.

"Roy?" Easton whispered, his eyes frantically scanning the room.

"Shh," Royal replied, his stare focused on glints of color twinkling in the nimbus, recognizing its deceptive beauty to conceal the danger pulsing in the atmosphere.

As the grotesque, smoky mass thickened, the foul smells of corrosive acid, sogginess, and infection mounted and hung in the air like primordial Grecian thermae, stinging and watering his eyes.

We have to get out of here.

Before Royal could voice a warning, a boll of fog swirled into the shape of what looked to be some type of claw with talons and launched toward Easton's throat, slamming his friend backward but not to the floor.

"No!" Royal yelled, heaving Easton to him. "You can't have him."

His words appeared either to anger or challenge

the force, because the weight yanking against him compounded. His biceps burned as he struggled to maintain his grip.

"It's so heavy," Easton gurgled. His shoes scraped against the wooden floor as he struggled to keep his head above the spectral energy and hang on to Royal.

A second claw emerged—this one digging into Royal's shoulder—and a steely pressure rammed into his chest. The blow forced a whoosh of breath from his lungs, and his shoulder smoldered as if glued to a hot iron. The pain almost masked the warm feel of the blood trickling down his arm and the alarming odor of charring meat.

Don't squirm. It'll make it worse.

The thought was easier said than done, and Royal writhed in pain. He screamed what he thought would be a litany of vulgarities, but he didn't recognize the words or his own voice, though he knew they had come from him. His throat felt scorched as if he'd been force-fed Carolina Reaper sauce, and his lungs throbbed.

Another claw formed, and Royal saw it more vividly. It resembled that of an eagle except it had nine talons instead of four and knobby overlapping placoid scales like a serpent. The tarsus was ashen gray with a purplish hue and the nails a pitch-black with gleaming pewter tips. The span of the claw looked to be approximately eight inches. It clamped his scalp from behind and yanked. The pull was enough to drag him and Easton several feet across the room. Splinters poked his legs through his jeans. He felt his grip on Easton loosen.

"Don't let—" he yelled but halted at the sight of Easton's bluing lips and ashy skin. Only the whites of his eyes were visible as he dry-retched.

This thing is going to kill us. Think. Think. His pulse quickened. *Someone must pay.*

Suddenly, Royal had his answer. His heart both swelled and saddened simultaneously.

"I love you, East." He took in his best friend and lover one final time before letting go and collapsing backward into the fog. His head fuzzed with fatigue as he drifted away from a distant female cry.

CHAPTER 34

EASTON

On a moan, Royal's eyes slowly opened, and Easton heaved a sigh of relief.

"Thank God you're all right."

"Where am I?" Royal asked, squinting against the light.

"Home. In your bed. How are you feeling?"

"Worse than the average Bruichladdich X4 Quadrupled whiskey hangover at a Chucky Cheese children's birthday party." He glanced at his bandaged shoulder.

Although Easton smiled, angst remained in his expression. "That good, huh?"

Royal pushed himself up on his elbows.

"No, don't try to get up. You need rest. That was some fool thing you did, throwing yourself into that carbonated vapor."

The corners of Royal's mouth curled upward. "You make it sound like a soft drink."

Leaning back in the chair he'd dragged beside Royal's bed, Easton folded his arms across his chest and scowled. Concern bunched in his eyes, and he no longer could suppress the torrid bounds of emotions lingering a fraction below the surface.

"You could have died, Roy. What were you thinking?"

"Someone had to pay the debt. You would have died if I hadn't."

Anger replaced concern. "Then you should have let me. It was my debt." And then the anger melted into tears. "How was I supposed to live without you? You were just going to leave me here alone."

"Oh, *sha*, don't cry."

Easton sniffed hard and swiped at his eyes. He hated this, despised sniveling like a child. Never in his adult life had he cried, and now he couldn't turn off the waterworks. Fat tears tumbled down his flushed cheeks.

"I'm okay," Royal reassured.

"You wouldn't be if Salethia hadn't shown up."

"Duchess was there?" He looked around the room.

"She's gone out for supplies. Said she needed more kalanchoe to help heal you, but she'll be back soon. She's brewing a potion." He swiped his eyes again. "I gotta tell you, for something so necromantic, it smells pretty damn good."

"Wait. Back up. How did Duchess know to come to the chapel?

"She said she sensed it. Something about bellows from the chapel cemetery and generational bonds." He shook his head. "I didn't understand everything she said, but the important thing is that she arrived in time and did what she did."

"What'd she do?"

Easton faltered, uncertain if Royal had recovered enough for the truth.

"Maybe you should wait for her."

"No, I'm asking you."

Easton's shoulders lifted and fell. He couldn't keep it from him.

"When you let go, I grabbed a piece of broken floorboard and struck whatever had hold of me. It let go, and I stood up. I tried to find you, but I couldn't see through the mist. No matter what I did, I couldn't shear it. It was so thick and had risen to my knees. Then, suddenly, your mother ran inside in total badass mode. I didn't understand what she was saying, but it drew the mist to her. Every time it would go at her, she'd chant something, and it would gather like a mushroom cloud and disperse. Then it began swirling as if it was being sucked down a drain and disappeared. When I finally could see you, you were barely breathing. We brought you here so she could treat you. She said you'd been exposed to toxins that a hospital wouldn't have an antidote for. That was five days ago."

"Huh." Royal's relaxed back onto the bed and stared at the ceiling as if contemplating. After a moment, his eyes lit with awareness. "Duchess," he whispered, barely audible. "Makes sense. Explains a lot." He looked back at Easton. "I've been out for five days?"

"Not entirely. Mostly, you've been disoriented and flailing about like Regan in *The Exorcist*, but *oui*." Easton nodded. "Salethia said it was a sign of her potion purging your body."

Royal rubbed his forehead. "I don't remember any of it."

"She said you wouldn't."

"What about you? Are you okay?"

"Peachy except for this sweet little hickey." Easton tugged the collar of his shirt to reveal the purplish bruise encircling his throat.

Royal's mouth fell open.

"No, no. Don't do that. It doesn't hurt."

"But what if it comes back? I didn't get rid of it."

"*Mais*, you did. It was like in the fairy tale. When it dragged you under, it told you its name. You said it when I pulled you from the floor. That's when it was sucked away. Salethia says it fears you now because by you knowing its name, it's enslaved to you in this world."

"You're...." Royal clasped Easton's hand and squeezed. "You're free."

"*Oui*, we both are. Free of all of our demons and free to love each other."

Speaking the words rejuvenated Easton, and the tension in his neck and shoulders released fully. A joyful and relaxed smile pulled up the edges of his lips. He didn't delude himself that being with Royal would be cotton candy and candy apples. In the same way leopards didn't change their spots, people didn't change their hatred and bigotry. He knew there still would be challenges but had the confidence it wouldn't be anything he and Royal couldn't face and defeat... together.

GLOSSARY

A

Allons – Let's go

Aseteur – Now

A l'ouvrage – To work/At work

Arrêté – Stop

B

Bahbin – Pout

Brasse mon tchu – Kiss my butt

Brasse mon cul – Kiss my ass

Bonne nuit – Good night

C

Ça marche – That works

C'est pas ma faute – It's not my fault

C'est tout – That's all

Ce n'est rein – It's nothing
Comprendez-vous? – Understand?
Couyon – (term of endearment)
Co faire – Why?

D

D'accord – Okay
Dors – Go to sleep

E

Eh bien, c'est ça – Oh well, that's it
Embrasse mon cul – Kiss my butt

F

Fais do do – Party/Social gathering

G

Gardez-donc – Look at that
Gris gris – (a hex/curse)

H

Honte – Shame

I

Il n'ya pas de quoi – You're welcome

J

J'ai ça – I got this
J'ai dit que ce n'était rien – I said, it's nothing

J'suis pas fou de sa? – Am I crazy?

Je fais – I do

Je sais – I know

Je ne sais pas – I don't know

Je ne suis pas bête – I am not stupid

Je suis de'pouille – I'm a mess

Je t'aime, aussi – I love you also

Je va vous voir plus tard – I'll see you later

Je vous salue Marie, pleine de graces – Hail Mary, full of grace

K

Kee-yaw – Wow!

Key awau – Wow!

L

Lache pas las patate – Do not drop the potato (i.e., Don't mess up)

M

Mais pourquoi? – But why?

Mais, ce n'est pas pour les enfants – But it is not for children

Mais là – Well, then

Merde – Shit

Mère – Mother

Mémère – Grandmother

N

Ne pas as la langue dans sa poche – Don't have your tongue in your pocket (i.e., Say what you think)

Notre Père, qui est aux cieux, que ton nom soit sanctifié – Our Father, who art in heaven, hallowed be thy name

O

Oi-vay – Uh-oh, Good grief

Olá – Hello

Oui – Yes

P

Papi – Father

Parfois tu montes sur mes nerfs – You get on my nerves

Pas rien – Nothing

Père – Father

Peut-être un petit peu – Maybe a little

Pooyah-ee! – WTH

Q

Que se passe-t-il – What's wrong?

Qui? – Who?

Qui n'a? – What's happening? What's the matter?

Quoi, ça dit? – What is it?

Quoi y a? – What's the matter?

Quoi? – What?

R

Rougarous – A Cajun folklore creature that has the head of a wolf or a dog and the body of a human, similar to a werewolf

S

Sa c'est assez – That's enough

Salleau prie – Doggonnit!

Sa me fait de la pain – I'm sorry

Sa mère – His mother

S'il vous plait – Please

Sim – Yes

T

T'es sur de sa? – Are you sure?

T'es bien? – Are you okay?

Ta mère – Your mother

Y

Y'ou t'es parti? – Where are you going?

ACKNOWLEDGMENTS

The list of people who have helped make *DEMON RODEO* possible is extensive, and my gratitude to them is immeasurable. Thank you to my family, friends, critique partners, editors, alpha and beta readers, ARC readers, cover artists, proofers, publisher, and bartenders. All of the words of encouragement, advice, honest opinions, sarcasm, humor, and cocktails have been invaluable. This journey has been long and complex. I wouldn't have made it without each of you. Thank you so much for sticking with me through it all. Also, a huge shout-out to everyone who read, shared, tweeted, blogged, followed, reviewed, or helped spread the word about *DEMON RODEO*. It is for you that I write and that this book is possible. Thank you so very much. *Merci.*

ABOUT THE AUTHOR

Genevive Chamblee is a Southern darling and resides in the bayou country where sweet tea and SEC football reign supreme. She is known for being witty (or so she thinks), getting lost anywhere beyond her front yard (the back is pushing it as she's very geographically challenged), falling in love with shelter animals (and she adopts them), asking off-the-beaten-path questions that makes one go "hmm", and preparing home-cooked Creole meals that are as spicy as her writing.

Genevive specializes in spinning steamy, romantic tales with humorous flair, diverse characters, and quirky views of love and human behavior. She also is not afraid to delve into darker romances as well.

facebook.com/genevivechambleeconnect

instagram.com/genevivechambleeauthor

tiktok.com/@creolegurlnola

x.com/dolynesaidso

ABOUT THE PUBLISHER

Hot Tree Publishing loves love. Publishing adult romantic fiction, HTPubs are all about diverse reads featuring heroes and heroines to swoon over. Since opening in 2015, HTPubs have published more than 300 titles across the wide and diverse range of romantic genres. If you're chasing a happily ever after in your favourite subgenre, HTPubs have you covered.

Interested in discovering more amazing reads brought to you by Hot Tree Publishing? Head over to the website for information:

WWW.HOTTREEPUBLISHING.COM

 facebook.com/hottreepublishing

 x.com/hottreepubs

 instagram.com/hottreepublishing